MANOLI

PEER REVIEW

emelissaris.wixsite.com/peerreview

Cover design and illustration by Dean Gorissen | www.deangorissen.com

For Lindy, my fellow escapee

Part 1

An affront to academic freedom

I had to go about this rationally.

I pressed the card down firmly on the small glass window.

The electronic barrier didn't budge.

I kept my cool. There had to be a solution and the only way to discover it was by experimentation, trial and error, verification and, falsification, elimination of possibilities.

The flip side of the card contained no information other than a return address; no barcode or photo or anything that looked of use in the circumstances. Still, I couldn't rely on appearances alone. Perhaps there was a hidden chip in there. How was I to know? I turned the card over.

For a second, I thought that the gate clenched itself shut just a little bit more tightly.

Yet I didn't panic. What to a layperson is an ill-thought plan, to a scholar is a hypothesis. If neither side of the card worked separately, perhaps both together would. It being impossible to scan them at the same time, the task would require agility and speed.

I took a deep breath, placed the card photo side down and then flipped it over as quickly as I could.

The result was the same – the barrier remained shut. My hypothesis had been neither verified nor falsified because in the course of flipping the card, I accidentally flicked it, sending it flying over to the other side of the gate.

Let down by technology, I was perilously close to being late for an important appointment, effectively locked out of the building. The little piece of plastic that should have granted me access lay just beyond my reach yet close enough to add to my frustration. All I could do was stand there, deep in contemplation.

I was about to swallow my pride and recruit the help of a passing student when I heard a sound that may or may not have been directed at me. At first it registered as mere background noise coming from nowhere, going nowhere in particular. On being repeated, it became a discernible mumble, the source identifiably human. Nigel Cole, Professor of Criminal Law, was standing diagonally across from me on the other side of the new electronic entry system.

He picked up the card and handed it over to me.

He said something, which I missed because of his impenetrable accent. Our acquaintance was limited to a shared membership of the Faculty of Social Sciences Committee for Postgraduate Studies. Having tried a few times to decipher his undoubtedly ground-breaking contributions to the structure of this or the other degree programme, I'd given up. Invariably, when Nigel spoke, I doodled.

Now that he was addressing me directly, I could hardly ignore him, pull my notebook from my satchel and start drawing concentric circles. I had to make an effort.

"I beg your pardon", I responded, lifting an index finger to my ear with a grimace that suggested I couldn't hear him over the surrounding noise.

Among the many unintelligible sounds that came my way, I caught the word "right".

Looking down at the gate and the scanners, I realised what my mistake had been. I had assumed that the reader on the left corresponded to the barrier in front of me when I should have been using the scanner on the right hand side.

When it was announced that the new system would be installed, many colleagues in the Faculty of Social Sciences were outraged at the prospect of being forced into a surveillance dystopia. The union organised a gathering to stop the machines from being installed. A seminar was hastily convened, titled "*Hold the door open for me: neo-liberalism and the biopolitics of movement restriction*". Rumours swirled about that the new system was a surreptitious ploy to keep records of when we clocked in and out.

Had anyone been indeed monitoring staff movements that first day the system became fully operational, I can well imagine their bafflement as I repeatedly opened and idly let close a gate without ever passing through it. I could only hope that from a distance it appeared as an act of playful disobedience.

"That's an affront to academic freedom, Nigel", I said as I waved goodbye and headed to the lifts.

The door was ajar. I knocked on it softly and stuck my head through.

"One minute, one minute", he said without taking his eyes off his computer keyboard.

"Yes, of course", I whispered and retreated back out into the hallway.

The office was in the corner at the end of the fourth floor corridor. It had been designated as the Head of Department's room because, in the Departmental Development Committee's view, it provided the requisite privacy. By that the Committee meant that one wasn't able to see what the occupant was up to without fully entering the room. The door faced a wall and one had to turn left upon entering to see the desk and the suite comprising a small coffee table and three easy chairs.

I rested against the wall and took a few deep breaths trying to control my shaking.

"Come on in, Michael", he shouted after a few minutes. "Sorry to keep you waiting. Endless admin. Sucks the life out of you. Take a seat."

He pointed at the easy chairs.

My hopes that he would join me at the table for a relaxed conversation were quickly dashed as he made himself comfortable in the sagging confines of his long-suffering swivel chair.

"So, I bet you're wondering why I asked you to see me."

I wasn't. He had already told me in his email. "Michael, please come see me tomorrow at 10am to discuss your promotion. Cheers".

What I *was* wondering, was why this man who by any standards enjoyed a decent income, a man whose position required his regular attendance at meetings with the high and mighty, why this man had never bothered to replace the teeth missing from the bottom left of his jaw. That gaping hole was most disconcerting at the best of times, but in the circumstances it was like a gateway to an abyss. I was also pondering why he would sign off his emails with "Cheers".

"It's about your professional development", he said. "The Promotions Committee was satisfied with your research, your teaching and your administrative contribution..."

I instantly knew what was coming. In academic terms 'satisfied' means 'found it little more than abominably bad'. Numbness was spreading all over my body as he paused to make sure that what he was about to say would sink in.

"...but we didn't feel that you're quite ready for a promotion. Your research is sound but it lacks, and these are the Committee's words not mine, *a vision*."

He stopped and looked at me, his locked fingers resting on his protruding stomach.

I turned my eyes away. Light-headed and lost for words, I stared at the bookshelves that ran the length of the wall from door to the desk end of the room. The shelves were surprisingly bare. Did he ever read? Had he entirely forsaken scholarly research and become a full-time manager? Ancient hard copies of journals occupied most of the shelves, and some textbooks and monographs were scattered here and there. Displays of tat were interspersed among the rows. A white rock on the very top shelf, a figurine in a Sevillana dress, a couple of commemorative plaques, a photo of Paul in his academic gown, some thank you cards, and, the academic equivalent of used train tickets, an assortment of conference participation certificates.

I turned back to face him.

"Paul, when I was first hired you told me that the appointments panel was so impressed with my profile that they thought I should be appointed at a higher rung of the scale but, bureaucratic obstacles not allowing it at that stage, you assured me that you would guarantee that I got promoted to senior lecturer within two years."

"Yes, I remember that like it was yesterday. What a bright thing you were."

"Only it wasn't yesterday. It was six years ago."

"Yes, well, you see, Michael, things have changed in these past six years. More bright young things have come through, some very bright indeed, with ground-breaking research, amazing teaching scores and what have you. They jump the queue, you know?"

"They jump the queue?"

"They jump the queue. So to speak but, yes, they jump the queue."

"So, what do I have to do to be considered for promotion?"

"As I said, vision. You need a vision."

"Can you be a little more specific?"

"That's the problem right there, Michael", he said leaning forward, wagging an admonishing finger at me. "You yearn for specificity when you need a vision. A vision!"

❖

That afternoon I only had one first-year tutorial. Of the seven students, only two had come prepared but that would suffice. I let them do all the talking while the rest spent a leisurely fifty minutes doing the social media rounds on their smartphones.

I hardly listened to anything they said. All I could think about was my conversation with my HoD.

That year it was "a vision". The year before it had been "inspirational teaching". The year before that "committed citizenship".

By any standard, I was doing everything that was required for a promotion. My publications were at the very least acceptable. Since my appointment, I'd published two articles in peer-reviewed journals, that were considered mid-table but decent, and a chapter in a volume of conference proceedings. My teaching was good too. Apart from the odd nasty anonymous feedback comment ("he makes social anthropology so dull that I've become a misanthrope"; "has he actually studied this stuff?"; "his voice is too soft and doesn't carry in the lecture theatre but that's just as well"), they seemed to rate me highly enough. I had been acting as Director of Postgraduate Studies for the past two years without any major failures, meaning that no student had died or been seriously injured on my watch and none had failed their degree without good reason. I wasn't particularly friendly with any of them and I avoided socialising on non-work-related occasions but I did look after them. I even kept paper tissues on my desk at the ready for emotional breakdowns. And I can boast that very few had to use them.

None of that was good enough for the Promotions Committee and Paul Digby. And it was becoming clear to me that it never would be. The noble dreams that had driven me to academia, the aspirations to help generate knowledge that would change the world in exchange for some modest reward, were to be crushed under the weight of an arteriosclerotic institution and other people's selfish, arbitrary preferences.

The last thing I wanted was to spend that evening with colleagues and students but I couldn't think how I might get out of it. I had no excuse for not attending the reception for postgraduate students that I myself had organised. Not turning up would have been transparently petulant.

Few euphemisms can take greater liberties with the truth than calling my Department's student-staff drinks events a 'reception'. They were held in the campus pub, The Scholar and Scroll, an establishment pithily so named by the first Head of the Classics Department back in the 1960s and the congratulatory growls for the academic tongue twister that his colleagues must have roared through pipe-filled mouths could still be heard in the walls. Younger generations were less impressed by the witticism and even less so by the nicotine-stained wallpaper, the beer-infused carpet that squelched at every step and the singularly unimpressive selection of beers, wines and spirits. So, everyone had taken to referring to it as The Scholar and Scrote or, more frequently, as simply The Scrote. Still, most nights of the week it was packed with students and staff. It remained the chosen venue for our events, always held in the harshly lit and rather bare first floor bar, which suffered from an even more depressing lack of character than the main saloon on the ground floor.

The fastest way to the Scrote from the McKenzie Building, where the Department of Anthropology was housed along with Social Work and Law, was through a field notable for two interesting features. First, it seemed to be constantly muddy no matter the weather. Second, no one knew why it was there. It was neither a car park nor a garden. It wasn't used for cattle (and, yes, cattle did roam elsewhere on campus). It was just a sodden muddy field.

The party was already in full swing when I arrived. Masters' students were queuing at the bar for their free drinks. Doctoral researchers were chatting among themselves, on constant lookout for the right opportunity to accost members of staff, all of whom were present and correct, never having been known to shy away from a free drink. Professor Alison Davies was encircled by a contingent of students and was being assailed by a ring of gratuitously dropped -isms. Professor Jeremy Allcock, coat on and battered rucksack over his shoulders as ever, wandered from group to group a forlorn figure, invariably ignored. Eventually, he would start the circuit of futility all over again as if the memory of his first attempt had been erased.

"Where have you been?", Doreen Williamson asked as soon as I walked in leaving a muddy trail on the squishy carpet.

"Sorry, had to finish some emails", I lied.

"I hope there's enough snacks", she said casting an anxious look at the tables.

She'd been the Department's administrator for almost as long as the institution existed and still she was never confident that she'd procured enough crisps and peanuts.

Dr Lucy Warburton, a bottle of white wine in each hand, came up to me to offer me a glass.

"I roped Lucy in to keep everyone well greased", Doreen said.

Only she would have been able to get Lucy to do something so out of character.

Professor Paul Digby, toothless, bald, and fat Head of the Department of Anthropology, was leaning by the far wall unsettlingly close to Dr Catherine Bowen. Dr Thomas Lusignan completed the small circle. Digby was laughing at something that only he appeared to find funny. He caught me staring and raised his glass of white campus plonk in salute. Catherine gave me a sideways glance, taking a sip of her gin and tonic. I returned a shy smile to her. Thomas took advantage of the brief intermission to sneak away and join Dr Horst Neuberg, who instantly button-holed him.

A heavy hand landed on my shoulder.

"Thought you'd abandoned me and dumped that damned speech on me."

The soft, upper-class, Fife accent of Duncan Erskine-Bell, thirty years my senior and yet my deputy as Postgraduate Studies Director, never failed to soothe me. Instantly, I felt more at ease.

"Actually, I was going to ask you to do the speech."

"No way, dear boy. Above my pay grade and all that."

"You're getting paid way more than me, Duncan."

"Not the point. Anyway, were you never taught that conversations about pecuniary matters are rude and unbecoming, dear boy?"

Duncan was never content using one word where ten were available.

"It was worth a try. Shall we get it out of the way now? It's as crap a time as any."

"Why not?"

He clinked his pint glass with the large signet ring around his little finger, which was the size of my thumb.

"Quiet everyone, quiet please."

The academic chatter died down. Once the gathering was looking in our direction, Duncan bowed and stretched out his arms offering me the floor like an MC in a mid-war burlesque show.

"Right, yes", I said.

"Can't hear you", someone said from the back of the room.

"Well, you missed the best bit", I said raising my voice. "OK, so I shan't keep you long. I bet all of you just want to go back to your wonderful wine, vintage of last week or so."

I had nicked that joke from a colleague at another University and it always raised a chuckle. People tend to hang on to anything half-amusing at events like that.

"One day you too will get to drink the good stuff", a voice said.

Was it Paul's? I couldn't be sure.

"Here's hoping", I said. "As most of you already know, I'm Michael West and I'm the person to whom you should feel free to pass on your congratulations for our terrific Master's and doctoral programmes. Complaints are welcome too but I've no doubt there won't be any. And if there are, they'll be locked away in the underground vault."

Another collective chuckle.

"When I was your age and in the same position as you are now, I wish my tutors had told me what I am about to tell you, in other words the truth. What *are* you doing here? A postgraduate degree in anthropology? Really? Can you really afford to piss all that money up against the wall on your way to the job centre for the privilege of spending a year in this godforsaken place? As for those of you embarking on a doctorate, where to begin? Do you honestly believe you'll get something at the end of this? Good luck to you but be careful what you wish for. Prepare yourselves for a lifetime of disappointment, aimlessness, being shat upon by others. Even worse, if, gods forbid, you ever find yourselves in a position of power, brace yourselves for turning into nasty pieces of work eager and willing to do your own share of shitting on the weak."

Of course, I didn't really say any of that but I certainly felt like speaking from the heart. Had I done so, everything would have turned out differently.

The reality is, I regurgitated some banalities about how exciting the year ahead would be, how important it was for them to balance work and play and how our Department was on the cutting edge of anthropological research.

When I said "that's all from me, I'll let you go back to your drinks", a collective sigh of relief spread across the room like a monsoon. The decibel levels rose back to maximum volume instantaneously.

In my expert opinion as student and meticulous observer of that which conditions and motivates human actions, what ensued in the following couple of hours in the Scrote determined the course of my life both in the short and the long run.

First, I was approached by Victoria Alvarez, a second year PhD student, who talked to me at length about her ethnographic research in some rebellious neighbourhood of Athens, Greece. To help me through that predicament, I set myself a private game. I would have a drink every time she mentioned these or their derivatives: neo-liberalism, agency ('agentic' would earn two bonus swigs), self-reflexive, performative, narrative.

I'd already had four glasses of wine by the time she told me that her Master's dissertation would appear in a relatively good journal the following year and that she had already published two book reviews and a couple of op-eds.

Her ridiculous overachievement made me quickly neck back another couple of refills.

Second, I tried to avoid Paul's gaze but mostly failed. Every time our eyes met, he raised his glass in what I took to be toasts to his success at bringing about my failure. Those brief incidents accounted for at least another few glasses of wine.

Third, Catherine Bowen, that queue-jumping, bright young thing who had been promoted to senior lecturer two mere years after joining the Department, squeezed her way through the crowd to come and speak to me.

"You're doing a great job with the pee-jee programme", she said.

"It's not exactly social science", I said, desperately attempting a bad joke that was made even clumsier by my drunken delivery.

I immediately downed another glass of wine in embarrassment.

"You're being too harsh on yourself", she said.

"It's not like it ever comes to anything", I mumbled.

"Well, I don't mean to patronise you but perhaps you should take things in your own hands, you know?"

"Take things in my own hands?"

"You're a bright guy, you know what you have to do, just do it without worrying too much about box-ticking. That's what I've been doing. It's paid off so far and long may it continue to do so", she said and raised her glass.

Perhaps it was the wine that I had already imbibed. Perhaps it was the fact that Catherine was the only academic who, with her confident, controlled air of authority, had shown me any empathy in longer than I cared to remember. Perhaps it was that from the very first moment I had seen her, when she had breezed through her interview for a post at the Department, I found her mesmerising. Every word she uttered had an impact on me and contact with her gave me a kind of pleasure, which I couldn't quite put into words.

Whatever the reason, right there and then, my feet sunk into the beer-soaked carpet of the Scrote, my ambitions crushed, stifled by the old and young egos and the naked ambition palpitating around me, I was overwhelmed by a strong sense of hope.

The abysmal hole in the plan

All the way across the non-purposed muddy field, the same few words and phrases were gyrating uncontrollably in my head: "vision"; "jump the queue"; "take things in your own hands". For some reason, "self-reflexive" was in there too but it seemed like the odd one out.

I hadn't quite formulated a detailed plan but there was no doubt in my mind that I was acting on one. The principle, still nebulous but powerful, the very vision that smote me in the Scrote told me to take things into my own hands and jump the queue. Without letting anyone know, I snuck away, fairly sure that my departure went unnoticed, as always, and soon found myself back at the McKenzie building.

Retaining the lesson of my morning grapple with modern technology, I managed to bypass advanced inebriation sufficiently to tap the card on the right-hand side reader and pass unimpeded through the electronic barrier. The nightshift guard was not at his post – presumably he was making tea or watching online videos on a teaching room computer.

I reached the door. It was unlocked. No surprise. We all kept our doors unlocked, if not wide open, even after hours. To the fixations of University management with security and surveillance, we, liberal and trusting academics, defiantly responded with utter recklessness.

I entered without breaking my by now somewhat erratic stride, confident that the room was empty. I'd left him behind in the pub, pretty sure that even if he decided to drop by the office before heading home, he could never have caught up with me.

Blindly, I felt my way through the dark room. In hindsight, I can understand how I collided with the first easy chair – it was straddling the narrow corridor between the shelves on the left and the sitting area on the right – but I have no idea how I managed to stumble into the second one. I must have circled round the coffee table. That second collision hurt more too, perhaps because it was entirely gratuitous. I hobbled about for a few seconds, holding my shin and trying not to make any noise that would add to the involuntary yelps I let loose on impact.

I finally made it to the desk and fumbled with the mouse. The monitor lit up. I squinted in the blue glow like a man who exits the cave of shadows to encounter true ideas for the first time.

He hadn't logged out of his account. The University really should start clamping down on that kind of irresponsible behaviour, I thought.

It was at that point that I knew exactly what I was going to do. I would access the files containing Paul's covering letters and the departmental recommendations he was preparing to send to the Promotions Committee and I would enter my name among those being recommended, attaching it to an already existing letter. Paul would never notice that he was sending one extra recommendation. All the work was done and he would not open the files again. He would just forward the contents of the folder lock, stock and non-smoking barrel.

Getting my application across to university management would not, of course, be the end of the story. It would only kick-start a process that would drag on for months on end and would involve endless to-ing and fro-ing between Heads, Committees, Managers, Internal Reviewers, External Reviewers and the gods only know who else. Sooner or later Paul would realise that my application had been snuck in somehow but my money was on him being too embarrassed to admit that it had been sent in error, let alone with mischievous and aggrieved intent. He would never retract it; he would just go along with it, wondering how in the name of publish or be damned it had ever happened.

The risks didn't cross my mind. As it turned out, even if they had, I could not possibly have been prepared for what followed.

Finding the folder was a piece of cake; Paul's filing was very systematic.

Negotiating the form itself, not so much. The text boxes were too small and didn't stretch to fit text longer than twenty of the allowable maximum of one hundred words. The tick boxes were untickable. The entire document seemed to have been designed as an infinite series of overlapping tables interlocked and poised to move in unison and in entirely irrational ways affronted at the slightest interference.

The format was bad enough but it was nothing compared to the bamboozling content. There were "metrics" (already a word I barely understood) and "indicators" of unimaginable "performance areas". Publications had to be rated narratively (that was fine; surely I could talk up my own work) and numerically but on a scale that referred to different elements of each when it made no sense to separate them. A note assuring that student feedback would not be taken into account by the University Promotions Committee was followed by an almost explicit contradiction in the form of a box requiring a detailed report of teaching evaluation results, the students' way of determining their teachers' professional futures.

I don't know why I thought that I would have been able to fill the whole form there and then but thinking I could, I made myself comfortable in Paul's swivel chair and started typing at a pace that fate dictated was too leisurely.

Had I been concentrating harder on the fact that I had trespassed in the office of the Head of my academic Department and was clandestinely forging a document and therefore in breach of most university disciplinary regulations and presumably several criminal laws, I would have heard the lift beeping and its doors opening and closing. I would not have missed the loud automated voice that sounded like an irate teacher forced to repeat the floor number for the millionth time to a group of disinterested students. I might even have heard the sound of Paul's worn out heels on the carpetless corridor floor.

I jumped up out of the chair, when he turned on the light.

"Paul!", I said, as if he was the last person on earth I'd expected to see in his own office.

"Hi. Wait, what, what are you, what?", he stuttered.

He was drunk. That gave me a little leeway. I discreetly switched off the computer monitor thinking that that would at least delay developments.

"Yeah, sorry", I said, not at all sure as to what to say next. "I saw this very interesting book on your shelves this morning that I've not read before, so I thought I'd just pop in and borrow it. I'd have let you know of course."

"A book? What?", Paul said.

He was squinting and constantly smacked and licked his lips.

He was not drunk. He was completely plastered. Set me to thinking that if that's what one looks like when drunk, then I'd foreswear alcohol for life. Not a pledge that I honoured.

"Yes, look, there, this book by someone called Malinowitz, Malinow or something."

Few outside academic circles know much about social anthropology but even they will have heard of Bronislaw Malinowski, one of the discipline's revered founders. And yet, in my confused state and my confusing estimation of just how confused and befuddled Paul might be, I somehow thought that it would be perfectly plausible to suggest I had not read much less come across one of the seminal books in the field.

Somewhere at the back of my head, I must have realised the abysmal hole in the plan so I sought to discombobulate Paul by employing the element of speed. I rushed to the shelves, stood on my toes, and reached for the book I was ostensibly there to borrow.

In the meantime, unsteady on his feet, Paul had stretched an arm to prop himself up against one of the lower shelves right next to where I was standing.

"This is, it's, strange", he slurred, wiping his brow.

"No, not strange at all", I said with a forced jocularity attempting to downplay our encounter to nothing more than a run-of-the-mill incident.

I pulled the book out from its nesting place.

As I retrieved the tome, the large rock came off the shelf too. I didn't make the slightest attempt to intercept it or to divert its trajectory. I stood there, Malinowski's *Crime and Custom in Savage Society* in my right hand, as the rock struck Paul's head.

He fell to the ground face down with a thump.

I crouched next to him. He was bleeding. I prodded him on the shoulder.

"Paul?", I whispered.

He remained still.

"Hello?", I said and gave him a stronger shove.

He didn't react.

I held my breath and frantically checked for signs of breathing.

There was none.

Paul was dead, killed with the help of Bronislaw Malinowski.

If ever there was a time to panic, it had just arrived. I twitched and jerked in all directions like some manic video game character compelled to catch items falling all around him from the sky.

This time I didn't fail to hear the lift.

I froze, still crouched next to the dead body, incapable of even considering what an outsider might make of the scene. For a split second, it crossed my mind to tweak appearances entirely. I contemplated hitting my own head with the rock and lying down next to Paul. That would throw everyone off the scent.

Perhaps I would have done that too but the hallway light came on and I heard footsteps approaching Paul's office.

It was too late to carry out my desperate plan of staging the most bizarre self-inflicted injury. If the inquisitive visitor entered the office, I would have had to accept my fate.

I closed my eyes and waited.

Nothing happened. When I reopened my eyes the hallway

light had been turned off again. Whoever it was had left without a word.

I stood and took a couple of steps back. From a distance the scene looked like nothing more than an accident. Paul walks in, he's blind drunk, stumbles, hits the shelf, the rock wobbles, it falls on his head, he loses consciousness and eventually, not exactly being the poster boy of the five-a-day campaign, succumbs to the shock and dies.

It appeared watertight to me. There didn't seem any good reason to complicate things. No one needed to know that I had been there when he died. All I had to do was to get rid of all conspicuous traces of my presence.

But there was plenty of time to do that. It was almost ten in the evening. No one else would turn up and whoever had just come by had already left.

I could finish what I'd gone there to accomplish in the first place.

I turned off the lights, and careful to avoid stumbling into the dead body of my Head of Department, I made my way back to his desk. I still had an application for promotion to senior lecturer to complete.

No actionable decisions

The Department Meeting had already been scheduled for the day after and Alison Davies, now acting HoD, saw fit to go ahead with it.

The first hour and a half was devoted to business as usual. Minutes of each Committee meeting, circulated well in advance, had to be approved.

Not without a fight, not in our Department. Jeremy Allcock, meant to have retired a decade ago but somehow the relevant forms fell by the wayside leaving him to fly under the radar ever since, had come fully prepared with a handwritten list. First, he picked up on three spelling mistakes in the minutes of the Research Committee. Then he felt compelled to point out a factual error.

"Paul appears to have been present according to the minutes but no contributions of his are recorded. I cross-referenced that to the minutes of the Departmental Meeting before that, in which it is recorded that he would miss the following Meeting, that is the latest one, due to a prior engagement in London", he said.

"Noted with apologies. Probably my mistake", Doreen said.

Trying to keep my exposure to pointless bureaucracy to a manageable level, I too had missed that Department Meeting by making an excuse so implausible that I'd already forgotten what it was.

Next, Jeremy took issue with a couple of orphan lines in the pdf document, which he considered to be an intolerable eyesore. Jeremy lived his life through paperwork and what was happening in the three-dimensional world beyond made little impression.

Dr Lucy Warburton concentrated on what she deemed to be important points of substance such as whether doctoral students should be allowed to use the departmental kitchen and, if yes, whether they should procure their own coffee and tea. That triggered a thirty-minute debate about hierarchy, equality, the importance of inclusiveness in building a healthy research environment, the relative advantages of English Breakfast over Earl Grey, and how much we'd be able to reduce our carbon footprint if we used loose leaf rather than tea bags.

Of course, no actionable decisions were taken. Department Meetings were for show. Everything was played out at Committees. There were plenty of these: Development, Research, Undergraduate Studies, Postgraduate Studies (I had to chair that one), Promotions, Undergraduate Student-Staff Liaison, Postgraduate Student-Staff Liaison (I chaired that too), Doctoral Student-Staff Liaison (me again, as an *ex officio* member in my capacity as Postgraduate Studies Director), Housekeeping (comprising just two members – Doreen and Jeremy), and Community Engagement and Outreach.

But even Committees, if carefully manipulated, easy enough since very few people, other than Jeremy, bothered reading documents or participating in the discussion, always went along with whatever their Chair desired. That, in turn, was almost invariably in line with the HoD's wishes. Still, everyone pursued the illusion that they were participating in decision-making in a democratic and meaningful way. Our perfect system of democratic centralism would have put Lenin to shame.

"Any other business?", Alison asked once all the agenda items had been exhaustively discussed and hung out to dry.

She looked around the room. Jeremy had his hand up.

"There is an issue with the photocopier", he said.

"Jeremy, if we could leave this for later or, even better, if you could take it up with the Housekeeping Committee, that would be great. There's something else, something very important not on the agenda that we need to talk about."

Jeremy conceded defeat, jotted one of his memory prompts on his notebook and sat back in his chair.

Satisfied that no more interruptions were forthcoming, Alison said:

"I'm sure you're all as devastated as I am at what happened to our dear colleague, the tireless Head of our Department, Paul Digby."

"What happened to him?", Jeremy Allcock whispered.

"I'll tell you later", Duncan, who always sat next to him, whispered back.

"I have spoken to Paul's wife Geraldine and passed on the condolences of the whole Department. The funeral will take place in three weeks' time. I will circulate the details once the arrangements have been finalised and we will be suspending teaching on the day to allow all students and colleagues to attend since I'm sure everyone would wish to be there. The Senate will pass a motion in Paul's memory and the Vice Chancellor has agreed that Paul's work for the University should be honoured in due course."

Alison was well known for being very matter-of-fact, come what may and all the way to her attire. With her short hair and two-piece suits, she looked like a bank manager.

Now she had taken her detached manner to a whole new remove. And yet, I didn't think there was anything remarkable about her unemotional delivery. I assumed that, having had a day to register the tragic event, she and everyone else had collected themselves and were ready to move on without any unnecessary sentimentality.

After all, even I was almost ready to carry on as normal.

The morning after the night before, I had woken up groggy, so much so that it had taken me a while to make sure that I hadn't dreamt the whole thing up. The truth of my recall was confirmed by the fact that I was clutching Malinowski's *Crime and Custom in Savage Society.*

As soon as a relatively complete memory of the previous night's events reconstructed itself in my head, I was overwhelmed by a burst of intense restlessness. I paced up and down my apartment for much longer than would be expected of a sane person as I repeatedly mulled over the same two questions.

The first was: "Why did I keep the book?". The only explanation I could think of was that when I left Paul's office, I must have thought it wise to stick to the story that I had invented to explain why I was there in the first place. This, despite the fact that the story in question had been devised for an audience of one, and he was lying dead on the fourth floor of the McKenzie building.

The second question was: "What have I done?". In hindsight, that was a misleading way of putting it. I knew full well what I'd done. What I couldn't come to terms with was how I could have brought myself to do it. How could I have thought it a good idea to forge a promotion application? Why hadn't I come clean to Paul when he turned up? Why hadn't I said it was a silly thing to do and just leave it at that? He was off his face enough to buy it. Why had I remained on to see through my ill-thought plan? And how could I have just left him there?

The one saving grace was that with no teaching on my schedule, I'd 'work from home'. Only no work would be involved and my apartment could hardly be described as home.

I had rented it as soon I'd been offered the job, thinking that by living on campus, I would have easy, round-the-clock access to the library. As always, expectations exceeded reality. In the six years that I'd lived in that apartment, I'd visited the library less than a couple of dozen times and not always for the purposes of studying or borrowing books.

But there I was, still in an institutional, red brick block of flats in a state of perennial temporariness. Most of my belongings were scattered all over the living area. The kitchen was equipped with two saucepans, one kitchen knife, a cheap half-dozen cutlery set and a few glasses. My suitcases lived in the hallway. Deep down, I harboured hopes that the arrangement would be transient and that I'd soon build up my profile and move to a more prestigious university.

After a few coffees, a long shower and a big lunch, I was ready to take stock of the situation. I concluded that for anyone to connect me to Paul's death would require a leap so fantastical as to be almost absurd.

So, the sense of panic at having done wrong began to abate as I set about distancing myself from the event. Do we all not regularly do things that we regret, then sweep them under the carpet and wait until they fade away along with our embarrassment and guilt? That day I was determined to prove that the same applies not just to trivial matters and issues of moderate gravity but also to homicide.

"What exactly *did* happen to him?", Horst Neuberg asked.

"Everything points to it being an accident, a tragic accident", Alison said.

I've often thought about why I then did what I did next. The first thing to remember is that, for all my latter day disenchantment and embitterment, I was, nevertheless, a scholar, and, for me, the discovery of truth took precedence over all else. A vague and inconclusive answer to an important query was sufficient to compel me to dig deeper and, having scrutinised the matter thoroughly, to share the results of my scientific investigation with the community at large.

Perhaps it was also my technique for managing my guilt. After lengthy deliberations in the solitude of my apartment, I had reached the conclusion that coming clean would serve no purpose. If anything, my tardiness in doing so would create a completely false impression and bring my honesty into question. Paul was dead. Nothing would change that. A confession would only cause needless harm.

Nevertheless, despite keeping my feelings of remorse in check and not allowing them to determine my actions, I found that the knowledge that one has played a part in someone's death was rather difficult to keep to oneself. The urge to speak to someone about Paul's death was quite powerful. I can only explain it as a drive to share what I knew like a neutral witness itching to let the world know that he had been present at an important event. Twice, I almost called Nikhil, my closest friend with whom I had shared most things since we first met as doctoral students, but both times I changed my mind. Still, the itch wouldn't leave me.

My reaction was also influenced by the fact that I was sitting next to Catherine.

The day before, when I wasn't revisiting the details of the previous evening's ghastly incident and grappling with what I ought to do next, I had been gripped by thoughts of Catherine. The promotion application to which I had attached mine was hers; the difference being that hers was for promotion to full Professor. Reading the detailed report of her many achievements had made me unbearably envious. She had been in the job for half as long as I had, yet she had published twice as much – including a book. Mine remained in draft stalled at chapter one, by which I mean the only thing in black and white consisted of the words "chapter one". Adding to my pique, she had delivered keynote lectures all over the place, securing competitive funding for her research in the process.

I realised that, jealous as I was of Catherine, I was growing more and more attracted to her. Her determination, her intellectual ability which, and this cannot be said of many academics, did not come at the expense of her social skills, all this and her clarity of thought, I found irresistible and sexy.

Like everyone who's ever been smitten, I wanted Catherine to notice and accept me. I wanted us to have a secret language, a code to which only we were privy. And yet, throughout the Department Meeting, coy and awkward as a boy emerging for the first time from an all-male boarding school and being thrown into a room-full of girls, I hadn't said a word to her. So now, sitting alongside her, I thought here was the ideal opportunity to open my big mouth.

"I guess we'll never find out who's responsible", I whispered in her ear.

She turned around and looked at me. In her eyes I saw alarm and inquisitiveness in equal measure. She could only have seen regret in mine.

❖

The McKenzie building cafeteria was managed by the Students' Union, which probably explained its name: Butty Call. Nevertheless, and against all expectation, it was an oasis of gastronomic quality on campus. The coffee didn't come out of a sachet and the sandwiches had fillings other than butter and bacon.

I sat on a bench by myself, as I often did, savouring my favourite brie and cranberry baguette sandwich. The student traffic around me was so heavy that it seemed improbable that seminar rooms and lecture theatres were ever in use. Some were pacing with a sense of urgency across the Atrium, laptops clutched to their chests, only to be seen within minutes walking just as briskly in the opposite direction. Many more were sitting on the, decidedly uncomfortable but inexplicably popular benches fiddling endlessly with their phones, tablets and laptops.

The architects responsible for redesigning the McKenzie Building a few years back had wanted to *"re-colonise and infuse non-structured communal spaces with a buzzing sense of publicity re-imagining the university as a locus of horizontal other-selfness, where knowledge circulates rather than being harvested, flows rather than being quarried"*. No one had the faintest idea what they were on about but, judging by how many students were stretched out on the benches and the floor, the project of making the place more horizontal was clearly on track.

Catherine gave me a sideways glance as she emerged from the lift and headed towards the Butty Call accompanied by Lucy Warburton.

Having re-entered the Atrium, they parted and Catherine walked in my direction, salad box in hand.

"May I join you?", she said.

"Of course, please do", I said, all the while trying to retrieve the bit of brie I could feel stuck on my bottom lip with the tip of my tongue.

"I wanted to ask you", she said as she struggled to settle herself comfortably on the curved surface of the oval bench, "why did you say that at the meeting earlier?"

"Well, it's just that English Breakfast is richer. I find Earl Grey too weak", I said.

Feigning ignorance didn't buy me as much time as I had hoped. Instead of joining me in engaging in an evaluative comparison between types of tea, Catherine said:

"That's not what I mean. You said we'll never find out who's responsible."

"I did?"

"You did."

"It's been quite a shock, hasn't it?"

"Absolutely, a massive shock. One minute he's there drinking his favourite Sauvignon Blanc with us, the next he's lying dead on his office floor."

"A shock", I muttered.

"Tell me though, do you really think someone is responsible?"

As far as I could see, two options were opening up before me. The first was to play it stupid, say that I didn't know what I was talking about, that I was so affected by the event that I wasn't thinking straight, that it had been a rash thing to say. The danger in that was that I would be so good at playing it stupid that I would actually appear entirely cretinous. That was a risk I couldn't afford to take, not if I wanted Catherine's attention, respect and, eventually, support.

My second option was to stick to my guns, for lack of a better expression, and reiterate my suspicion that there was something fishy about Paul's death but without making too much of it. The upside of that plan was that I would probably get to spend more time with Catherine, whose allure was becoming more magnetic by the second.

"I don't know, maybe what I meant was..."

I wasn't allowed to complete my phrase. She sprang up, grabbed my hand and pulled me to my feet, in a surprising show of body strength.

"Let's go", she urged.

"It's a bit spooky, isn't it?", she exclaimed as we stood outside the door.

She had no clue of the precise extent of the spookiness of the matter. Less than thirty six hours previously, I had exited, leaving that door ajar behind me with Paul's dead body stiffening on the floor.

"Very", I said.

"It was even worse yesterday, with police tape all over the place. They sure know how to make their practices as disruptive as possible to emphasise the extraordinary nature of an event."

Once an anthropologist, always an anthropologist.

She turned the handle and entered the room cautiously.

"Are you sure it's OK to just go in?", I asked.

"Yes, it's fine. They're done."

The room was more or less as I'd left it. The easy chairs that I had kicked aside were still facing the wrong way – I should have thought about rearranging them but it was no big deal. The desk was as tidy as I'd found it. Not a sign remained that anyone else had used it since Paul had sat in his chair for the very last time prior to attending the Scrote reception. The obvious differences were that he and the rock were missing.

Catherine looked around the room.

"The police said it was an accident", she said.

To my surprise, she proceeded to act out a reconstruction of events. Like a caricature of a drunken person, eyes rolling, neck loose, she wobbled into the room with her arms flailing left and right. When she neared the unit on which the rock used to rest, she bumped into it with a thud.

Straightening up, she stared at the shelves for a few seconds. I knew exactly why. The collision had not caused the structure, which was more or less part of the wall, to move one nanometre.

My earlier impetuousness was coming back to bite me. I had to undo it.

In the long years I have spent in universities, I have learnt that the most fool-proof way to trivialise something is to give it an academic veneer. Tragic losses, happy communions, art that makes the heart quiver, take any of them, subject them to academic analysis, corrupt them with jargon, and you drain them of all joy. And that proved to be my way out.

"Listen, I guess what I meant to say earlier was that responsibility is so fluid a concept that ascribing it is always arbitrary. I've no doubt that Paul hit the shelves serendipitously, or whatever the opposite of serendipitously is. He rocked the rock, the rock rolled off the shelf and hit him. What I was saying", I waved my arms around in the way I did when delivering lectures to students, "is that if we don't look for an explanation but we really try to understand Paul's death, we have to cast the net wider. Right? We can only capture it, if we look out, out of this room. In a way, we're all responsible and there's always foul play."

Catherine turned around and looked at me intensely. I not only found her intellect and accomplishments impressive. I was falling under her physical spell – the curly auburn hair, those bright green eyes enlarged by her myopia-compensating glasses, her full lips, her professionally fashionable outfit of high-waisted trousers and a tucked-in statement top that read *Nasty Woman*. The combination was intoxicating.

"Perhaps", she said. "Perhaps."

I devoted the next few days to establishing a sense of order and control. I delivered my scheduled lectures and classes; held my regular office hours with students, most of whom ostensibly wanted to ask me "a few clarifications" about the readings when in fact they were fishing for content for their essays. I worked on some admin, much of it to do with organising an upcoming weekend away from campus with postgraduate students and staff. I even peer-reviewed a textbook proposal on behalf of a publisher, in return for fifty pounds worth of books (such are the perks of the job).

I also tidied up my apartment. To ensure my entire wardrobe was clean, I went through every last item, worn or unworn, washing everything that I found whether neatly hung or draped over furniture. I even gave my woollen jumpers a whirl in the washing machine for the first time in our long-lasting relationship and took my coats and winter suit to be dry-cleaned.

I re-arranged my books, not that there were that many since most were in the office, in thematic order and then alphabetically arrayed within each category. At the end of the tidiness blitz, the flat didn't feel any more like home than it used to but at least I didn't have to tiptoe around coffee mugs, studies of rituals in Punjabi villages or circle-reinventing treatises on agency.

I even opened the document file of my perennially forthcoming book and managed to type the first sentences: "*The bias of ethnographic research is not incidental and contingent upon methodological choices; it is inherent to it. Or at least so will I argue in this book.*"

I was one of those anthropologists who, without ever having set foot in the field, without ever having actually interacted with people, had the temerity to tell those who did empirical work that they were getting it all wrong. I was correct, of course, but even I could concede that, coming from me, a critique of that sort was a bit rich.

It wasn't just a newfound love for the book's subject matter that drove me back to it but rather a renewed sense of purpose. I reckoned that, with Paul out of the way, my clandestinely, self-sponsored promotion would be in the bag. Once Alison found my application attached to Catherine's, she would never question Paul's decision to put me forward regardless of the recommendation of the Promotions Committee. To do so wouldn't merely be dismissive of his judgement; it would be disrespectful to his memory. All in all, if I concentrated on writing the book, which I was determined to do, then completing it, finding a publisher and taking it through to production would require about a year and a half. In that time I would be able to plagiarise myself by carving out chunks of the monograph for publication as freestanding articles. With all that under my belt and barring any extraordinary obstacles, I should be in with a strong chance of being promoted to full Professor in two years' time or, better yet, a move to a Chair at a more prestigious university.

My feelings for Catherine hadn't waned one bit. If anything, they were getting stronger. I knocked on her door more frequently than ever, employing all sorts of implausible excuses – asking what word limit she'd set for student essays, letting her know of a new article that I'd been made aware of, offering her tea – anything to gain her attention. I referred students to her for help making sure to copy her in emails where I had sung her praises for her formidable scholarship.

I could sense that these intrusions were not considered a nuisance. Catherine seemed agreeable to the increased level of contact between us. If anything, I had the impression that she too approached me more often and, it seemed, with growing fervour. In an unprecedented move, she offered *me* tea, English Breakfast too, one day when we happened to bump into each other in the departmental kitchen (of course, it wasn't a coincidental – I'd seen her make her way there and quickly followed).

So it didn't come as a complete surprise when I received an email from her with nothing but "drink tonight?" in the subject line. I replied, perhaps too enthusiastically, "Re: Sure! Where and when?". "Re: Re: The Montgomery Arms, 6.30".

I cannot overstate my excitement at her suggestion that we meet outside campus. I wasn't getting my hopes up but surely the choice of venue made it more of a date than a meeting between colleagues.

The Montgomery Arms was located along the B-road that led to the village closest to campus. Whoever designed its interior must have modelled it on their very shakey impression of what they believed historic pubs in ancient and much more famous university towns looked like – ye olde inns and taverns they'd never seen, much less visited. The room was wood-panelled from carpet-covered floor to tiled ceiling. The Mock Tudor effect (Pseudor as I liked to call it), the last thing a novice punter walking up the gravelled, cigarette butt-littered pathway to an 1980s building would have expected, was replete with copper cooking pots and pans that hung from the ceiling. Some were so low that they posed a real threat to the physical wellbeing of anyone above average height. The walls were decorated with photos of literary and academic figures, none likely to have ever visited the area, let alone patronise the pub their portraits bedecked. The gallery of mock regulars ranged from George Orwell to Iris Murdoch and from Isaac Newton to Stephen Hawking.

Catherine placed our drinks on the small round table and sat next to me on a sofa sticky with past spillage.

"Thanks", I said, moving my leg almost imperceptibly in hopes that it would brush up against hers.

"To our health", she said and clinked her glass against mine.

"How was your day?", I asked.

Such a wonderful, casual, after-work meeting between two people with a lot more than work to share this was turning out to be.

"Fine, I guess", she said.

"Is something wrong?"

"I can't pretend I'm not still rattled by what happened."

Elated as I was about our one-to-one, everything else had receded into the background, so much so that I was about to ask what had happened when, fortunately, Catherine spoke first, saving me from what would have been an inexplicable faux pas.

"And I'm still thinking about what you said the other day", she said.

"Are you?"

"I am", she said followed by a contemplative pause, which I thought wise not to interrupt. "You know my first book, right?"

Her hand landed on my thigh sending an anticipatory quiver sprinting through my nervous system.

"Of course I do", I said, cool as possible, given the circumstances. "It's a brilliant book. Brilliant."

I hadn't actually read it but that is never an obstacle when passing along academic praise where praise might or might not be due.

"I thought you didn't much care for empirical work", she said.

"Yours is different, yours is good empirical work. In fact, it goes well beyond the empirical."

"Right, anyway, you know it was an ethnographic study of the professional end of the criminal justice system in a London borough. I looked at the practices of police officers, coroners, magistrates, lawyers, pathologists, the lot."

"As I said, brilliant."

"But I've been blind to something very important, something that became painfully clear to me after our conversation the other day."

"What's that?", I said, a slight sense of trepidation offsetting the puff of pride that swelled in my chest on learning that somehow I had illuminated her.

"The discrepancy between lay and official perceptions."

"Oh, that", I said.

"Yes, that. It's massive, don't you see? It is now crystal clear to me that officials only see one side of the story and their perspective is skewed by the fact that they have to operate within systemic, institutional constraints. People, however, experience crime in a completely different way.

"That is absolutely true", I said.

It really was.

"That asymmetry has to be accounted for. Otherwise our anthropological knowledge of crime will be incomplete at best or altogether distorted and wrong at worst."

"We wouldn't want that now, would we?"

"I've been looking for a long-term project for a while and all of a sudden it presents itself to me."

"What's that then?"

"I told you."

"I mean, can you tell me in some more detail?"

"I propose to study the perspective on crime that agents on the ground assume. But this time I will take a phenomenological tack. Are you familiar with the recent phenomenological turn in the field?"

"Sure, yes."

She gave me a disbelieving glance that was not altogether unjustified.

"The point is to recover the body as the locus of all experience and enquiry into the world. Our situatedness, our immanence is both a constraint and an emancipatory conduit into the world of appearances. See the paradox there? We can only view the world through this body and yet this body will never be the same as the world nor can we have an independent perception of the body."

"Your body, my world", I let slip.

"Precisely", she said, unfazed. "And when there is a disruptive event, such as a crime, the continuity between body and world is put under stress. What is the unmediated perception of crime? What are its limitations and what does it produce? That's what I want to find out."

My word, it all sounded so incredibly clever.

"So what do you propose to do?"

"I'll use Paul's death as a case study."

"Hold on", I said possibly a little too hastily. "I thought that wasn't a crime."

"Exactly. That's what the police say. But look at your reaction to it; the exact opposite. What was there that made you doubt it?"

"I don't know. Nothing in particular. I didn't exactly doubt it anyway."

"Only it wasn't nothing, of course, and you did express a doubt. That was caused by something, by your embodied perception of phenomena."

To be accurate, it was a book and a rock that had made me question the official story but I got her gist.

"Yes, I see your point", I said.

"Which is why I want us to do this together."

Be still my beating heart and the rest of my anatomy! She wanted us to experience the world together with our bodies. If that was not a thinly disguised message, I don't know what would be. 'Yes, experience my body!', I wanted to shout but contained myself.

"That'd be great", I said with as much professional sangfroid as I could muster.

It really would be great not only because I would get closer to her than ever but also because working on a project with one of the foremost rising stars of the discipline might do more for my career even than finishing my own book.

"Fantastic", she exclaimed with her arms stretched. "I've already been in touch with the editors of the *Journal of Phenomenological Anthropology* and they're enthusiastic about the idea."

"Excellent", I said, trying to disguise that I had never heard of the *Journal of Phenomenological Anthropology*.

"How about we meet one of those days and crack on? The sooner the better."

"Sure. So exciting."

We need a trajectory

I meant to read up on phenomenological anthropology before Catherine and I embarked on our joint research project. And, like every time in the recent past when the opportunity to learn something new had arisen, my best laid schemes went agley and straight down the toilet.

Not exactly out of laziness; but I had developed a scholarly manière, a personal style that entailed flogging to death the same literature that had seen me through my doctoral student years. It involved regurgitating the same point in a sustained stream of microscopically different variations, while taking the same tack on every imaginable question under the sun.

I wasn't alone in that. Once their youthful ambition of Renaissance all-roundedness subsides, most academics become one-trick ponies. In a way, this makes academia a more predictable, and therefore slightly more bearable, place. Go to any academic seminar and, if you know the participants, you will know in advance what they will say, the questions they will ask, even the manner in which they will deliver their points. Professor This will invariably want to hear more about the interdisciplinary implications of the research presented. Dr That will express outrage at the absence of the sexuality angle. Dr Suchandsuch will dub everything 'performative'. Professor Other's question will inevitably be introduced with a self-deprecatory ode redolent of false modesty ("I can't be trusted to understand such clever points" or "I hope I'm not misconstruing your excellent argument") before proceeding to bore all and sundry with the specifics of his own most recent article. Curveballs are only ever thrown by junior colleagues yet to find their niche and I was well past that exploration stage. I had a voice, such as it was, and was sticking to it. In my defence, at least I wasn't one of those who make a virtue of being typecast, pretending that being set in their ways was the true mark of commitment to a lifetime project devoted to making a lasting contribution to knowledge.

I also couldn't get past the word 'phenomenology' itself. Whenever it did occlude my thoughts, I felt the urge to pronounce it by holding my nose and that ensured I couldn't take it seriously any longer.

There was one more thing that accounted for my failure to do any background research. Catherine would do it for me and she would do it much better than I ever could or would have been able to. She was also much more likely to understand it.

"The idea", she said at our first research meeting, "is to revisit the topos."

"The what?", I interrupted.

"Sorry, it's Greek for place, location, scene."

The gratuitous use of Latin or, even better, Greek is always guaranteed to add gravitas. And, by the gods, was Catherine good at that.

"And record our reactions, our lived sense of time and space, gauge how our embodiment..."

Every time she said 'embodiment' I felt the same tingle in undeterminable parts of my whole being.

"...is placed in that environment, becomes part of the scene..."

I was concerned that she kept using the word 'scene' but I told myself not to get paranoid about what must surely be nothing more than a mere placeholder.

"...reimagines it and, in doing so, performatively transforms it."

"So, we will be observing ourselves? Isn't that a bit unusual?"

"But that's the point, don't you see? Two birds with one stone. By employing methodological heterodoxy..."

More gravitas.

"...we will transcend the limits of anthropological knowledge through the ever-increasing but doomed never to be completed convergence with experience."

"Genius", I said, making a mental note to consider later what any of that might mean. "So where do we start?"

"At the Scrote, of course."

I doubt there are official statistics attesting to this but I would not be surprised if it transpired that most academic ideas are initially conceived in a bar. In our case, it seemed perfectly fitting that we should start where we started.

The Scrote was a little too busy considering that it was still early afternoon. The usual patrons were lined up next to each other leaning against the bar. Barry, owner of the campus bookshop that sold way fewer books than he bought pints; Dom, a builder who had worked on the McKenzie Building reconstruction and had somehow forgotten to leave once the job was done; Ed, whose employment status no one, not even Barry and Dom, knew. A few students were having an animated discussion as they sifted through the academic papers on the table in front of them. Two academics, too old and cynical to even pretend they could keep up with the developing demands of the job yet still compelled to be campus-bound while idly awaiting an even less rigorous retirement, sipped cheap cognac and spoke not a word.

"My round", I said.

"We're not drinking", she said.

"Aren't we?"

"Actually, there is some disagreement in the methodological literature as to how far in the topos one should immerse oneself. On reflection, I think we should stay sober."

"Maybe on the way back", I said.

"So, look around and consider the space. I'll do the same. Remember that we're not trying to capture our subjective experience but become part of the scene."

Scene.

"I'll try", I said, not having the least clue about what I was meant to do.

"What's your initial reaction?"

"The smell of stale beer is stronger in daytime."

"OK, that's a good start. It's true too. Quite overwhelming."

"I guess the smell of the evening crowd disguises it."

"Maybe. Anyway, concentrate on our task."

"What about you? What's your perception?"

"There's an intensity about the Scrote that I hadn't felt before."

"Maybe it's Barry's eau de toilette or Dom's absence thereof."

"Don't be silly. There's something different about the place."

"Is your knowledge of the past not prejudicing your impression?"

"Not consciously, that's for sure. But even if it is, that's fine, we're not here to erase the past but to capture it, relive it and paradoxically turn it into the future through a new narrative."

"OK, I'll give this a go. The pub is a leveller, it conceals inequality and injustice."

"Carry on", she said with interest.

"Everyone has the same resources and needs: alcohol and a desire to drink."

"So, it would follow that external conflict cannot be imported into the pub. Pub fights are either entirely primordial or rooted in events in the pub itself; a brawl over a spilled drink, an inappropriate look, that sort of thing. Otherwise they're entirely out of place, absurd."

"I guess that would follow."

"Revenge does not square with leisure."

"Revenge?"

"I'm using it as shorthand. You know what I mean."

I didn't but nodded anyway.

"Crime as a private matter is not intelligible here. The pub is the pure and original public space", Catherine continued and pulled out her notepad from the canvas tote bag in which she always carried her belongings. "I like that idea, let's keep it".

She jotted something down and snapped her small notebook shut pulling the elastic strap over the cover.

My contribution that far had been minimal and I felt embarrassed. I had to step it up.

"We need a trajectory", I said.

"Good idea", she cut me short and headed to the exit, which was just as well because I would have struggled to complete my thought.

The rain had started again. Catherine produced an umbrella from her magic bag. It was obviously a struggle for her to hold it above my head, which was quite a bit higher than hers, but I didn't dare risking patronising her by offering a helping hand.

"You're absolutely right", she said. "Every instance of violence has a trajectory. Not just a causal, linear sequence of events. It is an experiential bundle of facts and senses and things both dimensional and non-dimensional, all seemingly isolated but connected in the shadow of the event."

"That's exactly what I meant", I said without a hint of sarcasm.

"The trouble is that our access into the event can only be direct and linear."

"You mean we should take the mudfield?"

"Fantastic idea", she said and wrapped her arm around mine. "Let's do it."

The more our feet sank in the mud at every step, the more firmly we clung to each other. So concerned was Catherine about soiling her shoes – ballet pumps were admittedly a bad choice of footwear for the weather – that she was almost hanging from my arm. I'd never thought I'd see her admit that much need for assistance. Not that I was going to complain.

"I don't normally go through here, do you?", she said when we emerged at the other side of the mudfield.

"When I'm in a hurry, which is pretty much always."

"Do you?", she said almost astonished. "Well, I can see now that it's a transformative experience."

"Especially for your shoes."

My jesting was met with a disapproving look and her facial expression turned stern.

"Every culture I can think of pictures death as a journey across a liminal space that defies definition, a space of fear, where matter loses its substance, it becomes weightless and yet real."

She really was exceptionally clever.

"The mudfield is a passageway?"

"That's how it feels. We have moved from the self-containment of the pub, where no conflict has sense, to the mudfield, where all conflict concentrates. It's an angry place, the mudfield."

I wanted to tell her that she was wrong, that the mudfield was a passage alright but that it was filled with hope, not rage.

It didn't best please me that for the second time since Paul's death, I was back standing in his office, again with Catherine by my side. It had to be done though.

"They haven't cleared it yet", I said.

"Geraldine will tell us after the funeral what to do with his belongings. There's no one designated to move in yet anyway."

"Is Alison not keeping the gig for good?"

"No way. She's just taking care of things until we select a new HoD."

Paul, eight years in the post, had had no plans to step down nor had anyone in the Department or the University made any noises about replacing him. Much as he complained about being drowned in admin, he enjoyed being Head. True, his research had grown atrophic, to put it generously, while as an administrator he was effective, to put it even more generously. This combination of talents, if such they were, was rare, so replacing him would not be easy. I, for one, could not think of anyone who might want to take on the HoD job.

"So, here's where the trajectory peaks", Catherine said suddenly reverting to our mission. "This is a place that is not a place."

"Not for Paul anyway", I said on compulsion but was wise enough to mumble it so as not to provoke Catherine's wrath.

"And time, can you feel it? Time here is suspended."

"Is it?", I asked resisting the temptation to check my watch.

"Yes, absolutely. Death is timeless."

"Gotcha."

"But crime isn't. Crime is an act that cannot exist outside its temporal limits."

"So that means there is no crime, I guess."

That ontological contradiction could have brought our brief adventure in phenomenological anthropology to a beautiful end and signalled an even more beautiful beginning to our partnership. If only we were on a stage for me to draw the curtain or on a book page for me to write THE END underneath us.

"That's strange", Catherine said staring at the floor.

"What is?", I asked.

"The stains."

She was gripped by our muddy footprints on the floor.

"Why is it strange? They'll come off eventually. They deep-clean the carpets twice a year", I said.

"Yes but..."

"But what?"

"Nothing, nothing."

The Law Department liked to affirm its possession of the whole first floor of the McKenzie Building, as well as a substantial section of the second floor, with passive aggressive notes affixed to every possible surface from office and meeting room doors to kitchen cabinets. Without quite telling you so, it was quite clear that use of facilities by outsiders was prohibited or permitted on a strictly short-term basis. Whenever someone dared question their entitlement, Law people repeated ad nauseam that they attracted the largest number of students and therefore generated the highest income among all other Departments in the University. Invariably the Medical School would take issue with that claim and then scalpels and gavels would fly all around campus while the rest of us innocent and generally disinterested bystanders ducked and watched.

Nigel's office floor was stacked with decade-old literary-cum-political periodicals, a couple of piles of criminal law textbooks which an A4 note atop them declared were OUT OF DATE, and a mound of empty cardboard boxes discarded from book deliveries.

Fairly certain that what he had mumbled was an invitation for me to take a seat, I took one of the easy chairs opposite him.

"I need your advice on something", I said.

He said something unintelligible, which I assumed to have been no more than a pleasantry.

"It's about a criminal law matter."

"{mutter mutter mutter} anthropologists {mutter mutter mutter} advice {mutter mutter mutter} crime {mutter}."

"Well, you know anthropology deals with non-compliant behaviour a lot so it makes sense to come to you for help", I said taking a wild guess at what he had said.

Seeking Nigel's assistance in my situation might seem an odd decision given that I could barely understand where his sentences began and ended. Yet what choice did I have, where else could I have gone? I was hardly going to navigate the murky waters of the law by myself. I needed the kind of clarity that only an expert could provide. Seeing a practitioner would have been an option but a risky one. Speaking to a colleague would allow me to disguise the question as something academic-related. Plus, I could claim that I knew Nigel reasonably well. All things considered, it was worth the effort of trying to decipher his answers.

"A friend of a student of mine is in a bit of a tight spot. He was involved in a tragic event and now he's worried about his legal position."

"{mutter mutter mutter} details."

"My understanding is that he had gone into his flatmate's room to do something entirely innocent. I think it was to borrow an electrical appliance of some sort. By an unfortunate twist of fate, he dropped said appliance in the tub while his friend was having a bath. I'm afraid that the friend died."

Nigel scratched his chin. I was becoming a tad anxious that the scenario I had made up stretched credence and the listener's capacity for credulity beyond the realms of reasonableness.

"I should have clarified that the appliance was still plugged in", I added.

"{mutter mutter mutter} mean to drop {mutter mutter mutter}."

"What if he did?"

"Murder!", he said clearly and unequivocally.

"And if he didn't?"

"{mutter mutter mutter}"

"Sorry, Nigel, could you say this more slowly please? The law bamboozles me a bit."

"I'd need more details but the way you describe it, it sounds like an accident."

I was dumbfounded at the unexpectedly perfect elocution. So, he could actually enunciate when he applied himself. Or perhaps I had cracked the matrix with my heightened concentration.

"So, he'd be in the clear?"

"That's the thing with criminal liability, you see. It's not fine-tuned enough. It can't capture the subtle permutation of..."

I had to interrupt him before he went all academic on me. What I needed were concrete answers.

"Sure but can we concentrate on the boy's trouble? Would he

be in the clear if he only accidentally dropped a live appliance in the bath with his friend?"

"What did he do after the incident?"

"I think he fled."

"Bad idea."

"Why?"

"It's an evidential matter. Easier for prosecution to prove intention that way."

"I see", I said, though, in fact, my eyesight was getting a bit blurred.

"What's the penalty for murder, Nigel?"

"Life. Minimum fifteen or thereabout. Does the boy have any defences?"

"Meaning?"

Nigel let out an exasperated sigh, which he must have perfected over a lifetime's teaching first year law students.

"Was he hard done by the victim? Was he angry for some reason?"

"How angry are we talking here?"

"Very."

"And for good reason?"

"That'd help."

"Not sure."

"Did he have any mental health issues?"

"Not really", I said. "I mean, I don't know. I'll have to ask my student. Would it help if he did?"

"Could have it reduced to manslaughter. Much better."

"How much better?"

"Not life, to start with."

"I guess that is better. Anyway, Nigel, I don't want to keep you any longer. You've been tremendously helpful, thank you."

As I was about to exit the room, I turned around and asked:

"Nigel, just out of interest. Where are you from?"

I didn't catch the answer.

I tended to avoid conferences. I had come to find them insufferable. The atmosphere was always thick with a combination of self-assurance and earnestness, which, being incompatible polar opposites, caused a series of explosions, mainly in the souls of participants.

Conferences weren't even particularly informative either. If I ever wanted to listen to doctoral students reshuffle other people's words in ways that they considered original never stopping to consider whether they were meaningful, or hear established scholars microwave and serve reheated a recycled mush of the ideas they first built their reputations on... Well, the unadorned answer is no – I would not want to witness either, ever.

There was, however, an expectation, almost an unwritten contractual requirement, in my Department that we all attended at least one conference per year. Something to do with maintaining an active research presence, a policy that I of course resented but grudgingly allowed that it was best that I comply with. So, as I did every year, I duly registered for the annual meeting of the Anthropology and Social Theory Association in London, arguably the least painful of such occasions.

It had been six months since I'd signed up, snapping up the early bird discount. As the prospect of delivering a paper at the approaching conference loomed nearer and nearer, I would shoo it away with a convulsive jerk, busying myself with a thousand ways of draft-dodging.

Now that the moment I had been dreading for so long had arrived, I was actually relieved and grateful for the convenient timing. My conversation with Nigel had forced me to look at my situation in a different light. There was something about describing things in the technical language of law that was particularly scary. It left very little room for moral argument. Putting some distance between events and myself would afford me the time to think things over.

I was still unprepared for the academic obligations associated with conference participation but, not for the first time, I planned to wing it.

Being in London always makes me wonder why anyone would want to be an academic in such a magnificent city rather than actually living it. I could half-understand wanting to brain-stray in a leafy, muddy campus such as mine but hiding away from London was just inexcusable. There were, of course, the perks: the flexi work hours; the London allowance upping one's salary as academics rarely need to use it on daily commuting or any of the other mundane necessities that normal people have to face; the seemingly infinite number of cafés, where one could sit and look ponderous, preoccupied with refining the intricacies of one's latest earth-shattering theory. Still, these were unconvincing and admittedly less than noble reasons for wasting one's time in London in a University.

The tube spewed me out along with hundreds of commuters whose existence was confirmed by their instinctual ability with which they negotiated the London public transport system and tourists whose sense of self-worth was challenged by their inability to do the same. When I surfaced I felt like I had just been hatched and, like every newborn, excitement and apprehension coursed through me as I prepared to face that vast, overwhelming world that awaited me. And I relished the feeling.

On the short walk to the conference venue, I must have been surrounded by more people than I had seen on my campus in the past year. Add to that an insane number of cars and buses. It took me a good half a minute to cut through the pedestrian traffic on the footpath in order to turn left off the main thoroughfare.

When I finally succeeded, I was transposed to a different world, one not altogether different to mine, just busier and less muddy. Every building bore a University logo and most of those entering them seemed propelled by a bored air of futile urgency.

The building in which the conference was being held was heavily signposted – no doubt the result of many hours of free student labour – but it would have been impossible to miss anyway. The anthropology crowd, instantly recognisable, had already congregated in front of the venue door. As always, they were reluctant to walk inside when they could cluster like vampires waiting for an invitation. Some were smoking, by far the most plausible procrastination tactic, and the rest were pretending to keep smokers company.

Academic expertise and status tends to correlate directly to sartorial styles so one knows that those wearing hiking boots work in the field, men sporting open neck shirts and women in vintage outfits do theory, usually of the critical variety, and those in ill-fitting suits are students.

"Michael", Nikhil shouted jumping out of the crowd. "How's it going, buddy? Long time no speak."

"Sorry, too busy. All's well. Good to see you."

"Wouldn't miss this for the world, you know that."

"But will happily miss the world for it."

"Still not taking your cynicism medication, are you?"

"It's terminal so what's the point?"

"Which session are you in?"

"I've no idea. Haven't even looked at the programme yet."

"Come on, let's go register", Nikhil said and pulled me by the arm.

The doctoral students staffing the registration desk were eager to give us our name tags, goody bags and instructions. So wide were their smiles that I had little doubt that that very evening they would get together in the pub and dissect and disparage every single conference participant for our academic worth, our clothes, our table manners. One has to live with that. Nikhil and

I and all our contemporaries did it at that age and so did people before us and now it was the turn of the next generation. The succession game is brutal and bloody.

The first session was a keynote lecture by one of the iconic professors of the host Department. The marker of good academic speakers is how well they can deflect attention from the banality of the content of their talk. She excelled at that. Her address was full of anecdotes, which she weaved through some arguments that she'd been making all her career, and reminiscences from her time as a researcher in North Africa. Hats off to the organisers for a perfectly anodyne opening.

As it turned out, my presentation was scheduled for that afternoon so I skipped the sessions after the keynote to check into my bed and breakfast and finish cobbling together the ideas that I'd jotted down on the train to London.

I returned to the conference for the 'light sandwich' lunch. Had it not been for the fact that I'd been on the road since six that morning and hadn't eaten anything, I wouldn't have bothered joining the queue of people congregated at the counter, comparing the spread to the food available at their home institutions and, having finally settled on what met their dietary requirements, continued their conversations, their mouths full, as they clogged the service area in a bottleneck no one dared challenge out of misplaced collegial courtesy.

Having finally secured a few sandwich quarters on my wobbly paper plate, I went looking for Nikhil. He was with colleagues some of whom I vaguely recognised, others I'd never met before. I quietly ate my lunch while they chewed on more substantial fare such as the effects on academia of the UK's withdrawal from the European Union, the anthropology of Facebook and Twitter and the latest developments in their respective fields, in other words the current gossip at their Universities.

"I'm sorry to hear about Paul Digby", said Ursula, the tall, wholesome and rather striking German.

I knew that Alison had spread the word via one of those indiscriminate international mailing lists, where anyone can post anything (and where a disconcertingly large number accidentally circulate personal, often embarrassingly so, emails) but I'd never had imagined that anyone so far afield would care enough about it to remember the news.

"Thanks. It's been a hard time for us", I said.

"Has it? My understanding is that at least one of your colleagues is nonchalant about it."

"Who would that be?", I asked.

"Horst and I were post-docs together a few years back. I remained in Germany but he left."

"Getting an academic post is a dog-eat-dog affair in Germany", Nikhil said.

"I wouldn't say that. It's simply a meritocratic system of job allocation. If you're good enough, you stay in Germany. If not, you go abroad", Ursula said.

I wondered whether she was even aware of how many people she had managed to offend in one breath. It was really quite admirable.

"Horst is a very good colleague", I said.

"Is he? We two don't see eye to eye, to put it mildly. His news reaches me through common acquaintances", Ursula said.

"What did happen to Digby anyway?", asked the man who sounded like Captain Hastings from a 1980s radio adaptation of Poirot and whose name and affiliation I'd instantly forgotten after having been introduced to him.

"An accident", I said. "A rather tragic accident."

Generally speaking, there are three reasons for choosing one session over the several parallel ones at an academic conference. The first is that you are genuinely interested in what the speakers have to say. That applies only to the inexperienced and still earnest conference-goer. Second, one of the speakers is a big cheese and you want to impress them with a clever if sycophantic question, which has the added benefit of granting you the liberty to accost them about your work for the rest of the conference. That accounts for roughly sixty five per cent of session attendees. Third, the flipside of reason number two. You want to establish or assert power by targeting the weaker. Not the obviously vulnerable, however. Everyone would consider it bad form to maul, say, a first year doctoral student, fragile enough to crumble under the pressure of your difficult questions.

I assumed that those who had turned up at my exceptionally well-attended session were there for reason two. Of the three of us on the panel, one was the editor of one of the most prestigious journals in the field.

During the first talk I went over my notes. I would mitigate the rudeness of not paying attention to the speaker by catching up with what she had said in the joint q&a session at the end. I would then tell her how fascinating her work was by bringing up one of her points as proof of my alertness. All that was required was that someone ask her a question giving her the opportunity to ramble on about her paper all over again.

"Our second speaker this afternoon is Dr Michael West. Michael has published on...", never having heard of me before the panel chair looked down at his notes, "...a variety of themes over the years. Today he'll speak to us about 'Responsibility and Anthropology'. Michael, the floor is yours."

I had provided the non-committal title at sign-up without giving it much thought at the time. My vague plan was to come up with some gibberish on theory about theory, meta-theory as it is called in our circles, opening the door to an infinite room of mirrors, a meta-meta-world of navel-gazing.

While thinking things over the night before and on the way to London, however, I had realised that I could perhaps make more of the occasion. The more I thought about it, the more the conference seemed like a perfect opportunity for me to jump out of my niche and to launch my new research agenda. And when I say 'my' agenda I mean it, and there's no better word for it, performatively. It would become mine because I would announce it at the conference rather than the other way around.

"Social and cultural anthropology has, from its very inception as a discipline, been preoccupied with the question of responsibility and blame. Too frequently, however, we focus on institutional attitudes to holding people accountable. In doing so, we fail to consider something of the first importance, namely the embodied experience of crime and responsibility. What I want to do today is to outline the theoretical framework of my work in progress on precisely that matter."

The audience shuffled forward in their seats and clicked open their goody bag pens.

"Your presentation made ripples. It's the talk of the conference", Nikhil said.

"I'm glad people enjoyed it", I said.

"Your false modesty is too transparent. I didn't know you were working on phenomenology. When did that start?"

"Recently."

"What brought it about?"

"Impatience with the same old crap. How was your session anyway?"

"Can't forget it quickly enough. Too much postmodern rambling about seeing the unseeable and speaking the unspeakable and doing the undoable. And now we have to drink the undrinkable."

He raised his glass of institutional plonk that was fuelling the conference reception.

"So, tell me all about Digby's death."

"There's not much to say", I said.

"Don't be so bloody blasé about it. It's the most exciting thing to have happened in social anthropology since that guy from Norway was researching a BDSM club and was left tied up to a bed and ball-gagged for two days."

"I thought that was the stuff of myth."

"It's true. I've met him."

"What was he like?"

"Twitchy. So, tell me about Digby."

"Everyone at my Department is composed. Life goes on."

"How about that Horst?"

"What about him?"

"How did he take it?"

"I don't know. Dispassionately, I guess. Like he takes most things."

"He was all but dispassionate talking about Digby last time I saw him."

"What do you mean?"

"We had him over to give a seminar a few months ago."

"How was his talk?"

"Fairly inoffensive but that's not the issue. After having had a few at the after-talk dinner, he let loose."

"What was he saying?"

"Neuberg had this article that he couldn't get published anywhere and he maintained that it was because Digby had blocked it. Putting pressure on editors and all that."

"Why would Paul have done that?"

"Apparently Neuberg criticised him in said article."

"Criticised what? Paul hadn't written anything worth criticising in over a decade, if he ever did."

"Maybe that's why he wanted to suppress Neuberg's piece. Just as he thought he had found his safe haven of unnoticeable mediocrity, along comes one of his own to turn the spotlight on him."

"It's interesting that Horst saw it fitting to tell you about it."

"Not just me. There were a good ten people at the dinner. And he pulled no punches, I'll tell you that."

"For example?"

"He started off rather gently, all things considered, calling Digby a vulgar functionalist or words to the effect."

"Fightin' talk", I said with a chuckle.

"It got worse. In the end he was so angry that he became almost incoherent. He called Digby a dictator and accused him of all sorts of transgressions."

"Of what kind?"

"Of *all* kinds. Sadly, he didn't divulge any details."

"Interesting."

"Do you believe it?"

"There's little I have difficulty believing these days", I said.

The precise extent of how impressed the conference audience had been by my talk was only revealed to me when, on my return home from London, I was met by over fifty new emails, mainly, but not exclusively, from conference participants. They were asking for more information, suggesting things to read, sending me their own work because they "thought that it resonates with your research project". Ursula had written with as much enthusiasm as her character allowed her to muster, asking me for the text of the talk, however rough and bullet-point riddled it might be. So few had taken against it ("egocentric drivel", "where's the anthropology in all that?") that it didn't even bother me. The torrent of interest that my paper had attracted made the haters negligible.

I replied to every single email, even the negative ones, and with each reply I came up with something new, if fairly modest, to add to the original idea. I then fastidiously recorded those ideas, as well as colleagues' suggestions and references to the literature, all of them in separate, thoughtfully titled documents classified under subfolders of exponentially increasing specificity.

For the first time since completing my doctorate, research was not a chore. I was enjoying it without worrying as to whether it would be liked or approved by the powers that be. But, as ever, there was no shortage of wet blankets to dampen my mood.

First of all, in the quiet time of calm and uninterrupted contemplation that the trip to London had afforded me, I had weighed up my options. On the one hand, there was the value of spending time with Catherine, while also trying to wrong-foot her and dispel any possible suspicion, for which I only had myself to blame, that some kind of wrongdoing played a part in Paul's death. On the other hand, there were risks involved in revisiting the events of the night of his death even if using the false pretence that it was for purposes of research. Caught in the eye of the storm, there seemed to be no daylight between the two options. Now, after London, light years separated them in my mind. The most sensible thing to do would be to drop the whole matter and somehow try to persuade Catherine to do likewise.

Yet, what had started as pretence had now gained a new dynamic. Appropriating Catherine's ideas was reinvigorating my career. It was an unexpected turn of events but I relished it so much that it made my mouth water. I couldn't bring myself to give it up without at least seeing how far I could take it.

The trouble was that, to pursue my new research programme, I needed Catherine. I was making modest progress with my own input but there were no two ways around the fact that I could never match her erudition and imaginativeness.

There was also the question of whether I should tell Catherine that I had jumped the gun and spoken about our research at the conference. If I did, I would also have to disclose that I hadn't once mentioned her name. I hadn't meant to plagiarise her, it just seemed easier to present everything as my own work. The response, admittedly, had been flattering and I was now reluctant to understate my role and relinquish the success. So, the consequences of either telling Catherine or continuing to withhold all that information were each potentially disastrous.

Therefore, after painstaking consideration of all the options, I did what every proper academic would do: I didn't change a thing and carried on as before, kicking the dilemma as far into the long grass as I could.

"My dear boy, how are you?", Duncan Erskine-Bell said, walking into my office without bothering to knock.

"I wish you didn't call me 'my dear boy', Duncan. It sounds like you're grooming me."

"But I *am* grooming you, my dear boy. Not for the vulgar pursuits you might have in mind obviously – you know I'm not that way inclined – but for greater things, much greater things."

"Which way are you inclined then?"

"Nosiness is not becoming, dear boy."

"I thought it was our job to be nosy."

"I fear you might have misunderstood the meaning of intellectual curiosity."

"A bit rich coming from you, that. Anyway, you're early."

"Only a wee bit."

"Ten minutes."

"I had nothing better to do than spend an extra ten minutes with my favourite colleague."

"You mean you had nothing else to do."

"You're so brutally uncharitable."

"I thought that was part of the job too."

"Now now, we're a Department in mourning, we must be nice to one another."

"I'm not so sure about that."

"Which part?"

"Both."

"Is that so?"

"I can think of at least one person who might be happy about Paul's death."

"Surely it is not I, Rabbi?"

"You said so."

"I did? I don't recall doing so."

"No, Duncan, it's not you. But perhaps not everyone is as upset as you might think."

"Pray tell, dear boy."

"Is nosiness unbecoming no longer?"

"Touché."

"Anyway, forget about it, it's nothing."

Duncan looked intrigued and, if his frowning and staring out of the window was anything to go by, now pensively preoccupied.

"Well, Paul was HoD for such a long time that it's not unimaginable that he would have displeased some people. But enough for one to welcome his demise? I don't know", he said eventually.

"Have you started without me?", Doreen said as she knocked on the door and walked in.

"No, do come in, Doreen. Duncan popped in early for a catch-up, that's all."

"Is there a lot to catch up on?", she asked.

"More than I had imagined", Duncan said.

"Anyway, I only have quarter of an hour so let's get cracking. Some of us have real jobs, you know."

"You're in employment thanks to us, my dear, don't forget that", Duncan said.

"Have you not been keeping up with how you're not supposed to speak to female co-workers?"

"Change is not my bag."

"Alright, let's get started before the Union barges in on us", I said. "Doreen, would you like to tell us where we're at?"

"So, the venue's been booked for the last weekend of January."

"We'll freeze again", Duncan said.

"It was the only slot they could give us."

"The only slot they ever give us", I said.

"That place is beastly", Duncan said.

"It's a stately home and students love it", I said. "Plus it's our cheapest option."

"Quelle surprise", Duncan said.

"Duncan, if you wanted weekend junkets at the Ritz rather than mildly uncomfortable charitable organisations, you should have gone into banking", Doreen said.

"It's not the Ritz I'm after. Just a place with heating suitable for human beings and keys on the doors", Duncan said.

"The lack of locks is for safety reasons", Doreen said.

"Let's carry on", I interrupted. How many colleagues have signed up?"

"Quite a lot already, actually. Jeremy..."

"Has he requested the room with the bathtub in the middle of the humongous bathroom yet?", Duncan interrupted.

"Of course he has."

"That bathroom is bigger than my flat", I said.

"He loves that bathroom", Duncan said.

"So, as I was saying, Jeremy will be there, Alison, Horst, Catherine..."

"Catherine is coming?", I asked.

"She said she's never been and felt bad."

"Thomas is a maybe and so is Lucy. And the pair of you naturally."

That was a surprisingly high number of takers. In fact, it was everyone.

"How about the academic programme?", I asked.

"Oh must we have one of those? Can't it be an entirely social occasion?"

"You know the deal, Duncan", Doreen said. "The Director of the Mansion will go berserk if we don't have educational activities and we'll never be allowed back."

"And that's a bad thing, is it?"

"Don't start again. Doreen, academic programme, please?"

"I'm still waiting for you to suggest a keynote lecturer. The other sessions are more or less sorted. We'll have a 'meet the researcher' event with our staff showcasing their work."

"Who's volunteered for that?", I asked.

"Horst and Catherine so far but we need one more. Duncan?"

"I don't research and tell, darling."

"Catherine?", I asked.

"She told me just yesterday actually. We'll also have presentations by doctoral and Master's students. The president of their society is herding them. He'll send me a list soon."

"Ghastly, ghastly", Duncan said.

"That will be a bit ghastly, I'll give you that", I mumbled.

"I can work with one snob but two is too many", Doreen said.

"Quite, sorry", I said. "Right, bottom-line is we're on track. I'll send you a name for the main lecture soon. I have someone in mind."

"Anything you would like me to do?", Duncan said.

"Anything you're willing to do?", Doreen asked.

"I'm enthusiastically willing to be absolutely sloshed on free booze around the clock, entertain students with side-splitting anecdotes, irritate speakers by giggling or snoring, and subsequently earn myself a proud position in the Mansion's barred customers list."

"The booze is not free", Doreen said. "The Department's paying staff bills."

"Free to me", Duncan said.

"Do any of you have any sense of responsibility? Do you even know how a budget works?"

"How do you spell that, pet?"

"Incredible. Michael, is there anything else?"

"I suppose we have to address the elephant in the room."

"Just a bit of winter coat, dear boy. Don't be so cruel."

"Shut up, Duncan", Doreen said. "I suppose we do. What do you have in mind?"

"I don't know. Maybe a commemorative session?"

"The Mansion weekend is two and a half months away. Surely we will have flogged his memory to a new death by then", Duncan said.

"Insensitive but maybe you have a point."

"The thing is", Doreen said, "Paul kinda wanted to come along this time."

"He did?, I asked.

"Not a long time ago, maybe a couple of weeks, he came in the office asking about the details of all social events involving students. He said he wanted to be more proactive at engendering a welcoming community."

"And?", Duncan asked with renewed interest.

"He was really eager to come to the postgrad welcome drinks, which, as we know, he did. When I told him the draft programme of the away weekend, he seemed pretty keen on that too."

Was that because Horst would be speaking? Did Paul want to humiliate him in public? To make sure that he'd be kept in check? How serious was that vendetta after all?

"Perhaps we could get one of his doctoral students to say a few words about his work", I said.

"Few being the operative word here. There's hardly anything to say", Duncan said.

"How about Jeremy?", Doreen said.

"That's an idea", I said.

"A very bad one", Duncan said. "You know how Jeremy can ramble on with no discernible destination."

"I disagree", I said. "Jeremy is a treasure trove of information. I'll speak to him and make sure that he understands that he needs to keep within the time limit."

"Going, going, gone", Doreen said.

One thing about campus living that perhaps many people fail to appreciate is how difficult it is to get basic provisions in. You could, of course, sustain yourself without ever leaving but then you would have to make do with chocolate bars, milk, alcopop, and mainly salt-based meals from the staff restaurant.

Pretty certain that a campus diet would drive me to an early grave, I have to regularly summon the courage to venture to the neighbouring town and go on a supermarket shopping spree.

Perhaps many think of town versus gown as a struggle of underprivileged locals against spoilt, rich students and snobbish dons. Not in our purlieu. The roles here are reversed. The town, now host to several new big tech companies that have taken advantage of the available space to build their HQs and the good connections to various airports, is much richer than the university. The construction industry is booming, countless SUVs roam the streets, restaurants and bars crop up at every corner and brazenly charge unaffordable prices.

Not needing the measly income that our students bring in, locals consider it a no-brainer when balancing the benefits of having gormless hordes loitering in their streets looking for traffic cones to misplace for comic effect, against the cost of such visits. Completely indifferent to how close to the wind of human rights law they are sailing, most bars hoist 'NO STUDENTS' signs up on their doors. Establishments that have the decency not to be so openly exclusive, make sure to achieve the same effect by providing as rude and standoffish a discriminatory service as they can get away with.

Not that university staff are any more favourably treated. The sight of corduroy alone is enough to make shopkeepers and taxi drivers pull disdainful faces of haughty revulsion.

This class hatred and, considering how many of our students were not from a white background, covert racism used to outrage me when I first joined the university. Every trip into town was like a march into battle. Not infrequently I stepped in to defend students or I pre-emptively snapped at locals when I felt they were giving me funny looks.

With time, however, my sensitivity, like most traits of my youth, had been blunted to the point where I had taken on the perspective of the social scientist – observing the goings on around me in the detached manner of someone who is not affected by anything.

That attitude was somewhat difficult to sustain laden with six heavy bags of groceries while sprinting to board a bus with just seconds to spare, the prospect of a thirty-minute wait for the next one looming, to see the mirrored reflection of a smirking driver gleefuly about to shut the door and drive away nanoseconds before I could reach the door. Thankfully, his sadistic plan was thwarted by an elderly woman who shuffled her way in front of the vehicle delaying him sufficiently that my race was now against her. If I got to the door before her, I'd earn my place on regional public transport.

Once on the bus I inconsiderately kept the woman behind me waiting on the steps to punish her for all the wrongs she had undoubtedly done to the University community over her long life. I lay all my bags on the floor, opened my satchel, rummaged for the exact change. Then, having paid for the ticket, which the driver begrudgingly issued, I loaded myself with my shopping again and aimed for a seat. My mistake was in my choice of row. I was still walking to the back of the bus when the driver, having finished with the woman and making sure that she was seated safely, drove off with a jerk that sent me rocketing down the aisle, shopping items scattered all around me. I cursed under my breath, gave a couple of giggling students a menacing look, picked up my wine bottles, mayonnaise, and packet of quinoa off the floor, and took a seat.

With the wounds of defeat still stinging and my shoulder sore from the bang it took when I fell into the pole that separated the aisle in two, I slumped by the window and stared out. The road to the campus at the other end of town runs across the centre and, because of the town's wealth, it still retains some individuality. Chain stores haven't yet managed to turf out the independent shops. If anything, the independents are very successful as wealthy locals prefer the aura of exclusivity they get when paying top of the line prices charged by small but tasteful businesses or, when dining out, for the privilege of having their mash called purée and their gravy jus. The well-off are always desperate to stay ahead of the games that they themselves invent.

The high street was flooded with office employees in orderly queues alongside food purveyors. Then, clutching their lunchboxes, they strode back to their workplaces driven indoors again by a light drizzle. Those with more time on their hands were enjoying leisurely sit-down lunches.

Amongst them, sitting near the café window and leaning towards each other over the table in a posture of mutual confidence, were Catherine and Alison.

"I've been busy while you were away", Catherine said.

"I'm all ears", I said.

"I've been working on the theoretical framework. It needed tightening, we knew that."

"We did."

"So, I've put together a few pages. I'll forward them to you for comments and additions."

Her trust in me was so disarmingly enchanting.

"What I wanted us to talk about was the practical upshots of the theoretical groundwork."

Her office was like a reverse image of mine, the lower levels tidy; minimal furniture, no clutter on desk or table, a litter-free floor. Look higher and it was a different story, busy and loud, her shelves bursting with books, article printouts, loose papers, overflowing box files. The walls were lined with posters from art exhibitions and old conferences, some reproductions of famous paintings (Jean-Michel Basquiat featured heavily), greeting cards and postcards, and photos, lots of photos. Photos of her in various settings and poses. Catherine delivering a paper at a conference; Catherine graduating in her doctoral gown; Catherine in summer clothes at a restaurant by the sea; Catherine cuddling a dog; Catherine playing netball.

Invariably, she was the sole subject in each snapshot. Where others figured in the frame, they were there as background, as props – people on the beach, a Dean handing over her degree, spectators at the netball court. Had it been anyone else, I would have thought it dreadfully self-centred. But it wasn't someone else, it was Catherine, and her look in the stills, conscious of her surroundings but distant, instilled sadness in her dominance.

There was also something else that troubled me about those photos but I couldn't put my finger on it.

"There was one thing that has been escaping me", she continued.

"That's unlike you", I said in a clumsy attempt at flirting, which she didn't seem to mind.

"We started off hoping to juxtapose institutional perceptions of crime..."

I didn't take issue with the use of terminology because it was more important to me that I heard where she was going with this.

"...to the embodied perception of those who occupy the same time and space as the crime."

"Yes, precisely", I said.

"What has to come into the equation though, you'll find it quite obvious when I say it, is the truth."

"Does it?", I said, tensing up.

"I mean the concept of truth", she said.

That was a bit better. Concepts are generally much more innocuous than their applications to the real world.

"But not in the abstract", she went on. "To talk about truth in a meaningful way, we have to talk about the truth of the matter."

The emotional seesawing to which she was subjecting me was making me nauseous.

"To do that, we must explore where and how exactly institutional, official truth converges with or diverges from experienced truth."

"And how do we do that?"

"We speak to people."

The pathologist's practice was in the same building as the public library, a concrete structure that had been embellished with incongruously colourful cladding most likely in an attempt to disguise its only charm, a brutalist sincerity.

"It's like putting make-up on Jeremy", I said.

Catherine laughed. It was monosyllabic laugh but a laugh nonetheless.

The drive to the city had taken us the best part of an hour, the most relaxed stretch of time I had ever spent with her. In fact, the seclusion of the car, protecting us from motorway traffic raging past us and sheltering us from the incessant rain, made it quite the cosiest experience I had had in months.

We chatted about things unrelated to Paul's death or academia generally for that matter. We spoke about music, film, literature, favourite cities, childhood memories. Catherine had grown up in a rural town in the south, in a farming family. I was the product of a city, the son of a civil servant and an accountant. Between us, we had a full set of skills. She was good at picking crops and slaughtering animals, I was better at figuring out public transport. She enjoyed walks in the countryside, I was good at finding the most convenient shortcut to my destination.

Dr Pepple was a tall, lean man in his mid-50s. His grey hair, implausibly erect posture, and crisp white coat made him look like a character straight out of a medical soap opera. All that was missing was a stethoscope draped over his neck, not that he would have had much use for one in his line of practice.

"Can you explain to me again what the purpose of this meeting is, please?", he said. "My familiarity with the social sciences is rather limited."

Catherine outlined the hypothesis with lucid succinctness.

"Sounds as airy fairy as anything but, fine, whatever. How exactly can I help you?"

My dislike of scientists developed when I was a doctoral student. I had shared a flat for a year with a couple of biologists and met many more on campus. With few exceptions, they displayed an unwavering certainty that they were the chosen ones, custodians of the definitive truth about everything. Unperturbed that their conclusions were repeatedly falsified, they held firmly to the belief that theirs was the science that held the key to the meaning of the universe. Everything else, morality, politics, art, the emotions, amounted to little more than frills, imaginary add-ons.

Pepple's attitude seemed seeped in that oozy confidence. As far as he was concerned, the only interesting thing about the world was that it is an assembly of physical facts. His expression was one of arrogant bafflement as to why he should be expected to participate in what he clearly considered to be no more than a silly charade. Beyond the loathsome stereotype I so disliked, I also found him personally offensive. He was staring at Catherine with a smirk so intent that it verged on harassment.

I was pretty sure that Catherine felt the same but she pressed on regardless.

"You examined the body of our deceased colleague Paul Digby in his office. Can you please repeat to me what your thoughts were?"

"My thoughts? I don't have thoughts, Dr Bowen, I have facts, from which I infer conclusions."

"Isn't that in itself a thought?", I intervened.

He gave me a homicidal look.

"So that's the approach. Very well. I was called in by the coroner to examine the body of a man, fifty-five years of age found dead by the early morning cleaning shift. His identity was known since he was in his own office with his university staff card hanging from a lanyard around his neck. Being social scientists, I assume you are not interested in detail so I'll cut to the chase. The cause of death, which had taken place some seven to eight hours previously, was internal bleeding caused by an open cranial fracture, which was in turn caused by impact with a relatively blunt but heavy object. There's no speculation as to what said object was because it was lying next to the man's body. It was a rock. Toxicological tests did not reveal anything of note other than that the deceased had consumed a significant amount of an alcoholic substance. White wine, to be precise, and a lot of it. Can't really take a guess at the grape or the vintage. That's the long and the short of it."

"How did you feel when entering the room?", Catherine asked.

"Feel?", Pepple asked, taken aback.

"There is no right answer", Catherine said. "No template or protocol. We're just interested in your reactions to the scene."

Pepple considered that for a few seconds. When he spoke again his tone had altered.

"Fine, here goes. When you're called to an unexplained death scene, you don't know in advance what you'll come across. Not exactly, anyway. So you're always prepared for the worst. The best way of preparing, and this is not done consciously, it's just something you develop over the years especially if you've worked in places as volatile and violent as I have, is to maintain your belief that intentionally inflicted harm of the sort you deal with day in day out is exceptional, extraordinary. Otherwise, you'd lose all trust in life having a value or meaning. But to do that, you must first dismiss the very possibility of crime's normalcy at every opportunity."

"That sounds paradoxical", Catherine said. "You try to tell yourself that crime is exceptional but then your first assumption is that there is wrongdoing involved."

"You find it paradoxical? I find it necessary. It is something that has to be constantly confirmed without normalising it in the process. At the same time, one has to maintain one's professional integrity. It's hard to explain and even harder to understand when you're not in this game. Anyway, when I walk into a scene..."

He drew a long breath.

"No, let's be specific. When I walked into the late Professor Digby's office, my first reaction, to use the vernacular of your choice, was to draw the parameters of the situation. It was clear to me that the event was contained in that room; that whatever had happened had happened there. You just know when you're on the scene of a violent death. I then examined the body. I had no doubt about the cause of death and the later lab examination confirmed my initial impression."

"Did you consider at all how the rock might have fallen on Paul's head?", Catherine asked.

"Don't believe what you see on the television, Dr Bowen. My job is not to solve murders. It is to do pathology reports. The police have forensic teams for that kind of thing."

"And you never stop to ask yourself who did what?"

"No, never. I am only interested in causes of death, not the people creating those causes."

"Why did the police pronounce it an accident?", Catherine asked.

"Only their reports can answer that for you", Pepple said curtly.

"That was a waste of time", I said in the car on our way back to campus.

"Not at all", Catherine said.

I had appeared stupid again. The sensible thing to do was to keep quiet and let her lead the way.

"We got exactly what we were after from him. Think about it. 'I'm only interested in causes', he said. His perspective is completely determined by his job. So is ours. We, and I mean anthropologists, look for agency. We're interested in how the rock ended up on Paul's head, whose actions brought that result about but also how these actions were determined by the system in which they were played out."

"Are we?", I said.

"We are. You're the one who first opened my eyes to this when you spoke of diffused responsibility."

"I did?"

I wished I could have mustered more than confirmatory questions.

"But the non-professional, and that includes us minus our anthropology hats, crave a complete story."

None of these perspectives made me feel any more comfortable and I feared it showed in the way I was staring ahead without blinking as if we were about to drive into the core of the earth.

"What next?", I asked finally.

"I'm not sure", she said. "We have to think about it."

"Do you think we need to talk to the police?"

"They've closed the case and they will not be willing to waste any more time on it."

"Even for a research project?"

"Especially for a research project."

Some relief, at last, even though academic me was perplexed as to why we shouldn't persist a little more. We'd already started going down the road of approaching institutional players and it seemed odd that we would give up that easily and leave that thread hanging.

"What I find fascinating is how the truth is established", Catherine said. "It is nothing but the product of negotiation and power relations. Expertise only helps to place people in the game, it determines nothing beyond that."

I expected her to continue, as she customarily did when she got excited about something. Instead, she paused.

"You seem uneasy about something", I said.

"I *am* uneasy about something", she said.

"What is it?"

"Not quite sure."

"I was very honoured to be asked to speak about Paul", Jeremy said.

"Who else would I have asked?", I said. "You're the soul of this Department."

His old chest puffed up a little but perhaps it was not out of pride but rather that we were walking up the slope of a long hill that led from the car park to the crematorium.

"Dear mother of god, do they want people to die on the way to their own funeral?", Duncan panted.

"Keep up", I said and put my arm through his.

We were trailing well behind the rest of our colleagues, who were walking in pecking-order file: academics, administrative staff, post-doctoral researchers, doctoral students, Master's students, undergraduates. Alison had circulated a three-line-whip email to all students but, with no way to enforce attendance at the funeral, I had assumed it would be generally ignored. And yet, people had turned out in significant numbers. Being thus proven wrong was testing my lack of faith in the academic community's capacity for empathy.

I can't deny that I had been of two minds about attending. I had managed relatively effortlessly to pretend to others and myself that nothing was out of the ordinary since Paul's death but whether to attend his funeral presented a steeper challenge. In the days leading up to the event, I had tried to systematise my thoughts employing my full arsenal of rational argument. I kept telling myself that while I might have done what I had done, a look at the big picture would show that I was only one link in a long chain of events that happened to culminate by chance in the moment of my contribution. And that, I never tired of emphasising to myself, was in large part due to my advanced inebriation. My only mistake was that I had left the 'scene', as Catherine insisted on calling it. If, instead, I had notified someone, I would have been able to explain. I would have gone through the undoubtedly taxing process of being questioned by the police and probed even harder by colleagues but, in the end, some kind of order would have been established. I didn't see why the same order could not be achieved without having to go through the intermediary steps, which would have been an unpleasant experience for all concerned.

In short and in sum, and this was most important, there was no reason for me to feel bad about offering my condolences to Paul's widow. Nor was it inappropriate for me to bid him a final farewell. In fact, there was something about his death that only the two of us knew, and with a bit of luck would ever get to know, and that ironically made me the most appropriate person to perform last rites.

So, there I was, sporting my freshly dry-cleaned suit and badly ironed shirt, an indispensable and inconspicuous member of the Anthropology Department contingent paying tribute to our departed colleague.

The ceremony took place in a room not unlike a large seminar room, the difference being that it resonated with the quiet satisfaction of survival, of staying alive, as opposed to the pulsating throb exuded by the misplaced confidence young people have in their own immortality. Also, instead of a whiteboard there was a curtain, behind which lay a coffin.

I sat between Duncan and Jeremy. Doreen and a couple of administrators from central University offices were two seats to my left. Behind me, a few academics, including Horst Neuberg. Catherine and Alison were in the first row.

Celebrants have the tendency to sound patronising and flat as if they think their audience is dumbfounded that death occurs. They also seem to think they're in the business of marketing. They send off ideal representations of the deceased when the point is to treat them as someone who until recently actually existed. I am of the opinion that funerals should match in tone and atmosphere the life of the dead. Death is a powerful leveller already and it just adds insult to pretend that we were all the same in life and deserve identical curtain calls.

"And now", said Hades MC in the dulcet mannered monotone that made me hotter under the collar than the furnace awaiting Paul's remains, "I would like to invite Professor Alison Davies to say a few words on behalf of Paul's colleagues."

Catherine gave Alison's arm a squeeze as she got up to take the lectern. Our acting HoD didn't look like she needed any encouragement or consolation.

"Geraldine, dear friends and colleagues", Alison began in her familiar business-like tone, "when I first joined the Department, Paul was still a relatively young lecturer. And yet, one could already see that he was destined for greatness. He had already produced the work that would be his lasting legacy to the discipline. His series of articles on modern urban mating rituals, consolidated and completed in his book *The Anthropology of Seduction*, earned him a place among the great pioneers of the paradigmatic shift in social anthropology. But his ambition was even greater than that. A firm believer that the context in which scholarly production develops is just as important as its content, he set his eyes on a series of important administrative posts. He led the Department as Head for three years before taking up the post of University Vice-Dean for Education. During that time, his revolutionary policies aimed at enhancing and making more efficient the student experience. He instigated the introduction of the University post of Director of Betterment. *Stellarise*, our immensely successful flagship programme for helping students to make the most of their potential, was also his brainchild. After his term as vice-Dean came to an end, he took over again as Head of our Department. He stayed in the post for eight years, until his untimely and tragic death. As Head, Paul was encouraging and strict in equal measure. I still remember his visits, on evenings that we both worked late, to my office to talk about my research and administrative contribution when my time had come to apply for promotion. Many colleagues will attest to how aware he was of the impact his decisions had on our lives and how that was reflected in his firm running of the Department.

"Our professional lives will never be the same without Paul. Rest in peace, dear colleague."

When the coffin, apparently the environmentally friendly cardboard option as the cadaver-whisperer celebrant informed us, slowly trundled and disappeared into the hole in the wall, the auditorium stared in silence. Only Duncan was slapping his knee to the beat of the anodyne music that accompanied Paul on his purgatorial journey.

"What did you think, Michael?", Horst asked me with an excessively heavy pat on the back. "You never tell us what you think."

Was that true? As far as I was concerned, I always spoke my mind. Perhaps it was just that I didn't have a mind to speak frequently enough. I could certainly have given him my view about him turning up at a funeral in his customary, all-season sandals, chunky cardigan and collarless shirt.

"Think about what, Horst?", I asked, with a reciprocal comedic punch to his arm.

"About Alison's obituary. Wasn't it perfectly back-sided?"

"I think you mean backhanded, Horst", Lucy corrected him.

"Naturally I do."

"You reckon?", I asked.

"Naturally I reckon", Horst said.

"Would you have done it differently?", I asked.

"I wouldn't have done it at all."

"I'm looking forward to your talk at the postgraduate away weekend by the way. Thanks for offering to do it."

"I'm looking forward to it too, I have to say."

"It's a shame Paul won't be there to listen to you."

Naturally, he knew what I was implying. I was not expecting him to wonder how the news had spread; he couldn't delude himself that his quarrel with Paul would remain a secret very long especially after his drunken outpouring to Nikhil and his colleagues. All the same, I had not expected him to look so smug, almost victorious in fact.

"Michael, I wanted to talk to you about something too", Lucy Warburton said.

"Sure, I'm all ears."

"There's an issue with the doctoral students' common room."

"Has it flooded again?", I asked.

"What? No. They're too loud. You know my office is right next door to it..."

"It's a few doors down, isn't it?", I interrupted.

"Still, it's very close to it. And they're so loud that the noise reaches me even a few doors down."

"What kind of noise?"

"Chairs scraping, computers being turned on with that awful sound they make, the door creaking every time it opens and closes."

"I'm sorry, Lucy, but those seem to be much like ordinary office sounds. I'm not sure what I can do about it."

"You could move the common room."

"That'd be an overreaction, don't you think?"

"That's what Paul said too."

"You went to Paul with this?"

She blushed at the realisation that she shouldn't have by-passed me on a matter that fell within my jurisdiction, not to mention that she was showing some bitterness about the person whom we had just seen off to his farewell incineration.

"I only brought it up in a casual, brief corridor conversation."

"Did you now? Thomas, what do you think? Your office is right opposite the common room, isn't it?'

Thomas shrugged. I thought it funny that Horst would have reprimanded me for not speaking my mind when we were in the company of Thomas, who hardly ever spoke at all. His default position was with his head lowered, his nose nearly touching the lapel of his designer jacket, arms tightly pressed against his rib-cage, hands buried in his pockets, his legs slightly bent at the knees. It was as if he was making himself smaller, trying to occupy as small a part of the world as possible.

"Lucy, I suggest you keep your own door shut and if the problem persists, come speak to me again. Now, please excuse me."

I left the small group to go across the room where Catherine was standing with Alison and Geraldine Whitmore-Digby. The conditions for offering my condolences were optimal.

The pub was full. Everyone had braved the short walk through waterlogged streets. I scrummed my way through the student throng waiting at the bar for their free drinks. Realising their motivation for attending the funeral, I felt silly for prematurely dismissing my lack of faith in the goodwill of the student body.

"I'm very sorry for your loss, Geraldine. Paul was always enormously supportive of me until the very end", I said.

I hadn't calculated my words in advance, I honestly hadn't. Everything I said had come out spontaneously.

"Thank you", Geraldine said hesitantly.

"Michael West", Catherine said, "is a valued member of the Department."

"Paul often spoke about you."

That was a blatant lie but it didn't surprise me. Grief makes people mendacious. It's the price to pay for rehabilitating the departed as the perfect member of a perfect, happy and completely imaginary community.

"Actually, perhaps Michael can help", Alison said.

"Help with what?", I asked.

"Paul donated his books to a charity in East London..."

"How thoughtful. I'm sure that'll change a lot of lives", I said.

"...but he requested in his will that the Department organise that."

"Paul didn't keep an awful lot of books in his office, did he?"

"No, someone will have to go through his collection at home."

"I'll rope a PhD student into doing it, it shouldn't be a problem. It'd help if you approved a small fee for it."

"No, I shan't have any students come to the house, PhD or otherwise", Geraldine said.

She had almost panicked at the prospect.

"I meant that you should do it, Michael", Alison said.

"It won't be difficult. He was very well organised", Geraldine said.

I made a polite, if entirely untruthful excuse to turn down Jeremy's offer for a lift back. Having experienced his driving on the way to the crematorium, I didn't fancy meeting my maker in a ditch off a country road. I caught the bus instead. I had left the pub session with a nagging feeling without being able to discern its cause so was now in need of some down time for meditative introspection. All I managed until I got to campus was to eliminate the most obvious reason for my restlessness. Everything had gone well. Guilt had not kicked in. If anything, taking up the chore of sorting Paul's books for a worthy cause went some way towards atonement.

It was only when I returned home and I put my feet up facing my own bookshelves that it clicked.

Something evanescent

With dawn a good hour off and red bricks illuminated only by the faint, yellow streetlights, there was something evanescent about campus. The buildings felt like mere facades, empty and deceitful.

It wasn't necessary to complete my task before the crack of dawn as I set out. Now his official librarian, I had permission to enter Paul's office and could have done so inconspicuously in broad daylight. Still, I didn't want to take any chances.

Once again, there was no security guard to be seen. The daily provisions had not yet been delivered at the door of the Butty Call. All the lifts sat idly in the deserted lobby of the McKenzie building. I entered one and ascended to the fourth floor, which was just as quiet. The lights flickered on as I stepped into the corridor triggering the motion sensors.

The office door was unlocked, as usual, but opening it required more strength than I had anticipated. Something was caught underneath causing the door to jam slightly. When I entered and turned the lights on, the obstruction revealed itself to be a small bunch of flowers, plant food sachet still taped to the nylon wrapping, no card attached.

There was no time to wonder who had placed it there and why with such haste. Evans-Pritchard was leaning against Margaret Mead. I propped him up with Malinowski. *Crime and Custom in Savage Society* was back where it belonged.

Shutting the door behind me and making my way back along the corridor, I sensed I was not alone on the fourth floor. It was still too early for the early morning shift cleaners and anyway it was highly unlikely that a cleaner would be there sobbing her eyes out at that hour.

I traced the source of the crying to the doctoral students' common room. Perhaps Lucy had a point about the noise after all, I thought.

"Victoria?"

She was crouched on the floor, head in hands, bawling, oblivious to her surroundings. It hadn't taken long to find out who'd left the flowers.

"Victoria?", I repeated.

She lifted her head and gave me a blank stare.

"How long have you been here?"

"I don't know", she stuttered.

"Are you alright?"

It was an awkward question, truth be told, but what else could I have asked her?

"No, I'm not", she said.

Her frankness took me aback. An English person would never have told the truth.

"What's wrong?", I asked.

"He's gone."

"Who's gone?"

"*He* is gone?"

"Do you mean Paul?"

Instead of an answer she started crying even louder, blowing her nose at the same time.

My duties as Director of Postgraduate Studies included providing pastoral care so, ever the professional, I dutifully sat next to her on the floor.

"I see you're very upset about it", I said, recalling the University Student Well-Being Office guidelines for dealing with students in distress.

She turned and looked at me again.

"You think?", she said.

There was no need for sarcasm but I had to let it drop.

"We're all distraught about what happened to Paul."

"You don't understand", she said.

"Would you like to talk to me about how you feel?", I said, now more intrigued than concerned about her welfare.

"I don't know what I'll do without him."

Paul had not been her supervisor, Horst was. Why would his loss have hit her so hard?

"We'll all have to plough through."

"You just don't get it."

That almost qualified as a scream for help.

"Why don't you explain to me?"

"I wouldn't be here had it not been for him."

"How's that?"

"He guided me, he gave me advice, he encouraged me."

"I see", I said.

I couldn't imagine how displeased Horst would have been about his supervisee's admiration for Paul.

"I met him when I was doing my Master's degree. He was so approachable. I wanted to speak to him but was too shy and yet he must have been able to tell how anxious I was, because he came to talk to me. He offered to read a draft of my dissertation. He urged me to apply to do my PhD here. He made sure I would be granted a scholarship."

How had he done that? The process of awarding doctoral scholarships was meant to be transparent and subject to all sorts of checks and balances, both internal and external.

"He helped me publish my thesis."

"Listen", I said, "obviously you thought very highly of Paul and you owed a lot to him but you, like all of us, have to move on. The best tribute you can pay him is to continue to excel and produce great work."

"Everything I ever write will be dedicated to him", she said.

"I'm sure he'd be delighted about that."

❖

She was so exhausted from crying and sleep deprivation, which I suspected had been afflicting her for a long time, that it wasn't too difficult to persuade her that it was best she not be seen in that state by others and that she should go home and try to get some rest.

Despite her manifest adoration of Paul, she hadn't attended his funeral. Instead, she had preferred to lay a clumsy bunch of flowers at his office door. Judging by her state that morning, she couldn't possibly have managed the funeral. As we parted, still drawing on my counselling expertise, I urged her to come see me to discuss ways of coping. As I did so, I made a mental note to drive home how overrated and dangerous it was to be so sensitive, for academics especially.

Work emails are hardly ever worth getting excited about. Perhaps that's why IT services have made sure that it takes a good five minutes for our computers to switch on, boot and connect to the network. The wait builds up a sense of suspense, but the anticipatory buzz fizzles out as soon as one accesses one's correspondence.

As a young member of staff, so zealous was I, and so much more zealous did I want to appear, that I accessed and answered my emails around the clock. Initially, when not in the office, I would try to be at home as much as possible in order to check my correspondence every few minutes on the oversized laptop that I had bought with my University research allowance money.

After a few years, I changed course. I now justifiably pride myself for having anticipated the work-life balance movement, by having imposed a self-ban on doing emails at home. I saved all the dull tasks for the office. There were so many upsides to it that it was a no-brainer. First of all, trawling through emails and responding to them from the office took so long that it gave me a sense of achievement and the semblance of increased productivity. Second, my delay in responding to messages projected such an air of busyness about me that those to whom I eventually responded would feel especially gratified that I had taken the time to acknowledge them with an answer.

There were a few dozen new messages in my inbox. Most were round-robin, admin-related emails; the usual ineffectual flurry that presaged the upcoming term meetings of various Committees in the Department and the University. Those I could file away immediately for future reference, in other words condemn them to recorded oblivion. Some were from students asking for extensions to the essay submission deadline. Most could be answered by a cut and paste job reiterating the formal requirements. The regulations could of course be easily found on the departmental website, and students had been told so from the beginning of the year, but that would require deliberation, preparation and a resourcefulness not characteristic of our precious cherubs.

The only interesting message was from a sender whose foreign name I didn't recognise but who had the foresight to grab my attention with the subject line, all in upper case: INVITATION.

I half-expected it would turn out to be yet another obscure offspring of some distant princeling importuning me to open an account with a deposit of a couple of hundred dollars into which he could transfer a multi-million dollar fortune for safekeeping.

But no, it was from a Professor of social anthropology in the Netherlands.

"Dear Dr West, I am writing to you in my capacity as editor of the Social and Cultural Anthropology section of the *State of the Art* series of Schrieke Publishers. I am sure you will be familiar with the series, as it is the most central point of reference in our field. As you know, the publication is periodical and appears every decade. The aim is both to record developments in social and cultural anthropology but also to set the agenda for future work.

"I recently came across your new research project on the anthropological phenomenology of crime and shared it with the rest of the members of the editorial board. Everyone found it absolutely fascinating. We would therefore like to invite you to contribute a chapter to the forthcoming volume, which is due out next year. Do not be concerned if it is still work in progress. We very much want to be associated from an early stage with such revolutionary material.

"I am of course at your disposal if you have any questions. I sincerely hope you will be able to accept our invitation and would be delighted if you agreed to contribute to the volume.

"Yours sincerely,

"Prof. Dr Dr Ambroos Bakker"

My first reaction was to think that it was a hoax, although I couldn't imagine why anyone would want to trick me like that. I had to reread the email a few times. I ran an Internet search just to be on the safe side and Ambroos Bakker really was the editor of the anthropology section of the State of the Art series and he really did have two doctoral titles, even if one was honorary.

Certain that the invitation was genuine, I leaned back in my chair and basked in the international recognition of my scholarly leadership. How everything had changed in the past few weeks!

I was of course going to write back to Bakker and accept the invitation with a gratitude mixed with a subtle hint of arrogance sufficient to suggest superiority without making me sound obnoxious. First, however, I had to make sure that I would have something to say in my contribution to the book.

I scrolled down my list of emails. There it was, two xs as sign-off, the attachment ready to be renamed from PhenomAnthro_prelim_ideas.doc to StateOfTheArt_chapter_MichaelWest.doc.

Muddy prints in a public building

Since speaking to Dr Pepple, our phenomenological research had lost momentum. Catherine had not instigated any new ventures nor, unsurprisingly, had I been inspired to come up with any fresh ideas of my own. On the one hand, that suited me to some extent, because a lot had piled up on my plate. On the other, I missed spending time with Catherine. And besides, I needed the material.

I was therefore delighted when she agreed to have a drink with me at the Montgomery Arms only for my elation quickly to be dampened by her aloofness.

She went through the motions as though nothing had changed, kissing me on either cheek, ordering her customary gin and tonic, sitting close enough to me on the shared sofa so that our legs touched ever so slightly. And yet, every topic of conversation that I ventured to open was soon shut down with a brusque one-liner. Every joke of mine was met deadpan and expressionless. My eager attempts to revitalise our joint research met with an indifferent shrug.

"What's going on?", I finally asked.

"What do you mean?", she said, staring straight into my eyes.

"You're not yourself tonight. You're quiet, distant. Have you lost interest in our research? Is something else going on?"

She took off her glasses and rubbed them clean between the pleats of her skirt.

"You can tell", she eventually said.

"It doesn't take a clairvoyant."

"Am I that transparent?"

"Not normally, no."

"Well, yes, there's something bothering me."

"Would you care to tell me?"

"I don't know. I mean, it's just a hunch, a mental irritant. It might be too embarrassing to share."

"I'm sure it isn't."

She bent her left leg at the knee, pulled it up on the sofa, tucked it under her right leg and turned to face me. The glint of the joy of enquiry in her eyes was unmissable.

"OK, here goes. We had assumed that Paul's death was an accident."

"Yes?", I said, with some trepidation.

"I mean, that's what the police said. What reason did any of us have to question them?"

My stomach roiled.

"None", I said.

"But", Catherine said, "you did, however intuitively."

"Yes, but I explained, it was just, you know, just a thought about responsibility. I wasn't disbelieving the police."

"Yes", she said, pausing to complete the thought, "but it triggered our research."

"Which is just research."

"What do you mean 'just research'?"

"Sorry, I didn't mean it that way. Please, carry on."

"Our fieldwork has been wonderful, everything's working just the way I'd envisaged it."

"I agree."

"But it has also yielded results that were unintended and went beyond my wildest expectations."

"It has?"

My hands were now shaking.

"Think about it."

Little did she know the speed at which my brain was processing what she was telling me as I weighed the possibilities of what was to come.

"Take the pathologist for one."

"What about him?"

"Why was he so loath to say outright that it was an accident?"

"A matter of professionalism, I should think. He can't vouch for something that he can't be certain of."

"That's precisely the point. He couldn't be certain of it. Then, there were the footprints."

"Which footprints?"

"On Paul's carpet."

"Our footprints?"

"No, not ours. The ones below ours."

"There were footprints below our footprints?"

"They were faint and smudgy but, yes, they were definitely there. Did you not see them?"

My head was beginning to numb. I tried to run events back as quickly as I could. I had scraped the excess mud off the bottom of my feet, when entering the building, I was sure of that. I also had checked that I hadn't left any prints on Paul's carpet. I must have underestimated my drunkenness, my adrenaline and the dim lighting.

I had to stay composed.

"No, I can't say I did. But even if you're right, that's unremarkable, isn't it? Muddy prints in a public building surrounded by fields?"

"I'd been in Paul's office just before he came to the Scrote. I hadn't noticed any muddy prints; the carpet was clean."

"Why would you have noticed anything, if you weren't looking?"

"I just think I would have. Those new carpets are so dazzlingly bright, you know? And Paul was terribly house-proud like that; he'd never have abided a dirty floor."

"Still, maybe they were left after you know what."

"Out of the question. The police were wearing those protective plastic shoe covers and the room was cleaned straight after they finished and hasn't been cleaned since."

"I think you're making too much of this."

"You don't even yet know what I'm making of it", she said with a frown.

"That's true. What are you making of it?"

"There's one more thing, before we get to that. The shelves."

"What about them?"

"You saw what happened when I threw my weight on them."

"What happened?"

"Exactly. Nothing happened."

"I guess you're too slight to move a whole bookshelf unit."

"I'm not weak, you know."

"Paul was much bigger than you."

"Trust me, I know that. Nevertheless, he was not big enough to shake the shelves and make the rock roll off."

"That's all conjecture."

"Maybe each element by itself is but taken all together they're more than that, much more."

"So, what are they?", I asked, hoping that an answer would never be offered.

"I think it might not have been an accident. I think someone was in that room when Paul died."

She paused for a second.

"I think someone killed Paul with that rock."

I was shocked, of course, but more than that, I was taken aback by the ontological complexity of the situation. Here was Catherine talking to me about none other than me, accusing that someone, not knowing it was me, of killing Paul. The consequences of her joining the last two dots were of course intolerable so I found myself awkwardly yet explicitly having to refute part of my own existence.

"Wow", I exclaimed in an attempt to kick-start this process of self-denial.

For emphasis, or perhaps to distract her or simply driven by my lust which was mounting the more precarious my position became, I placed my hand on her leg, wrapped my fingers around her bare ankle and caressed with my thumb as much of the top of her foot as was left uncovered by her Mary Janes.

A shackle-like grip

Since its inception, academia had for centuries kept itself locked up in its ivory white tower. With the odd exception, scholars pondered over their divining thoughts within the heady confines of their lofty quarters. The outside world was of little consideration to them beyond serving as a sometime stimulus, intriguing at times, but mostly irrelevant. Self-respecting dons had little interest in what impact their work might have beyond the ornate walls of their institutions. Why should they? Salaries were guaranteed. The more a university education became an attainable aspiration for growing numbers of people, the more the market demand burgeoned and once the ordeal of tenure was overcome, academic jobs were secure for life. Positions in academia multiplied exponentially and new blood came pouring in. I know because I was a beneficiary of the boom.

It is deeply to be regretted that the corrosion of that refined system of ineffectual isolationism and flexible working hours began from within. Some academics started making noises about the university needing to be active in the community; that it had a duty to enlighten lay-people, to participate in the humdrum management of things and subject itself to the hurly burly of everyday life. These same academics deluded themselves that theirs was the responsible way to go, that the old ways were somehow dishonest, that it was incumbent upon all of us to make amends. While this was obvious nonsense to anyone in their right mind, the instigators behind the move to shake things up were blind to the foolishness of their views. Above all, they craved attention and gratitude. So much so, that they were willing to reduce the scope of their research activities and focus instead on trivialities that anyone, even university middle managers and social media account administrators, could understand. It is of course no coincidence that those same academics produced sub-standard, unimaginative stuff.

The ripples these turncoats generated became a tidal wave once those in charge of the purse strings caught on. They, being much wilier than their academic accomplices, saw the new movement for what it was: an ingenious way of controlling finances and forcing universities to generate more revenue by selling patents and attracting corporate funders. They enthusiastically rode the new wave in the name of 'engagement' and 'impact', anything, in fact, so long as it was catchily trendy.

It was all perfectly abhorrent.

I harboured the same strong feelings about what Catherine was to suggest next on that evening we shared at the Montgomery Arms.

To be inspired by the circumstances of Paul's death in order to illuminate the darkest niches of the human condition and to further our understanding of ourselves was nothing short of noble. To have suspicions about Paul's death on the basis of some fragmentary and circumstantial evidence was understandable as an instinctive and human gut reaction. If anything, it emphasised the need for our research. But to suspend our research and deal in vulgar empirical problems was simply beneath us as scholars. Who cared about anything else when we had the unique opportunity to explain humanity itself? Now she was proposing to turn our abstract research, with all its potential to change the course of the history of social anthropology forever, into something unfathomably vulgar.

Considering her suggestion from my own perspective, enriched with all the complexities embroidered into my life over the past few weeks, my academic outrage gave way to a wave of extreme anxiety; an anxiety that was exacerbated by the context.

Catherine placed her hand on top of mine. That she was not simply acquiescing to corporal intimacy but was also actively contributing to it herself had given me a jolt of joy so unprecedented as to be almost unrecognisable.

With our hands intertwined, the look she bestowed on me went deeper and had an effect on my body more powerful than I ever imagined possible for something intangible. With baited breath, I waited, eager for her to say something that would seal and sanction our physical union. Instead, she said:

"We have to find out what happened to Paul."

"Do we?"

"We owe it to Paul", she said. "We owe it to our colleagues."

"We do?"

"You're the only one I trust blindly."

I deferred for later consideration whether that trust boded good or bad.

"But the police have closed the case. What's the point in us asking further questions?"

"Remember what our research has taught us about the truth. It's all a matter of power relations."

Her combination of sweet-talking and critical social anthropology had me cornered.

"Say we agree to do this", I said. "I still don't know what *this* is."

"I haven't thought through the details yet."

"It's OK, I shan't pass it through blind double peer review. You can share the rough draft with me."

That irritated her and she jerked her hand away.

"Don't joke, this is very serious", she said.

Too serious to even tell me what she had in mind.

The exchange with Catherine played tricks with my head more devious than the exam questions I tended to set when I was hungover or in a bad mood. Later that evening, as I stared at the bookshelves in my flat, I cross-examined my state of mental flux.

Was Catherine toying with me? Did she suspect me? Did she trust me? Was she drip-feeding me information in order to gauge my reaction? Or, worse still, to catch me out?

That was succeeded by a flush of guilt or something like it at any rate. I couldn't be sure and not because I didn't know what guilt felt like; although hardly an expert, I'd had my fair share of guilty moments over the years. It was just that on this occasion, I was not certain what it was I was feeling guilty about. It wasn't for what happened to Paul – that much I knew. I was well beyond the point where even the possibility of remorse vanishes into defiance and defensiveness. What troubled me most was not having come clean to Catherine when the opportunity first presented itself. If our relationship were to blossom and become more than a shackle-like grip around the ankle, I should have been frank with her.

Of course, telling her the truth might have backfired. No, scratch that, it certainly would have. Be that as it may, the alternative would be even worse. Revealing my secret after the fact would mark the end of everything. It would render our modest, brief but bursting with meaning embodied perception of the phenomenon of each other meaningless, hollow, seemingly hypocritical and calculating on my part.

For sake of affection alone, I could not confess anything to Catherine. I had to play along. Only, of course, I also had to do the exact opposite.

Regrettably shelving our scholarly plan to explore the lived experience of crime, we turned to amateur sleuthing. The first step was to look for witnesses. It was, as always, Catherine's idea.

"We need to be subtle", she said. "We can't divulge the purpose of our questioning. We can only trust each other."

I found not being able to voice my objection to that inaccuracy rather frustrating.

"Gotcha", I said.

The first person we needed to approach was the security guard who had been on duty the night Paul died. To find him, we had to consult the duty roster and that meant speaking to the University Chief of Security.

"Has he done something wrong?", Amina Okafor asked.

"No, not at all", Catherine reassured her. "It's just that our Department has asked us to draw up a pattern of staff movement so as to optimise space allocation."

"A brave new world", Amina said.

"Nothing sinister about it", Catherine said. "Just a question of economy."

"And you're sure he's not in trouble?"

"Absolutely", I contributed.

"Let me have a look."

She pulled a bulging ring-binder from the Dexion shelves behind her desk. Her office space, not much larger than a stationery cupboard, was diminished further by the paperwork piles and files that spread litter-like into every nook and cranny. The symbiosis of humans with security intelligence would have been an interesting research project, if it didn't conceal so many risks. Amina lived amidst a thousand secrets in a fragile state of peace.

"We'll digitise everything eventually but it's taking us awhile", she said apologetically.

From the folder, she removed a piece of paper and ran her index finger down the lines.

"OK, Ed was at Engineering, Tracy at the Med School and at McKenzie it was Liam. Liam Daly."

"Brilliant, thank you. Is he on duty now by any chance?", Catherine asked.

Amina tunnelled into the clutter on her desk and excavated the day's duty sheet.

"Nope, but he's on in half an hour. You'll probably find him in the common room. Extension 1602."

"Thanks", Catherine said.

She rushed to the door, fishing her mobile out of her tote bag to dial the number of the locker room shared by the security guards and janitors even as she walked away.

"Thanks, bye", I said, about to follow Catherine out the door.

"You don't have to do that, you know", Amina said.

"Departmental orders", I explained.

"No, I mean you don't have to speak to the guards. Not for the McKenzie building. We're all 21st century now, aren't we? We've got the system."

"What system?"

"The new entry system. It records and stores all data – who comes in, who goes out, the lot. It'll be a lot more helpful than Liam. He forgets what he had for lunch the day before. And he always has the Yorkshire pudding for lunch."

I thanked her with a hasty nod and exited the box room. Catherine was already on the phone so she wouldn't have heard what Amina had just volunteered.

In my head I cursed neo-liberalism and the biopolitics of movement restriction.

❖

Liam Daly was a large man. Countless gravy soaked Yorkshire puddings had arranged themselves alongside the meat and trimmings in overlapping folds in his abdominal area. Had he not been as tall as he was, and he was very tall indeed, he would have looked like a blob on sticks.

"That was a long time ago, you know?"

"I know but it was a memorable night, wasn't it?", Catherine asked.

"Not at the time it wasn't, you know? Just an ordinary night."

I can't deny taking secret delight in Liam beating Catherine at her own game of time and space social theory.

"OK, let's start again. Do people often enter the building in the evening?"

"Not really, no."

Catherine drew a breath to move on to her next question but Liam wasn't done.

"Maybe a stray student sometimes", he said.

"OK, so you would..."

"Sometimes Professors."

"Right, so it's..."

"Especially after evening events."

"It sounds busy", Catherine said.

"I don't know, you know?"

"Do you remember Paul Digby coming in that evening?", I said.

Liam paused to think about it.

"Yes, yes, I do remember him. Very nice bloke. Always said hello."

"Did he?", Catherine said.

"But you don't remember anyone else entering or exiting before or after Paul?", I said.

"What's this about anyway?"

Catherine rushed to dispel Liam's suspicion.

"Just an administrative thing that the Department has asked us to do. Checking movement and all that."

"So why don't you...?"

"I guess you would remember if anyone else had come in, wouldn't you?", I interrupted in a haste.

Catherine threw me a look thorny with bafflement and irritation.

"I guess I would, yeah", Liam said, pausing. "Actually, now that you mention it, maybe I do remember one or two people come in, yeah."

"Did you recognise them?"

"No, not really, sorry."

"Do you remember what state Paul was in, when he came in?", I asked. "He looked drunk, no?"

"Yeah, now that you mention it, maybe he was a bit."

"But he was well enough to go through the new gate system, right?", Catherine said.

"I guess. Now that you mention it."

"I mean, you don't recall opening the manually operated gate for him", she pressed on.

"No, I guess I don't", Liam said.

"That's all, isn't it? No need to mention anything else", I said to Catherine.

"It looks like it."

"Well, we'll let you have your tea then, Liam. Thanks", I said and stood up.

"Actually", Catherine said raising her right hand, "one more thing. How often do you do the night shift?"

"Once a week for sure. Sometimes twice a week, when Amina is short of staff. I'm not married, you see, so nothing to go back home to. The others all have families. They do it for the overtime but they prefer..."

"Right, sure, I get it", Catherine cut him short. "When's your next night shift?"

"Day after tomorrow", Liam said.

We left the room that smelled of tea and granulated beef soup and resonated with conversations about football, politics, television and the price of petrol. We were as blissfully ignorant as we had been on entering.

The architecturally soulless façade of Paul Digby's house was thankfully semi-hidden by an ivy cladding that had crept up to cover all but the door and bay windows. I had been there only once and that was for a dinner party shortly after joining the Department. In Geraldine's absence, Paul had done the cooking. The blandness of the steamed salmon had stayed with me much longer than any of the conversations with host or guests. Alison was definitely there but the identity of the rest had faded, leaving just a dim memory of bad academic jokes and stale recycled gossip. The only saving grace was the wine, nothing like the premium vintage Paul had talked it up to be, but, unlike the conversation, at least it flowed freely – so much so in fact that it loosened my tongue sufficiently to contribute to the chat with a series of lead balloons.

Not having seen the study on that stultifying occasion, I now found myself contemplating the task that lay ahead of me. So he did have books after all and presumably this was where they had been left to die a slow death of neglect. A famous philosopher, once asked whether he'd read all the thousands of books in his collection, answered gravely that he had read only four but assured his questioner that he had read them very carefully. Paul, I suspect, must have taken his cue from the philosopher but had missed out on the "carefully" bit.

"Here's your tea", Geraldine said, entering the room and setting a tray down on the kidney-shaped Edwardian side table alongside the worn-out Chesterfield armchair. Was that where Paul used to sit to not do any reading?

"I appreciate your doing this", she said.

"My pleasure", I responded.

I immediately regretted my choice of words but it was too late for a retraction so I opted for distraction.

“Paul had quite a collection of books”, I said.

“Did he?”, she said.

I found making small talk with her difficult enough already without her transforming herself into a brick wall.

“Well, I mean, we all have books. Part of the job and all that.”

“A waste of space, if you ask me.”

It would have been dishonest to disagree with her too passionately.

“I take it you’re not in academia?”, I asked instead.

“Of course not. I live in the real world.”

There was the old cliché again delivered with the all too familiar and condescending edge non-academics adopt when presenting an unreflective and obvious fallacy as a profound truth that they have single-handedly grasped and articulated. Obviously I am not in the front line of those willing to defend academia but I cannot help taking issue with the nonsense that academia is not the ‘real world’. What is that ‘real world’ anyway? People obsessed with their self-interest? Being judged by people patently inferior to you in every way at every corner? Having to bend over backwards to please those who do not deserve to be pleased? Making gains at the expense of others?

The ‘real world’ gang wouldn’t last a day in academia.

“I have my own company”, she volunteered in an attempt to reboot the conversation. “We make the robotic system that controls how bin lorries tip wheelie bins.”

“That’s very niche.”

“That’s how technology works. I guess you too are too busy looking at the big picture?”

“I wouldn’t put it that way. So, did your company develop the system?”

“No.”

“Who did, if you don’t mind me asking?”

“It was patented by Markos Delatollas.”

That name rang a bell.

"Markos Delatollas from Electrical Engineering at our Uni?"

"Yes."

"And the patent was the result of his University-funded research?"

"I assume so."

"And you bought it."

"It was up for sale."

The hypocrisy was staggering. It was best to drop the conversation.

"How should I go about this? Any instructions?"

"Yes", she said and picked up a folder from a shelf. "This is Paul's catalogue. You'll find separate lists for books he owned, borrowed ones, ones he had lent out, valuable copies, what is here and what he kept at the office, everything."

"Sorting it should be easy then."

"I'd appreciate it if it were also quick and thorough. I don't want any of it left here at the end. I'm planning on refurbishing and repurposing the room."

When she left me alone with the books, even the mustiness of the study offered some warm respite from the superior Geraldine's chill presence. I was used to outsiders not having an interest in what goes on between red brick walls but her loathing was deep-rooted and visceral despite her having profited handsomely from academic research.

I thumbed through the list of books looking for one title in particular. It was there alright, in the office list. I smiled at the thought that the physical counterpart of the entry was sitting comfortably on its shelf too.

The task was relatively easy. The books were placed in sequence. The list didn't make any library science sense but perhaps he just recorded and stored books in order of acquisition. All I had to do was take them off the shelf, box them and tick them off. In some cases, I took liberties exercising my academic judgement. Some titles were so dated that they wouldn't pass basic equality and diversity tests for bigotry. Others had been superseded by more recent research.

I was on the second last shelf when, between a book about the constitution of the social (a good book) and another on religion (one I'd never heard of), I found, wedged in, a pink envelope. There being no recipient, stamp or postmark on the front, it didn't take a great deal of thought to figure out that it had been hand-delivered. The envelope had been torn open.

The note paper inside was also pink and was covered in hand-drawn love hearts and smiley faces, also in another shade of pink. The colour coding left me in no doubt as to the nature of the content so I pushed the door shut before reading it.

"Mi amor,

How can I ever thank you for what you've done for me? All my wishes have come true thanks to you.

But I'll try. Not in words but in actions.

I look forward to our next trip so much. You should brace yourself for more fun than you've ever had.

I love you, mi amor,

Your Carmencita"

There was much I could have asked Geraldine when I'd arrived. Why, for instance, had Paul never bothered to fix his missing teeth when he could clearly afford a crown? Why too was it that she resolutely resisted allowing any students to set foot in the house?

Now, as I left, I had the answer without having had to ask, an answer that Geraldine Whitmore-Digby must have known too well. He didn't need the dental work because his bite was as good as ever.

❖

"Are you sure it was from her?", Duncan asked.

"Short of being there when she wrote it, yes. I mean, come on. 'Mi amor?' Twice over as well? 'Your Carmencita?'"

"I suppose so."

"I can't believe you went through his personal belongings", Doreen said.

"I most certainly did not. I was only performing my duty as the executor of that part of his last will and testament."

"Artful canine specimen", Duncan said

"It's unbecoming to speak ill of the dead", Doreen said.

"Which is why I do so unsparingly while they're still alive", Duncan said.

"Who would have imagined?", I said.

Duncan and Doreen sipped on their wines. Barry, Ed and Dom, our next door neighbours at the bar of the Scrote, bent to their pints and I followed suit. There we were, six in a row, quaffing side by side in perfectly synchronised choreography.

My theory is that drunks like the company of drunks not for the conversation but for the element of complicity, for the blessed relief that comes with the diffusion of responsibility for doing what others tell them is wrong. Though best achieved in silence, Barry, Dom and Ed put that assumption to the test. During their long, daily sessions at the Scrote, they were habitually engrossed in conversation with each other and on occasion with other patrons. Their ability to refresh and change the topics of discussion was rather admirable. It probably helped that they occupied a campus intersection abuzz with information and speculation.

"Please don't tell anyone, OK?", I said.

"Of course not", Doreen said.

Her attempt to show how appalled she was at the very suggestion that anything said could possibly go beyond the porous walls of the pub was too forced and self-conscious to reassure.

"Have you noticed anything different about her since you know what?", I said.

"Now that you mention it, she's not been in as much", Duncan said. "And when she is in, she's a bit subdued. The fourth floor used to boom with her precocious avidity."

"She was late submitting her term report too", Doreen said, "but perhaps that was Horst's fault. The online system does not send a notification until the supervisor enters notes and approval."

"Damn those online systems", Duncan said. "Whatever was wrong with the informality of the supervisor-supervisee relationship? It's not about box-ticking, it's about transfer of wisdom."

"You've never actually had a PhD student, have you?", Doreen suggested.

"Beside the point."

"Speaking of Horst", I said, "do you think he knew?"

"If he did, it didn't show", Doreen said. "His relationship with Victoria has been alright. Her first year report was in on time, he was happy with it, they've had their regular supervision sessions, nothing out of the ordinary there. Why do you ask?"

"It's just that Horst strikes me as quite territorial."

"That he is", Duncan said.

"He wouldn't be best pleased to find out that his one doctoral student was, how to put it, involved with another member of staff. The HoD no less", I said.

"Wouldn't you be?", Doreen asked.

"Perhaps but I'm not one to hold grudges."

"And you think Horst is?", Duncan said.

"Isn't he?"

The most important technique that any teacher should possess is making the student feel that they knew the answer all along. It's manipulative, of course, but in a benign, end-justifies-the-means way. The same technique also works outside the classroom.

"I am happy to say that our relationship has never exceeded the limits of courteous and entirely unemotional professionalism."

"Not words I would associate with you", I said.

"What on earth are you suggesting?", Duncan snapped.

"Alright, alright, untwist those big knickers. I didn't have you down as so irritable."

"You have us all down as something, do you?", Duncan said.

"It was just a joke."

"Humour has its limits."

"Oh yeah? And what are they?"

"No one can question my courtesy and collegiality."

"I wouldn't dream of questioning either your courtesy or your collegiality. Your professionalism on the other hand ..."

"That's enough", Duncan said and climbed off the bar stool as quickly as his robust frame allowed him.

"Duncan, sit back down. Michael is just being stupid", Doreen said. "Michael, get some bloody awareness. Apologise immediately."

Being chastised by Doreen could only be ignored at one's peril. The Department had consumed all her working life. After the best part of three decades of dealing with students and difficult members of staff she had fine-tuned the lines, the tone of voice, the posture. She had also acquired the wisdom of invoking her disciplinary ways only when absolutely required.

Her de facto and unshakeable authority was supported by the fact that she was in complete command of how the whole institution operated – from the Vice Chancellor's office to the basement of the Scrote. She was the Department's one and only administrator. Even as the volume of business grew to meet proliferating targets set from above, it never crossed anyone's mind that we might need more admin staff. Doreen was manager, secretary, social events organiser, nanny and agony aunt to academics and students alike. She juggled everything successfully and that's the way she liked it too. She had a family but her true life was the job and it seemed to give her self-fulfilment, self-esteem, and a smug sense of satisfaction that I found both enviable and a little pathetic.

I dutifully apologised and we returned to our drinks observing the time-honoured convention that every quarrel has to be swept under the carpet by switching to less contentious topics.

All in all, it was a good after-work drinks session. Duncan's surprising and, I thought, unjustified outburst had been an unexpected glitch but it still didn't detract from the fact that some seeds had been sown.

An inexcusable trespass

Universities are like monasteries. Some find shelter in them because they have already achieved serenity in their, invariably misguided, certainty about what is valuable in life, their intellectual ability, the meaning of the world. Some are there for the modest perks; the inexpensive institutional meals, free books, sponsored conference trips complete with three-star hotel breakfasts. Others, the relatively noble ones, join academia out of confusion about the world and their own lives. And then there are those who fit into academia less badly than they would fit in the world outside.

If the last category did not exist, it would have to be introduced to classify Lucy Warburton. On the surface, one would describe her as socially awkward to the point of belligerence. But, like everyone, she deserved the benefit of the doubt, so over the years I had tried to be more charitable in my efforts to fathom her. I had come to the conclusion that her life, or at least what I witnessed of it, was a continual struggle to stake out her rightful place. The trouble was that she herself didn't know what that place might be or what she wanted it to be.

As a result, in her view, no matter what others did, it was always an inexcusable trespass. No matter how lightly one trod, those were her toes one stepped on. However mundane or innocent a remark, or meaningless a look, every response and action regardless of motive would be perceived and responded to as an act of aggression.

"How are things?", I asked making myself comfortable in one of her easy chairs.

There were so many photos of her children on every available surface in her office that I wondered if she was working on a longitudinal research project designed to record each day of their lives.

"What do you mean? Why shouldn't things be good?"

She crossed her legs under her long floral skirt. She adjusted her glasses and then promptly crossed her arms. The shield was now in place.

"No reason. Could go either way really."

"Did you want something in particular?"

Pleasantries were a minefield with Lucy so I was happy to cut them short.

"I'm just a bit confused about the teaching allocation."

"What about it?", Lucy said.

"Did you happen to speak to Paul about your postgrad seminars before you know what?"

"No, why should I have?"

"It's just that I had a brief chat with him a few days before you know what. Well, I say chat but actually it was only a passing exchange in the corridor, you know the kind. Anyway, he sort of implied that he was reconsidering the hours on the Anthropology and Social Change course."

"That's my course. That's always been my course. I introduced that course."

She was already beginning to brew.

"Of course, of course. But, you know, the numbers have to be balanced."

The prime context for the practical application of the concept of justice in academia is the allocation of teaching. Whoever takes on the thankless task of setting staff teaching loads, and in our case it was the HoD because, of course, Paul would reserve for himself any job that gave him power over others, has to take into account more parameters than the Lernaean Hydra has heads. Who introduced the course? What has each been promised on being appointed? Who has the expertise to teach the course? Who is on leave? Who is going to go on leave or sabbatical over the next couple of years? Who has an administrative load that must be offset against their teaching load? Who will be most upset if their expectations are disappointed? Such matters can only be settled by universal compromise sealed with an iron fist. And even then the ensuing arrangement remains a fragile peace.

"Also, apparently, and don't quote me on this because as I said it was only a passing conversation with Paul, a colleague was giving him grief."

"About my course?"

"Said colleague, please don't ask me who it was, felt that the course is a bit dated and that a component on late capitalism and neoliberalism should be introduced. That would be taught by him, I mean said colleague, because it's his, said colleague's, expertise."

"Was it Horst?"

"Yes, it was. It was Horst."

"That's preposterous. I already talk about late capitalism in the course."

That was true. She did. For a full ten minutes. The course was terribly thin on that ground. Horst would have been justified to make the complaint. Only, he never had.

"Anyway, I don't mean to alarm you."

"You should mean to alarm me."

"I just wanted to ask you whether anything has happened in that direction."

"I'm calling the Union."

"No need to rush. You see, my impression was that Paul was having none of it."

"Really?"

Her surprise was as intense as her outrage.

"That's the sense I got. I think he explained to Horst that things cannot change, not halfway through the term anyway, and certainly not without consulting you."

"Paul said all that?"

"Words to that effect."

She paused to collect her thoughts, disproving my impression that defensiveness was her one and only default setting.

"I wouldn't have expected that. It changes everything."

Paul Digby had discontinued one of Lucy's courses a couple of years back. Lucy's fury at the decision was uncontainable. She more or less camped outside the Vice Chancellor's office, had the Union work for her around the clock, sent daily emails to all on the University staff mailing list. Her campaign was to no avail. That the course had only attracted three students or fewer per year in the first five years of running it had not helped her cause.

"It does, doesn't it? I mean it would, had Paul not passed away. I think said colleague was immensely peeved by Paul's refusal."

"I don't understand, how did you get all that information in a fleeting chat in the corridor?"

"We spoke fast. The point is that you should be alerted to the possibility of the teaching allocation changing under the new Head, whoever that may be."

"Yes, thank you, thank you very much", she said.

The invitation to contribute to the State of the Art series had come quite late into the production process. I couldn't blame the editors since I was the one who had left it so late to announce to the world my sensational new research.

I had to hurry. The first draft was due in by the end of January. What with the assignments I would have to mark in the weeks that followed, the intervening Christmas holiday, the last week of January already a write-off to allow for preparations for the Beauclerk Mansion off-campus weekend, I only had a few weeks to research, write, edit, re-write and submit the chapter. The relatively low limit of five thousand words did make things easier. Yet it also made my task harder because there would be no room for flab.

I spent all afternoon sending emails, editing teaching slides and watching videos of pets doing cute things as I waited for everyone to leave the Department. Once the noise had died away, I went for a check-out stroll along the corridors just to make sure that no one had remained behind.

I opened StateOfTheArt_chapter_MichaelWest.doc and began to read.

It really was quite masterful. It is only the best and most experienced scholars, who have such strong and extensive command of the field that they can build it into the background of what they have to say in an informative way but without endless expositions. They then construct their own argument on that platform so as to stand out as a novel contribution while still being part of an established body of knowledge.

Catherine was achieving that effect so effortlessly that it made my mouth water. One could see even in that early draft, a stage where most of us can only yap excitedly about an emerging idea that we do not quite yet understand, whereas here she was already pushing the boundaries.

Her point, now even more sophisticated than at the outset, was simple to the point of being ingenious. Anthropology has all too often explored crime as triggering rituals of justice, as holding the perpetrator accountable for his transgression. What if, however, we reversed the perspective and thought of crime not as anteceding justice but as being itself part of justice? And what if we didn't privilege the perspective of institutions but fitted the attitudes of all actors into the same picture? To do that, we would also need a new methodology, she explained. A methodology that would be able to capture the comprehensive aim of our enquiry and not fragment the data of experience in order to squeeze it into artificially constructed pigeonholes.

The more I read, the more impressed I was with Catherine's feat. Even so, much of it went over my head and I grew to realise that appropriating it would be a monumentally difficult task. There was a whole range of substantive and stylistic changes that I had to make. First of all, to make the whole thing credible, I would have to bring it into line with my own previous research. That would involve a self-reference here, an allusion there, an assumption further down the line. A very tricky task, not least because all my publications were of a completely different ilk and direction to what I was proposing to do in this chapter. Then I would have to scan it for recurring turns of phrase that might be readily identifiable as Catherine's and then edit the text so as to reflect my style, such as it was.

Submitting it as it stood, with only light-touch amendments was not an option. If there's one activity that academics apply themselves to with meticulous rigour it is peer review. When evaluating colleagues' submissions before publication they will happily rip to shreds whatever comes their way, emboldened by their anonymity and the fact that their word, whether justified or not, is final. But even if my manuscript didn't land in the inbox of a nit-picker, alarm bells would have gone off in the head of any half-educated reviewer, if I didn't conjure up the necessary changes.

Obviously, no matter how well I disguised and tried to appropriate the raw material, it was always going to be the product of Catherine's thinking and I would be, no two ways about it, guilty of plagiarising. I had presented it at the conference without giving it another thought because I assumed that it would be as unnoticeable and forgettable as many of my other conference performances. Publishing it as my own work, however, was taking it to another level. There was no way Catherine would not find out. For myself, I wasn't so much worried about my reputation and my academic integrity. She'd have no way of proving that the idea had been hers so it'd be foolish of her to make a fuss. What was more of a concern was the strain that it would put on our relationship. On the other hand, the pace of academic publishing was such that the book wouldn't be out for at least another nine months and nine months was a long time and there was no foreseeing how our relationship would develop.

So there I was, so engrossed in trying to grasp the nuances of the argument so as to appropriate it and so relaxed in the assumption that, at that time of the evening, I would work undisturbed that I once again failed to notice the lift stopping on the fourth floor or the footsteps on the corridor until I caught something through the corner of my eye and saw Catherine standing at the threshold of my office.

In my state of intense concentration, for a moment I thought that she had materialised in space through her writings. Maybe it was because I thought I was being confronted by a vindictive apparition that a strong sense of guilt overpowered me when she said:

"What are you still doing here?"

She turned on the main light to restore all dimensions to my perception of things. I hastily turned off the document. Luckily, the lecture slides I had been working on earlier were still open and they came to the foreground.

"Just updating some teaching material."

She approached me, stood behind my chair and looked at my screen.

"Malinowski?"

"What?", I said.

"You're giving a lecture on Malinowski?"

Of course, Malinowski did feature in that lecture. That's what Catherine was talking about. I had made the wrong connection.

"It's gotta be done, right?"

"Isn't it time to renew the curriculum? Make it, you know, less racist and sexist?"

"Maybe next year. What are you doing here anyway?"

"I'd forgotten a couple of books in the office and I'm working from home tomorrow so I thought I may as well come pick them up tonight."

That was some commitment, considering she, unlike me, lived in town.

"How about a drink?", she said.

"Sure. The Montgomery?"

"It'll be last orders soon."

"True."

The Scrote would have closed already, as it normally did on weekdays, so there was only the one option left.

"Do you want to come to mine?", I said. "I've got some wine and gin. If you're lucky, there'll be a lemon in the fridge and the tonic will not have gone flat."

Trepidation trailed me as we left the building. With no shortage of things to be worried about, my predominant concern was whether I had saved the changes I had made to the chapter before turning off the computer.

She was lucky with the tonic but not so with the lemon, which was, as I had remembered, in the fridge but in such an advanced stage of disintegration, that its surface played host to an unwanted fungal culture. She didn't object to her G&T having only two of the three ingredients.

"I don't know how you can drink gin and tonic", I said joining her on the sofa.

"Why not?"

"I think of it as more of a summer drink."

"Stereotypes."

"Perhaps."

"Anyway, it's good to be reminded of the summer in this miserable weather."

"It's not that bad. It's been fairly dry, if you think about it."

"Listen to us", she said.

She removed her gaze from my bookshelves to look at me.

"I know, you're right", I said.

I made a mental note to revisit Paul's *Anthropology of Seduction* to check whether trivial waffle is invariably the first stage of the ritual of human mating. Was it only academics that were so awkward or was it just us? In any case, I was glad that Catherine had ended the weather conversation.

The problem now was finding a substantive but safe topic of conversation and there were none.

"Do you still suspect foul play in Paul's death?", I said.

"I do", she said with disconcerting determination.

"What are we doing next then?"

"We still need some way of finding out who else was in the building at the time."

"But we tried our only option and drew a blank."

"Not so sure about that."

"Perhaps we should try a different angle", I said.

"Such as?"

"We've been looking for opportunity, right?"

"Right."

"Even if we did establish opportunity though, it'd still be inconclusive."

"What do you mean?"

"Here's a thought experiment. Imagine that the building had been brimming with people at the time. Surely we wouldn't go around asking whether each of these people did it."

I felt grateful for the tried and tested distraction devices that are hypothetical thought experiments.

"OK, so?", she said.

"Maybe what we should be looking for is motive. That way we would be able to narrow down the list of possibilities."

"You think?", she said.

Had she drowned a chuckle? If so, I ignored it and continued.

"So, if we were to find that one of the people on the list was in the building, then we'd have more to go by."

"I see your point. And where do you suggest we begin?"

"What do we know about his personal life?"

She sighed.

"Not much. He'd been married to Geraldine for, I don't know, twenty-five years or so. A long time at any rate. That's about all I know."

"She doesn't seem particularly fond of academia."

"I hardly know her. Alison has known her for much longer."

"Did he have a life outside the university?"

"Does any of us?"

"Ouch."

"It's true, no?"

"Still painful to admit."

"Anyway", she continued, "if it's someone outside the university, how did they get in through the security system?"

"They could have entered on some pretence earlier and hidden somewhere in the building."

"And how would they know that Paul would be there at that time?"

"I don't know."

"If you ask me, it doesn't seem premeditated or planned."

"Why not?"

"The muddy footprints."

"I still think you're reading too much into that."

"I disagree. And if I'm right and they belong to whomsoever was there, then it suggests haste."

"You lost me."

"I assume that the killer rushed through the mudfield."

"Maybe there was mud everywhere. Wasn't it raining that night?"

"No, it wasn't."

"Are you sure?"

"Positive."

"You pay more attention to the weather than I do."

She gave me one of those patronising, disapproving looks.

"So", she said, "if that is the case, then it has to be a member of staff."

"We've been side-tracked again. Let's not forget that we're trying to establish motive."

"Maybe opportunity and motive are not as sharply separated."

"Still, let's try to be systematic. Motive. Who in the Department might want to kill Paul? And do it in a rush too?"

"I don't know", she said.

She sounded as if she was answering a different question than the one I had asked, perhaps one she had on her mind.

"I can think of at least one person who had a grievance against him", I said.

"How about you?", she said raising her head and looking straight into my eyes.

I had to play it a bit slow and more convincingly so than ever.

"What about me?"

"How did you get on with Paul?"

"We were colleagues, that was about it."

"He was more than a colleague."

"Not to me he wasn't."

"What do you mean?"

"I don't know. What do *you* mean?"

"I mean he was HoD."

"Oh that, yes, that he was. Still, our relationship was professional and courteous."

"I've no doubt. I don't know why I even asked you."

"Really?"

"You're a good guy, Michael."

Actually, yes, I was a good guy. Sure, I was a tad cynical, as Nikhil never tired of accusing me, but surely only good guys can become disenchanted. And could I really be reproached for trying to do something for myself in the infinitesimally narrow margins that others allowed me?

"Thanks", I said.

"No, I mean it. You're never involved in petty politics, you're not affected by trivialities. You see all that for what it truly is. You're focused on the big picture."

"Is that what good guys do?"

"If the big picture is about the welfare of everyone, then yes."

She took off her shoes, arranged herself horizontally on the sofa and stretched to rest her bare feet on my legs.

Our first kiss was like first kisses usually are: exploratory, uncertain, a little awkward. What followed was much better and I knew that because I didn't want to run away as soon as it had finished. Since she spent the night, I don't think Catherine did either.

Breakfast was minimal, consisting of only black coffee. I had offered to nip over to the Butty Call and fetch a couple of their chewy croissants only to have the offer laughed off.

"I thought you patronised the Butty Call."

"Only when absolutely necessary. I usually bring a packed lunch from home."

"Or you go to a fancy café in town."

"What?"

"I saw you in one of those new places once. You were there with Alison."

"Are you stalking me?"

"Don't be silly. I just happened to be going past."

"It couldn't have been me. I've never had lunch with Alison in town."

"Maybe you were just having tea and a scone."

"I've never had tea and scones with Alison in town. Or anywhere else for that matter."

"Maybe I was wrong. I'd just had a fall rushing for the bus so perhaps I was seeing things."

Maybe I *had* been wrong. I thought it strange at the time what with Alison not having been in the office that day and living in a village several miles over the other side of campus. I was becoming convinced that I had been making things up because of the fall.

"You probably were."

"Have you done this before?", I asked.

"Done what?"

"Been involved with someone from work."

"Why are you asking me that?"

"Sorry, I didn't mean to offend."

"So why are you asking?"

"I said sorry. Just being a bit apprehensive. You know what they say."

"What? Don't shit where you eat?"

"I wouldn't put it that way. It's a terrible analogy anyway."

"So how would you put it?"

"Listen, I'm sorry, forget I ever said it."

I pulled her close and kissed her.

"We have to go. Don't you have an appointment in, like, ten minutes?", she said.

"I do", I sighed.

I fetched our coats and her tote bag from the hat stand.

"That's very light. Didn't you get the books you came in for?", I said.

"I forgot", she said. "You distracted me."

It was her turn to come up to me, put her arms around my neck and kiss me.

"I've been trawling the Committee and Department Meetings minutes for material", he said.

"That's great, I'm sure it'll be a most fitting tribute."

"Yes, yes, but there's something I found rather odd."

Catherine rolled her eyes and smiled. We were in the lift and so was Jeremy Allcock.

Jeremy was capable of spending the entire day riding up and down in the lift obsessing over the minutes of a decade-old meeting in a vain bid to reconfigure the order of business.

"Your meticulousness is admirable, Jeremy. If only more colleagues were as rigorous."

"Thank you but there's something I really don't understand. Maybe you can help me with it."

"Jeremy", I said, "what with essay time coming up, term reports due and then Christmas and all, I'll be a bit too busy for this. How about you try to work it out and then maybe send me an email at the beginning of the year?"

"An email?", he said.

Jeremy was so old school that Doreen used to have to type up his hand-written notes. Eventually, she'd had enough, complained that that was not in her job description and Jeremy was politely asked not to expect Doreen to be his typist any longer. He'd taken it graciously enough but by odd coincidence hadn't published anything since. Everything he did write, which wasn't much, he wrote in longhand. To his credit, he applied himself and made significant progress at using the computer. He managed to read emails and occasionally print out attachments; how otherwise could he have access to his precious minutes? His attempts at sending emails, however, were doomed to failure.

"Yes, that's best", I said.

The door opened on the fourth floor. Catherine and I stepped out into the corridor. Jeremy, draped in his old grey coat, unstable on his weak legs and worn out shoes under the weight of his rucksack full of the same books that had become an extension of his back, stayed in the booth, pensive and anxious, before disappearing from view behind the closing door.

I said goodbye to Catherine with a fleeting touch on her hand. She smiled and headed off to her office.

I was a few minutes late for my appointment and Victoria was waiting outside my door. Apologetically, I invited her in and we sat at the coffee table.

"How are you holding up?", I asked.

"Not very well", she said.

Her bloodshot eyes had been drained of tears.

"Victoria, I'm not the right person to advise you about your personal well-being but I'm more than happy to refer you to the appropriate University services."

"Thank you."

"We'll make a phone call at the end of our meeting, alright?"

"Alright."

"What I can provide assistance with, however, is the academic side of things."

"OK."

"How do you feel about the progress of your thesis?"

"Not very well."

"Could you elaborate?"

"I'm alone."

"Why are you saying that?"

"He's gone."

"Yes, I know, but doesn't the Department afford you all the facilities and help you expected?"

"I guess."

"And you have a supervisor."

She scrunched up her lips to indicate little less than disgust.

The supervisor-supervisee relationship is quite special, its character formed back in the olden days when universities were few and doctorates even fewer and academic genealogy still mattered. Yet it had survived over-inflation and modernisation. The supervisor's formal task is to provide guidance, direct students to the appropriate literature, help them choose and formulate a topic in a manageable way, check what they write for accuracy, consistency and originality.

In reality, in most cases the supervisor is a combination of parent, lover and tyrant at the same time. If that sounds incestuous and creepy, the reality is that it can be even worse. Buckets of tears have been shed over a single word or even a misplaced question mark scribbled in the margins of a chapter draft. Supervisory sessions can be the intellectual equivalents of torture by cranial clamp. The skull is squeezed to the point of being crushed to extract all the bad stuff in order to make room for new intellectual dead-ends. Although rarely fatal, the damage done is permanent.

That's not to say that supervisors fare much better. A failed doctorate can be the end of one's career and a successful one can be career making. But be too successful and there's the associated risk of inducing patricide or matricide once the mentored student becomes an established academic.

Not that I speak from personal experience. When writing my thesis, I was pretty much left to my own devices. My supervisor had died (literally, not academically; those two kinds of death do not entail each other) just after I completed my first year. I was then reassigned to another, someone too busy to allow attention to me interfere with his need to trawl the Internet to see who might be citing him in their work. My doctorate should have come with some form of special commendation for resilience and resourcefulness.

"I don't know whether Paul...", I continued.

She welled up at the sound of his name again.

"Help yourself to a tissue", I said pointing at the coffee table.

She wiped her eyes and blew her nose so discreetly that it was unlikely to have had any effect in her emotion-clogged sinuses.

"What I wanted to say was that Paul raised the issue of your supervision with me not so long ago."

"He did?", she snuffled.

"I don't think I'd be misrepresenting him if I said that he thought it'd be best for you to be transferred to another supervisor."

"Is that possible?"

Puffed up as they might have been, her eyes could not conceal a mix of excitement and surprise.

"Of course it is. I think Paul might have taken soundings as to whether he could take over himself."

"Paul would do that?"

As if he would. He'd know better than to mix business with pleasure. In all probability that was the reason Victoria had been allocated to Horst in the first place.

"He was concerned about your welfare. Here, have another tissue."

"And now?", she said pausing her sobbing.

"It didn't go down very well with your supervisor but that was to be expected. Be that as it may, we can still go ahead with it. But first I need to hear from you how you feel about it."

"I'm not happy."

She was slowly learning the art of understatement.

"Are your differences with Horst academic or personal?"

"Is there really a distinction?"

She probably thought she was making some general point about scholarship consuming one's identity as a person but, still, she had unwittingly hit the nail on the head.

"He's making me take the argument in a direction that I don't like."

"He's your supervisor. He knows things and he guides you. That's his job."

Her eyes sparked with anger.

"He knows nothing", she snapped. "He doesn't understand anything. My arguments go over his head. He's fixated with the same two or three ideas that he's been talking about all his life. And he's boring. So incredibly boring. Has he ever talked to you about his pickling? He goes on and on and on about it. Half our supervision sessions are wasted on safe canning techniques and how a few weeks ago one can of tuna worked but the other didn't and how fabulous cauliflower is if you use a mixture of cider and white wine vinegar. He should write a book about pickling, not pretend to understand a book on the anthropology of rebellion."

Of course Horst would be into home pickling. He probably did some knitting on the side too and quite likely he was on a waiting list for an allotment.

"Your feelings about this are abundantly clear. I'll deal with the procedural side of things, although you should probably have a chat with Horst first."

"Is that necessary?"

"You can't just disappear into the night. And falling out with people is best avoided."

"OK."

"What we need to discuss now is to whom to allocate you."

"Anyone else will do."

"There's the logistics of it to consider as well. Some people are oversubscribed, others don't have the right expertise. How about Duncan Erskine-Bell?"

"No way", she said with a startling urgency.

"I beg your pardon?"

"Not him, no."

"I don't understand, you just said anyone will do."

"Anyone but him."

"Or Horst."

"Anyone but Horst and Erskine-Bell."

"I sense a personal dislike for the man. What accounts for that, if I may ask?"

"He's been awful to me."

"In what way?"

"The way he used to look at me, things he said."

"Such as?"

"Snide things. He used to make me feel inferior."

"Used to?"

"He stopped."

"How come?"

"I can't say."

She didn't have to.

I respected Alison Davies. Her scholarship was solid, if on the conservative side, and her management style effective. She didn't beat around the bush, talked straight and generally made the right call, at least on the rare occasions that Paul allowed her any discretion to make decisions. She was also relatively sensitive to the personal circumstances of each of us. It was a pity that she didn't want to keep the HoD job for good.

"It's about your promotion, Michael", she said before I had even landed in the chair.

I could only bring myself to nod. I wasn't quite prepared for this to happen so soon.

"Had Paul spoken to you about this?"

"No, no, he hadn't."

"That's strange. I see in his diary that you had a meeting the morning of the day that he you know what."

I thought I had taken into account all the important angles to the situation. I had deleted our email exchange regarding the meeting but not once had it crossed my mind that Paul would keep a diary with all his appointments. I kicked myself for denying so readily that I'd discussed the promotion with him. I had to stick to that story now.

"Oh yes, that's right. It was a brief meeting about something else entirely though."

"Here it reads 'MW re promo'."

"Does it?"

"It does."

"Of course, what I am thinking? We discussed the promotion of the away postgraduate weekend. He was keen that as many students sign up as possible. He was determined that we make a success of it. You know, the whole making students feel at their alma mater and all."

She looked far from convinced.

"Anyhow, it looks like Paul was putting you forward for promotion."

"That's nice to know."

"His recommendation is glowing."

"I'm grateful that he appreciated my hard work."

"It's a bit odd because there's a dissonance between this and what he'd said at the Promotions Committee."

I gave her a hurt look and she hastened to make amends.

"It's not that he didn't appreciate your work, just that he felt that you weren't ready yet. Inches away but not quite there."

"Maybe he had a change of heart."

"Quite a sharp one, if he did. Anyway, whatever accounts for that, it is what it is. The Promotions Committee only provides advice to the HoD, its decisions are not binding."

That was not strictly speaking true in terms of the rules but it was certainly true under Paul's rule.

"So, are we going ahead with it?", I asked.

"I don't want to go against Paul's wishes..."

"That's very thoughtful", I said.

"It's important that there be some continuity in the way that the Department is run."

"Quite right, yes."

"But, at the same time, I want to make sure that your application has the strongest possible chance of being successful at the higher level."

"Sure, I understand."

"I guess Paul had decided to take a gamble but I find that unnecessary."

My heart sank.

"I'm not sure what you're getting at."

"We need to strengthen your application a little."

There was no room for arguing against that. She was the HoD and she held all the cards. I tried to focus on the bright side, which was that she was not withdrawing the application.

"How do you propose that we do that?"

"There's nothing wrong with your research..."

I'd happily take that. Beggars can't be choosers.

"And your teaching, well, there's only so much we can do about that at this point. So that leaves us with the admin side of things."

"Are you not happy with my performance as Postgraduate Director?"

"No, on the contrary, you're doing a great job. It's just that you need to sink your teeth into something more substantial to make your application watertight."

"Such as?"

"There is currently one vacancy that ticks the boxes."

It didn't take much thought to know what she was talking about. It did, however, take a leap to believe that she was really suggesting what she was suggesting and still that wouldn't explain why she was doing so with a smirk.

"Are you saying what I think you're saying?"

"It would help your cause no end. Actually, if you agree to this, the promotion will be in the bag and after a few years of serving, so will the promotion to the next rung of the ladder. Plus, if you ask me, I think you'd be an excellent HoD."

"Shouldn't this be done by someone more senior than me?"

"Seniority has never been a formal requirement."

"Isn't it a substantive one? Isn't the idea that I should be concentrating on research?"

"As I said, your research is fairly sound already and there's no reason why you shouldn't be able to juggle it alongside the HoD-ship. I know it sounds daunting but I'll be here to help. We will all be."

"How about the Professors in the Department?"

"I'm the only one left. Discounting Jeremy, of course."

"And Catherine?"

Alison's puzzled and suspicious look underscored how inexcusable my slip-up had been.

"What about Catherine?"

"Nothing, it's just that she's the rising star and all that", I tried to patch things up.

"Listen, it doesn't even matter whether anyone else is suitable or available. The point is that this is for your own good."

"I appreciate that, thanks."

"So what do you think?"

"Can I give it some thought for a few days?"

"OK, take until the end of the week. I have to send my recommendation to the University Committee by this coming Monday."

"That'll do, thanks."

"Great. I hope you'll agree."

I was halfway out the door when she said:

"Oh and Michael..."

I turned around.

"Yes?"

"There's one more strange thing about this recommendation of Paul's."

"What's that?"

"It was appended to another one for some reason. Any idea why?"

"No, how should I know?"

"I guess he did it in a hurry. Who knows? Anyway, thanks for coming. Let me know your decision as soon as you can."

I'm not one to fall easily for psychobabble. I find the karma and 'everything happening for a reason' talk ghastly and clichéd. Still, experience has made me wonder whether events in one's life are all stored in some kind of metaphysical container, happily remaining there together, semi-strangers to one another, until a catalyst is thrown into the mix and boom, they all come to life, form connections leading to results, which none could have achieved had they stayed suspended in semi-isolation.

I have no scientific proof, or any other kind for that matter, of the connection between Alison's polite if forceful offer of the HoD-ship or everything that ensued in rapid succession over the following few days but I am convinced that a link and an explanation must exist.

To start with, it can't be a coincidence that I found Horst waiting for me outside my office and that, were it not for my meeting with Alison, he would have otherwise trapped me at my desk, leaving me with no escape route.

Seeing him from a distance, I made sure to catch his attention by saying hello to Doreen at the top of my voice. She was somewhat taken aback by the decibel level and the identity of her manic greeter. Having made sure that it was no one of importance, she rewarded me with a wave of her hand that acknowledged and dismissed me simultaneously.

As I came within a few metres of my office door the seething anger of my waiting visitor hit me like a nuclear shock wave prompting me to turn on my heels and head off in the opposite direction.

"Michael, Michael, I want to speak to you", he shouted at my retreating back.

Fully aware that pretending not to hear him was not credible in the circumstances, I widened the distance between us. I didn't care. Why should I? It was what I intended.

I heard him speed up, the rubber soles of his sandals slapping the floor as he chased after me. Nikhil was right. There was nothing dispassionate about Horst. All these years he'd been playing the cool, intellectually superior, hippy academic, the lofty one who remains calm and aloof amidst the tedium of trivial, mundane academic concerns. Look at him now. See how little it took to make him fume to the point of exploding.

"Come back here, come back", he yelled.

Lucy stuck her head out of her office and immediately pulled it right back, a little fearfully.

"Hi Lucy", I said as I ran past her.

"Who do you think you are?", Horst yelled.

I turned around as calm as the business of business-as-usual dictated.

"Oh, hi Horst", I said. "I didn't realise you were speaking to me."

I kept the volume pitched just above the threshold of bad farce.

"Naturally I'm speaking to you, whom else would I be speaking to?"

He was getting more aggressive by the second. His body was tensing up, his voice shrilling into an agitated higher note.

"What are you playing at?", he said.

"I don't know what you mean."

"I don't know what you mean", he repeated.

His imitation of my intonation and accent was pretty accurate, I had to give him that.

"I really don't."

"I really don't."

"Horst, this is getting silly. Can you please explain why you're so upset?"

"You know very well why I'm upset."

"I do? Please do refresh my memory then."

"Victoria."

"What about Victoria?"

"Why are you taking her away from me?"

"Now I see. Perhaps we should discuss this in private."

"The private is public."

"I'm not sure the slogan quite applies here, Horst."

"Shut up. Why are you taking her away from me?"

"As you wish. It's not a reflection on your performance as a supervisor but it's in Victoria's best interest to be re-allocated to another colleague."

"She's mine. She's mine!"

"No one owns doctoral students."

"Ha!", he let out a sarcastic syllable. "You can't be so naïve. You're bullshitting."

"Listen, Horst. This is out of my hands. Paul had already put the move on track."

Seeing him lose it the way he did next was vindication enough although it was also considerably scary.

"That fuckin' prick", he yelled. "That fuckin' prick."

His outrage was depriving him of all lexical capacity.

"It's what he would have wanted", I muttered.

"Is it? Is fuckin' it what he would have fuckin' wanted? I'll fuckin' tell you what I would fuckin' have fuckin' wanted. To see that fuckin' prick burn."

That seemed like a good time to press Horst's big button, the nuclear one.

"Now now, Horst. You can't talk like that about Paul. I know he took issue with your research but you know how intolerant he was with substandard work. No reason to hate the man so much."

Horst was not a bad scholar. He had something that the rest of us lacked, having been exposed to two schools of thought, Anglo-American and continental European. Unlike many, he combined the two traditions fairly well too. His work was neither too problem-oriented nor did it lean towards nebulousness. It was well-written and not merely for the sake of elegant prose. It had a point. Some of the time, anyway.

It was perhaps inevitable that it had all gone to his head. He never tired of boasting that the academic systems on both sides of the water were too small for his intellect and that everyone else was afflicted by such limitations as to render us incapable of appreciating his brilliance. He considered it absurd to be criticised for his work by anyone other than the few academic heroes that he held in high esteem (most of them conveniently dead, which precluded being criticised by them). When it came to feedback, Horst tended to gag on it.

Still, the punch that landed heavy on my shoulder was unexpected. Admittedly, it hurt a lot since he did hit my clavicle knuckles on but grunting and doubling over as I did perhaps overstated its effect.

"Fuck you", Horst screamed at me, undeterred. "You know nothing. You don't understand anything. You've no idea. You're a nobody. Everybody hated that bastard."

Still on my knees, I extended an arm to calm him down in the neutral manner of someone uninvolved in the altercation. I had barely touched his jacket sleeve when he swung his right arm and struck mine, pivoting me in a semi-circle until I eventually collapsed on my right side.

"Horst, enough. Go, now!", Catherine, who had been standing at the doorstep of her office with a front row view of the show, growled at him.

Her authoritative tones proved magical. Horst huffed and slunk away like a cowed beast.

Maybe to save face or because there was still leftover, bottled up, ungovernable fury that he had to vent, he stopped a few metres down the corridor and turned around and wagged a finger at me.

"She's not going anywhere, you hear me? Or I'll see you burn too", he yelled.

He turned away once more, mumbling to himself all the way to his office. I managed to straighten up.

"Incredible", I said.

"Yes, incredible", Catherine repeated.

Abnormal and misbegotten

Giving a lecture to first year undergraduate students at the beginning of the academic year and then again as the term enters its death throes just before the festive break is much like the experience of Dr Lanyon who, accustomed to sharing a pleasant dinner and good wine with his friend and host Dr Jekyll, on a subsequent occasion encounters something "abnormal and misbegotten in the very essence" of his dining companion, "something seizing, surprising and revolting". This very essence is true too of the mid-December ordeal the lecturer must face when the once shining faces of the student rows before him transform into glowering ranks of Mr. Hydes.

It was to be expected really. They were young and adjusting to life on their own was a struggle. Their early excitement drove most of them to binge on the good sides of independence early on but they were soon hit by the unrelenting reality of having to juggle studies, fun and making ends meet. That left them ragged in body and soul. Even the few that had joined our University out of choice (most came to us from the last chance saloon of clearing; they didn't have the marks, we didn't have the numbers so we did each other a favour) became tired and disenchanted.

So, standing in front of this ragged audience and talking about Malinowski's account of attitudes to crime and punishment of the people of the Trobriand islands, bore some resemblance to administering an antidote to an accidental overdose of the drug that had shaken their very "fortress of identity".

Not that it was easier for me. Term takes its toll at the best of times even without a violent death casting its shadow over everything. Even more dispiriting is recycling the same lecture for what feels like the thousandth time. I was among the few who tried to revise their notes and delivery every year but still the variation was minimal and, in any case, muscle memory unfailingly led me back to the same old turns of phrase, unfunny jokes and even some mistakes.

That year, however, rereading my notes and refreshing my memory of the book had rekindled an excitement that had been dormant for too long. Instead of looking at the clock every few seconds and despairing at how much longer I would have to bore them and me equally, I spoke about the Trobriands and their ways with all the enthusiasm of a young lecturer addressing a class for the first time. In fact, my exhilaration was not so much diminished by that morning's events as enhanced by what had transpired.

"That was your best lecture of the year, sir", Adeel Rahman said to me, having waited respectfully for me to turn off the computer, pick up my notes and move away from the lectern.

"Thanks, Adeel. I appreciate that."

"I find the significance of reciprocity and mutuality in the arrangements of the Trobriands particularly fascinating."

"So did Malinowski. In the next term we'll see that our societies are not all that different in that respect."

"Amazing, thank you, sir."

He lingered there for a few seconds without saying anything. He clearly wanted to table a request.

"Is that all, Adeel?"

He let out an embarrassed chortle.

"Actually, sir, I wanted to ask you, sir, could I do a long essay on the course instead of taking the exam?"

"Have you read the regulations regarding exams and essays?"

He lowered his head. Of course he hadn't. Students rarely did.

"Anyway, yes, you may do this."

"Thank you so much, sir! And do you think Dr Bowen would be agreeable to supervising it?"

"That'd be unusual; it's normally the course convener who supervises long essays in the course. That too is clearly stated in the regulations."

"Of course, sir, I understand. It's just that her expertise is closer to what I want to do."

When it comes to which kind of student is more irritating, it is a toss-up between the indifferent ones and those who, after half a term of instruction, think they already have what it takes to win a Nobel prize and judge the expertise of their teachers.

"It might be possible but you must talk to her first", I said.

Not having to supervise a dissertation weighed more than any dent to my ego that might be caused by a first-year student choosing Catherine over me.

"One more thing, sir. Do you think I could use my own empirical data?"

"That depends on the topic. What data do you have in mind?"

"My father is a police officer, sir, so I can draw material from his files."

"Is he really?"

"Yes, sir. He's stationed in the area, sir."

"In the campus area?"

"Yes, sir. He was actually the DCI at the scene of the death of the esteemed late Professor Digby."

I clutched my notes to stop my hands from shaking. My initial instinct was to make an excuse and flee but I regained control and pulled myself together enough to continue the conversation.

"I see. Well, you have to be careful with using sensitive data. In fact, we would have to check whether you'll have to take the ethics course first. Come to think of it, if this does apply, quite definitely the course convener must be the one to supervise the dissertation."

He looked disappointed.

"You should also know what to expect", I continued. "I am only allowed to give you general guidance over a few supervision sessions. This will have to be your own work. However, I am at liberty to veto material that I consider to be unpublishable for ethical or other reasons."

"I understand, sir."

"Now, if there's nothing else, I have to go. Come and see me after the break to discuss this in detail. There's plenty of time. In the meantime, don't speak to anyone else, because there's the risk that it might curtail your chances of having the topic approved."

"I mean, OK, it's a big deal losing a doctoral student..."

"Your first and only doctoral student."

"Still, it didn't warrant such a reaction."

"No, it didn't."

"I mean, physical violence in the workplace? Unprecedented."

"Maybe not unprecedented but I get your point. Are you going to do something about it?"

"I don't think so."

"OK."

Catherine looked relieved with my decision not to take any action, which was understandable, fair even. In academic circles, as in most areas of social life, quarrels of the sort I had with Horst are usually settled in one of three ways. The first is an apology. The second is terminal fallout, which only means a headache for the rest, who need to make an effort to keep the two parties apart in every conceivable activity so as not to risk any further embarrassing clashes. The third is to sweep the row under the rug by pretending that nothing ever happened and without involving any outside agencies. That, I felt, was the preferable option unless circumstances dictated an alternative course of action.

"How are you feeling?", she asked.

She held my hand, which was a little naughty considering that we were in the coffee queue of the Butty Call.

"I'm OK, thanks", I said. "All the better for having you by my side."

She tightened her grip of my hand.

"I'm just thinking", I said, "how easy it is to misjudge people. I knew Horst was a little up himself but I always thought of him as relatively low-key. And yet, he proved himself to be capable of awful stuff."

"Low-key, eh?", she said.

"Yeah, arrogant but harmless."

We had come to the front of the queue. Catherine ordered our coffees – it was touching that she knew how I took mine, easy as it may have been to remember that I liked it straight, nothing added.

"The thing is", I picked up where we'd left off when we sat on one of the oblong benches, "it makes me wonder what else he might have been capable of."

"What do you mean?", Catherine said.

"You heard what he said about Paul."

"I did."

"And it didn't shock you?"

"He was angry. He'd lost control. Happens to everyone."

"Does it? He lost control alright. And look what he did next."

"I know what you're implying. I'm just finding it hard to believe it."

"Why? Everything would fit."

"How so?"

"You know that Paul's been sabotaging his research, no?"

"I might have heard something. 'Sabotaging' might be a little too strong though."

"Not as far as Horst is concerned. So, perhaps they discuss it at the drinks, he gets agitated, runs across the mudfield, meets Paul at his office, bang. He could have been one of the people that Liam saw come in but didn't recognise."

She frowned and looked at the floor.

"There's something we need to find out", she said and necked down her coffee.

❖

Doreen was much as she had been that morning.

"Come in, have a seat", she said, eyes still fixed on her computer monitor.

"Oh it's you", she said when she turned to face us. "What can I do for you?"

"It's about that evening at the Scrote, Doreen", Catherine said.

"Which evening at the Scrote?"

"Fair question", I said.

"The evening that Paul died", she said.

"What about it?"

"Did you happen to notice what time Horst left the pub?", Catherine asked.

"We all stayed until the end, didn't we?", Doreen said. "Well, apart from you, Michael."

I felt Catherine's gaze cutting right through me.

"I was shattered. Went straight home", I said looking ahead at Doreen.

"You mean you were drunk", she said.

"Lucy was too conscientious a cupbearer."

"What time did you leave, Michael?", Catherine persisted.

"I don't know", I said. "Around nine maybe? I was in bed by nine thirty or ten. Doreen, do you remember how Horst behaved at the party?"

"I wasn't really paying attention to him."

If she didn't, it would have been a first. Nothing ever escaped Doreen.

"Did he spend any time talking to Paul?", I asked.

Doreen looked at Catherine. It was remarkable how she had managed to establish her authority, even over Doreen, in such a short period of time.

"Yes, he did."

"In a group or one on one?"

"Both."

"And when it was just the two of them, do you remember how that went?

"Was their conversation animated? Did it look fraught? Were they gesticulating?", Catherine asked.

"Are you serious?"

"You know what I'm getting at. Did they seem to get on alright?"

"I guess they had reasons not to."

"And did they seem affected by those reasons that evening?"

"Come to think of it, maybe. I can't remember anything in particular but it is a bit odd that they spent as long as they did chatting, just the two of them. I can't remember them fighting or anything though."

Catherine had remained quiet while I forced open Doreen's memory. She was still quiet when we left the office.

"See?", I said.

"I think we're reading too much into isolated incidents. If you think about it, they're insignificant."

"Maybe each element by itself is but taken all together they're more than that, much more."

"What?"

"Your words, not mine."

The sight of a blank page was no torment

A large part of academic research consists of staring at a computer screen incapacitated by despair. It's especially bad when you have to start from scratch. No matter how well you have formed the idea, how thoroughly you have studied the sources, how solid your empirical work is, nothing can justify one option going down in black and white over another, because there is nothing that comes before the opening sentence for it to anchor itself to. Given that in academic writing everything has to be grounded on something that precedes it, the first line is always arbitrary. That's why at the beginning of academic texts one should not be surprised to find pseudo-literary turns of phrase, clichés that cling on to something outside the text for their validation or vacuous, redundant summaries of the argument to follow.

In a sense, my task was a little easier, because I didn't have to start from nothing – I had Catherine's text to go by – so the sight of a blank page was no torment. At the same time, that made things harder because not only did I have to make an arbitrary beginning but I also had to engage in acts of arbitrary destruction.

There I was, slumped back into my creaky swivel chair, looking at my computer, typing random letters and deleting them immediately, sighing and groaning as if I were in physical pain.

The interruption of the phone ringing came as a welcome relief, soon tempered, however, when I heard Alison's voice at the other end.

"Are you busy?"

"It's OK, I can spare a few minutes."

"Can you pop by my office now, please?"

I couldn't refuse. I could only hope that she didn't want to see me about the HoD-ship. I still had a couple of days and I was certainly not prepared to give an answer yet. On the one hand,

I knew that she was right that doing it would all but guarantee me career advancement. On the other hand, being HoD required certain special and well-balanced abilities that I didn't feel I possessed. One had to be even-handed and ruthless, insightful and superficial, academically inquisitive and utilitarian, all at one and the same time. One also needed to be power-hungry and self-centred to an extent that I couldn't dream of approaching. Not at the time, at any rate.

I needed to exhaust every second of the deadline that Alison had afforded me.

I dropped everything to rush to her office. When I got there, it became clear that the reason she had asked to see me was different.

"Hello, Geraldine", I said. "Good to see you again."

I thought I had pitched the greeting with just the right amount of familiarity but it didn't do anything to soften Geraldine Digby.

"Hi", she said. "I'm here to help clear Paul's office."

"You haven't sorted the books yet, Michael, have you?", Alison said.

"I've not had the chance to do the office. It's been a hectic few days what with the end of term approaching and all that."

"Hectic?", Geraldine said with a snigger.

I expected Alison to offer a word of defence and support but none was forthcoming.

"There's not that many, I can do them now", I said.

"Here are the lists."

Geraldine produced a couple of A4 pieces of paper from her handbag and passed them to me.

"I'd like to have a quick look to see whether there's anything worth keeping", she added.

"Of course. I have a meeting now so I'm sorry I can't come along but Michael will help", Alison said.

I wished I too had had the foresight to invent a meeting and get out of that chore.

"Please follow me, Geraldine", I said.

She carried a cardboard box, as she moved about the room sifting through her late husband's belongings. She placed it next to her wherever she stood, selecting an item, inspecting it briefly, then tossing it in the box while muttering "rubbish".

Once she was finished with desk and tables, she moved next to me by the bookshelves.

"What's all that tat up there?", she asked.

I climbed up on a chair and passed her the Sevillana doll, the plaques, cards, conference certificates, Paul's photo in full don regalia.

She tossed it all into the box.

"Don't you want to keep any of it?", I asked.

"No, why should I?"

"I don't know. Memorabilia?"

"Not my memories", she said.

Somehow, consigning all traces of Paul's life to landfill oblivion had loosened her up. Her voice, hitherto an irate monotone, now had a tinge of colour, even a dash of joy.

She dumped the commemorative plaques in the box.

"You're quite friendly with some of our colleagues, right? Alison, for example. And Catherine."

"Wouldn't go that far. I've known Alison for a long time, that's all. I've only met Catherine a few times."

"Maybe it's best that way."

"What do you mean?"

"Work being work and home being home."

"Only it's more often the case that work is work and home is also work."

"It's a difficult balance to strike."

"No, it's not."

Her irritability was returning. Best to change the subject.

"There is a first edition of an important book here", I said pointing to *The Interpretation of Cultures.*

"How much is it worth?"

"I don't know. Maybe eighty to one hundred?"

"Give it away."

"Should I include a note that it's more valuable than the rest?"

"No, let them exercise their entrepreneurialism."

"You don't want to keep any copies of Paul's book?"

"The seduction one? I want to get rid of that the most."

The flicker of lightness was dimmed forever from the conversation and changing the topic was not going to help. In silence, I stuck to my task, going methodically through the books on the shelves, crossing them off the lists, placing them in the box.

"Hi Geraldine", Catherine said, poking her head through the door. "Alison said you're in the building so I thought I'd come say hello."

"Another few minutes and you'd miss me", Geraldine said. "I'm nearly done here."

"I'm glad I came then. How are you?"

"Fine. Getting ready for Christmas. I'm hosting lunch for friends and family."

She was trying to hammer home with every wrecking ball remark that she couldn't care less about Paul's passing.

"Stressful time, Christmas", Catherine said reverting to an old and reliable cliché.

"Not really", Geraldine said. "I should go now. Michael, thank you for helping out with that. I don't expect to see either of you any time soon so take care."

With Paul Digby's merry widow out of the room, Catherine and I looked at each other and laughed out loud simultaneously. Can there be a surer sign that two people are kindred souls than discovering that they find the same things funny and sharing the same thoughts at one and the same time?

"I thought you knew her better", I said.

"What gave you that idea?"

"You seemed more familiar with each other at the funeral."

"Don't believe everything you see at funerals."

"The dynamics of rituals, eh?"

"Exactly, the dynamics of rituals. Can I give you a hand?"

"Thanks. I'll pass books down. You take the list and cross them off please."

I climbed back on the easy chair to reach the highest shelves.

"This Geertz is a first edition", Catherine said thumbing through the *Interpretation of Cultures*

"I know. Made no difference to Geraldine. It goes."

"That's a shame", she said picking up another book.

"If you thumb through every single book, we'll be here all day."

"Go on, pass me the next."

I did so.

"Must've been a great time when you could make things up", she said flipping the pages of Margaret Mead's *Sex and Temperament in Three Primitive Societies.*

"She deserves a little more credit than that", I said passing down the next book.

The prolonged silence that followed made me turn around and look.

"Ready for the next one?", I said.

Catherine was staring at the flyleaf, transfixed.

"What's wrong?", I asked and came off my makeshift step-ladder.

"This is yours", she said.

"What? No way."

"Look."

She turned the book around for me to read the handwritten dedication: "*To Michael whose own big hit is only around the corner. Nikhil*".

My mind sprinted at several hundred kilometres per second into the past. I saw myself pulling *Crime and Custom in Savage Society* out of my shelf, shoving it into my satchel and then returning it to its original place on Paul's shelves. Back a little more. I'm sitting in my living room, still mixed up. I begin to tidy up, frantically putting clothes in the wash, matching up odd socks, rearranging shirts and shoes in the wardrobe. Next, the books. I place them all in alphabetical order. Every book that was in the apartment. Whether it belonged to me or not. Two copies of the same book find themselves side by side on my shelf. Forward again. One of the two copies had to be returned urgently, and far too early in the morning to allow for clear thinking, to its rightful place. I had picked up the wrong one. Here it was now, in Catherine's hands.

"Right, yes, that's right", I said and pulled the book from her. "I had lent this to Paul."

"Paul borrowed Malinowski from you?"

"Yes, why not?"

"Because he already had a copy."

"Did he?"

"Of course he did. Who doesn't?"

"I'm sure many people don't. Duncan probably doesn't."

"Well, Paul did."

"Yes, it's all coming back to me now. I think he mentioned that he'd lost it."

"No he hadn't. It was right there, where this copy was."

"How do you know?"

"Because I'd seen it a million times."

"Maybe it was my copy that you saw."

"No, it wasn't."

"How do you know?"

"I just do. Plus, it's not on his borrowed items list. It's in the list of his own books."

"He probably made a mistake. It's not unthinkable."

“It’s pretty unthinkable. Not to mention the coincidence.”

“What coincidence?”

Catherine looked up.

“The shelf location”, she said. “Anyway, take this one and pass me the next book. Haven’t got all day.”

A down-on-its-luck funfair

I hesitate to call my mistake with the Malinowski book a beginner's error, because to be a beginner implies the intention to repeat whatever activity one has begun and I certainly had no desire ever again to get involved in someone's death and then get embroiled in trying to cover things up by drawing suspicion to someone else.

I had, nevertheless, started and so I had to finish. There was no going back and, after my elementary blunder, the stakes were higher than ever.

But my progress had stalled and obstacles were proliferating exponentially to the point where I was losing the initiative, if I ever had it, and so, instead of calling the shots, I was struggling to catch up and minimise the possible damage.

I was concentrating on my State of the Art chapter when Horst walked past my office. The fleeting venomous look that he gave me sounded the alarm bells. I leapt from my chair, stumbling as I raced to the door to peer into the corridor.

I just caught a glimpse of him entering Catherine's office pulling the door shut behind him.

The circumstances in which any of us shut our doors are few: consoling a student in distress, holding an oral examination or a student disciplinary hearing, conducting a job interview, even taking a sneaky nap. To my knowledge there had never been call to expand that list to include discussing the possibility of having murdered a colleague. Now it couldn't be ruled out.

Sinking back into my chair, I began semi-consciously to weigh my rational calculations of the latest situation against my irrational instincts. Despite the lack of hard evidence, I took it as a given that Catherine had asked to see Horst about Paul's death. Other than that, I was lost in a daunting wilderness of unanswered questions. Why would she speak to him behind my back, without consulting me? What was she planning to ask him or, even worse, what was she about to tell him? Of all the snippets of misinformation that I had spread about him, which ones had flowered into suspicions? Which ones had reached Horst? Given his reaction to having Victoria taken from him, how was he going to respond to the campaign of character assassination that I had been waging?

My next moves depended on the answers to those questions and none were available. Whatever I did would have to be a stab in the dark, an experiment without protocols that could result in catastrophe.

But I could not let uncertainty incapacitate me. I could not allow things to happen in my absence. If taking action meant taking an incalculable risk, then so be it.

The time interval I allowed between knocking and pushing the doorknob was almost undetectable by standard time-keeping devices. I already had good reason to rush things but even if it hadn't been so, their conversation was so voluble that it permeated, muffled but unmistakeably heated, through the closed door and into the corridor leaving me in no doubt that it was the right time to strike. My only plan was to barge in; then I would have to improvise depending on what I encountered in the room.

None of that came to pass. An unexpected obstacle stood in my way. The door was locked.

Being stopped so abruptly in my tracks by an immovable object came as a shock but it would soon wear off. Less easy to shrug off was the unease, the underlying sense of dread that fuelled the accompanying adrenaline rush.

To start with, I was deeply offended on a professional level by Catherine's uncollegial attitude. It went against everything that our Department stood for – openness, inclusiveness, transparency, responsibility. On that score alone, I resolved to give her a piece of my mind as soon as the opportunity presented itself.

More pressing even, though I cannot really claim that this was a professional concern, what the hell was Catherine talking about with Horst that required a locked door in and such closely guarded privacy?

Then there was the question what to do next. The whole thing was turning into a game of chess – chess without rules.

Lost in a fog of conflicted thoughts, when I felt the door being unlocked and tugged from the inside, rather than letting go the handle, I instinctively pulled the door shut again.

Catherine's second tug was much more forceful and fingers still firmly gripping the handle, I tumbled into the room.

Horst was standing. I was busily processing the scene. Had they had a confrontation, toe-to-toe, face-to-face or had Catherine not bothered to offer him a seat at all in the first place? Perhaps my intrusion had forced them to bring their meeting to an abrupt end?

"What do you want?", Catherine demanded.

I told myself that the hostility I detected was more likely to do with the row she and Horst had been having than with my unexpected entry.

"Nothing urgent really. I didn't mean to interrupt."

"You always crop up where you don't belong, don't you?", Horst said.

"Shut up Horst", Catherine said. "Michael, I'm busy now. If you don't mind?"

With that one curt phrase steely with professional appropriateness, she left me defenceless. I had to affirm that we were on the same side, that I wasn't the one posing the threat to her, that the real menace was the man standing in the middle of her office.

I leaned towards her and tried to kiss her. She jerked back in horror. Then, straightening up and squaring her shoulders, she propelled me out of the office until we were both in the corridor.

"What the hell are you doing?", she snapped.

"Nothing out of the ordinary."

"This is our workplace, Michael."

"And that puts you off all of a sudden?"

"What's that supposed to mean?"

"Holding hands, fleeting touches. I didn't think our relationship is a secret."

"Oh, that."

"What else?"

"Nothing else. Now leave. We'll speak when I'm done here."

Embarrassed and in a state of consternation, somehow I made my way to the Butty Call in search of a cup of tea in hopes it would help me to calm down and concentrate.

That proved to be a miscalculation, though how and why only became apparent gradually.

The Students' Union had thought it a good idea to set up a miniature German-style Christmas market in the lobby of the McKenzie Building. It was as tacky and uninteresting as might be expected. The huts – all three of them – were little more than glorified makeshift portable ticket cabins. To temper the impression of a down-on-its-luck funfair, students had covered them in tinsel and baubles. Homemade chocolate truffles, or a rough approximation, were on offer in recycled nylon bags that had been clumsily tied with ribbon and had definitely seen better times and possibly even had wrapped better offerings in a previous life. Also on sale were handcrafted greeting cards, mostly featuring jaded and painfully unfunny memes. Most of the students present were queuing up at the third booth-cum-hut, where mulled wine was being ladled into paper cups as fast as it could pass for heated.

"That's very entrepreneurial of them, isn't it?", said a voice behind me.

Alison was smiling at the sight of the students with all the maternal pride of someone watching her own children selling lemonade from a stall in front of their suburban house.

"I'm surprised they were allowed to have a gas fire in here", I said.

"I'm still expecting something from you", she said, ignoring my point about fire safety.

"It's a big decision", I said. "I'll have to exhaust the deadline, if that's alright with you."

"Of course, I understand. You've another two days left then", she said and drifted away like the ghost of Christmas uncertain.

With most students circling around the ersatz Christmas market eager as dogs sniffing bums, there was scarcely a queue at the Butty Call.

"Hello, sir", Adeel Rahman called out from a table at the far corner.

I waved at him and his two fellow first year students, whose faces I recognised because they were paid-up members of the front-row disciples' club.

They giggled which was fine, since it meant that the interaction was both friendly and courteous and, best of all, over. They would not be approaching me, I reckoned.

I held my container of tea with my thumb under the edge of the base, where the cardboard was thicker, and my index and middle fingers on the rim of the lid to avoid scorching myself on the insufficiently insulated cup.

I successfully navigated my way through the growing crowd of students gravitating towards the gratis festive cheer, summoned the lift, boarded and pressed the button.

Feeling relieved that I would make it to the fourth floor undisturbed and alone, there to catch my breath and compose myself a little, my peace of mind was shattered when the metal door screeched open again. I did little to hide my disappointment holding onto the forlorn hope that it would be no one I knew.

As it happened, it was the next best thing. Thomas Lusignan stepped into the lift, a cup of mulled wine in hand.

"Hi, Thomas", I said.

He nodded, stood in front of me, face to the lift door and stared at the floor.

He was at his most awkward. I assumed he felt embarrassed to have been busted drinking on the job. I was tempted to reassure him that mulled wine doesn't really count and that a small, innocent transgression was permissible given the time of year. Not that I was being kind. It was more to see him implode with shyness. I didn't. It would have been cruel.

When we reached our floor, he leapt out even before the automated voice announced our arrival.

The encounter with Thomas improved my mood to the point where I was actually smiling. I wondered what it must be like to be so introverted. Does it really cause that kind of eye-avoiding anguish or is that merely a case of deceptive appearances? Perhaps Thomas was not shy; perhaps he had nothing but contempt for the rest of us. It would be difficult to blame him, if that were the case. Or maybe his wings had been clipped once too often and he had retreated monk-like into a vow of silence.

In my new state of relative jollity, things appeared not to be as bad as I had thought them to be. The fact that Catherine had given Horst so much benefit of the doubt might mean that it was the end of the whole story. He was the only one to arouse any semblance of reasonable suspicion. If Catherine was not prepared to believe that he was somehow involved in Paul's death, then she most likely would be inclined to suspend all investigation and we could go back to our lives retaining only the good bits of the past weeks.

I walked briskly to my office. When I got there, I wished I had taken my time.

Her tirade of insults

Catherine was sitting in my swivel chair, her eyes fixed on my computer screen.

"Did you really think I'd never find out?", she said.

She was calm and collected but there was no mistaking the underlying tension. My first instinct was to feign ignorance but I knew that would only make my position completely unsustainable and would enrage Catherine further.

"Listen, I was going to...", I began my defence.

"Shut up", she said, still in complete control.

"But you asked me a question", I muttered.

"I said, shut up", she snarled.

I did as I was told. She turned her attention to the computer screen again.

"You've not even made an effort to change the original text."

"I wasn't done yet."

"Shut the fuck up."

"Sorry."

"So, let me get this straight. I come up with an idea; I offer co-authorship to you, god knows why but I do; I write a methodological and conceptual framework; I share it with you, because you're my co-author so we have to trust each other, cooperate, that sort of thing; you nick my idea, you brutally plagiarise my working paper and try to pass it off as your own work and to the State of the Art series no less. You don't even have the decency to paraphrase."

"I told you, I wasn't done yet", I whispered.

"Shut the fuck up, Michael."

"Yes, sorry."

"Actually, no, it's not because of a lack of decency that you failed to appropriate rather than stealing outright. It's because of your utter incompetence."

"That's a bit harsh", I dared say.

She didn't even bother telling me to shut up. She just speared me with a look sharper and more painful than any stick, stone or word.

"I threw you a lifeline, Michael. Do you not even have the elementary insightfulness to see that I was trying to help you? Are you in complete denial about where you are heading professionally?"

"I'm up for promotion actually."

"Don't even get me started on that travesty. I brought you on board out of sheer pity. I thought that involving you in a worthwhile research project would resuscitate your career; that it would make you pull your finger out and drag you out of that drivel that you've been working on."

"My work is not that bad", I complained.

"Oh, yes it is. It's worse than bad. You're the only one who doesn't see it. It's nonsense."

The way she pronounced "nonsense", each letter delivered a separate and equally painful blow.

"Maybe some get away with doing that sort of bullshit pseudo-theory but at least they have flair, they can write decent prose. You don't even have that. Your writing is dull, self-indulgent, meandering."

"Some people like it."

"See? Complete denial. So I throw you a bone and what do you do? You go and steal it and chew it in your pathetic little corner full of cobwebs and dead cockroaches."

Tempting as it was after her tirade of insults about my writing, I couldn't really pick up on how ridiculously far she had stretched the bone metaphor after accusing me of poor prose.

"Let me explain."

"Explain what? Were you or were you not asked to contribute to the next State of the Art volume?"

"I was, yes."

"And why, of all people, did they ask you?"

"I take it you didn't receive an invitation?"

"Don't fucking push it, Michael. Tell me, why did you get an invitation?"

"That's what I wanted to explain. Will you hear me out please?"

She crossed her arms and waited.

"You know the Anthropology and Social Theory Association, right?"

It was out of embarrassment and nervousness that I paused expecting an answer. None was on offer of course.

"Of course you do. So, I had signed up for the annual conference and I was planning on presenting some of my other stuff..."

She pulled a face of olfactory irritation.

"...but then it occurred to me that it would be the ideal opportunity to present our joint work even in that preliminary stage just to take some soundings."

"Our *joint* work", she emphasised. "And did you present it as *our* work?"

"Well, no, that's the thing. I knew it was a risk. After all, the work was at a very early stage so, if it didn't go down well, I didn't want you to shoulder the responsibility."

"And you thought it necessary to keep that a secret from me as well?"

"You're right, I probably should have told you but I thought I'd wait until it generated some reaction."

"Carry on."

"I've no idea how but the news reached Bakker and out of the blue I got the invitation to contribute to the State of the Art volume."

"And still you said nothing."

"That's because I had hardly even started thinking about it. I was working on some rough ideas. I wanted to have something to present to you first. You accuse me of plagiarising when the truth is exactly the opposite. I felt I hadn't pulled my weight, that I hadn't contributed enough so I didn't want you to think that I was piggy-backing on your ideas. Your brilliance is intimidating, don't you see?"

She didn't say anything for a few seconds. I interpreted her silence as an indication that the ace that I had pulled out of my sleeve had trumped all her cards. So much for wishful thinking.

"You're something else, you know."

She was calm, the anger visibly dissipated, her voice softening. Once again, I mistook that as a good sign.

"To deceive me is one thing but to try to flatter me into acquiescence? What do you take me for? And do you really think that any of your shit is half-plausible? Extraordinary. Truly, mind-bogglingly extraordinary."

Her fury had been difficult to deal with but my instincts had kicked in and I had assumed a fighting position. Yet I was defenceless against the disappointment that now coloured her demeanour.

"I assume it was all a lie", she carried on. "Everything."

"No, no", I protested, "not at all. Everything was genuine."

She shut me up with a dismissive wave of her right hand.

"Perhaps I'm the naive one after all. First I share with you my research ideas and then, all of a sudden you give me long, melty looks, you seek me out all the time, more or less stalk me, you long for my company and go all touchy feely. And there I am stupidly falling for it, falling for *you*. I thought the unimaginable had happened, that I was actually in a healthy relationship with a fellow academic and a decent one at that, one with integrity, one who is not aggressively competitive."

"It was all true, Catherine", I said.

"Don't even call me by my first name", she said curtly.

"How should I address you?"

"Fuck, Michael. I don't know. Professor Dr Bowen. No more familiarity between us."

"Please, believe me."

"You are to write to Bakker immediately and pull out of the volume. Otherwise, your career is over."

She shook her head, came out from behind my desk and pushed me aside.

"Professor Dr Bowen, please", I called out as she stormed out of my office.

When she left, I didn't know what to do with myself. I was overwhelmed and restless. I wanted to run but flight was impossible. The only recourse was to pace up and down my office, weaving around the furniture, squatting with my head in my hands each time a hot flush of shame swept over me.

Catherine's full force, frontal assault had left me deeply ashamed. I had used her; that much was true. Not in the way that she thought, but I had manipulated her with deliberate intent to mislead her about Paul's death. It was also true that I had not been as truthful as I could have been about the phenomenological anthropology of crime business. Although I had not explicitly ruled out turning the project collaborative again, it was highly unlikely that I would, or could for that matter.

But I didn't think I had deceived her about my feelings for her. Every kiss and every touch had felt true and the longing in my eyes when I looked at her was not forced. Making love with her felt so natural that to call it simply enjoyable would do it an injustice. It was fulfilling, a moment of mutual completion.

Then again, Catherine was a much more accomplished student of the human condition than I was. She could read human behaviour and interpret it with remarkable accuracy, placing every dissected piece neatly into the big picture. She could detect what determined people's actions and had the acumen to separate motivations from systemic forces, psychology from social factors.

So, all in all, perhaps she was right. Perhaps she could see something that I couldn't. Perhaps my personal investment cluttered and blurred my view and it took her detached perspective to grasp what determined my decisions and whatever meaning they had.

That there was a chance that I did not understand my own actions as well as Catherine did made me feel even more embarrassed. Exceptionally gifted as she may have been, to be so transparent was humiliating.

That was almost as unbearable as the sense of emptiness that overwhelmed me. I was certain that I was experiencing loss and an inevitable one at that. I had only myself to blame, of course. I should have known that I would not have been able to reconcile lies with sincere feelings, that sooner or later something would have to give. Now that I was faced with the consequences to which, helplessly enamoured with Catherine, I had been blinded, my sorrow went so deep that it paralysed me. And it did so in every respect.

I spent the rest of Thursday morning at my computer. In an attempt to comprehend my feelings, I devoured information on the five stages of grief theory.

Did the stages always come along in the same sequence? Geraldine Whitmore-Digby seemed to work backwards from the end, acceptance. Or maybe she had skipped to the end of the list.

And how about Paul? Had he seen the end coming in those minutes before he was struck on the head? If so, had he gone denial/anger/bargaining/depression/acceptance at the speed of light? "It's strange", he had said to me and I had assumed he was talking about my being alone in his office so late in the evening. Could that have been him entering the state of denial having foreseen his impending demise?

Me? If what I was experiencing really was grief, how could I possibly feel anything other than depression and never go past it? I could hardly be angry, let alone bargain with myself or anyone else. As for acceptance, if I came to terms with losing Catherine, I would also have to accept losing everything else. And yet, there was little I could do about the former and that made the latter more likely. But little is not the same as nothing.

Then I stumbled on a piece of biographical information that sent my brain spinning in a different direction. I already knew that when it was first conceived, the stages of grief theory related to the terminally ill and those losing a loved one. What I didn't know was that the academic who devised the model had experienced a life riddled with bereavement herself. She was born one of triplets, which to me is already to have lost part of oneself. Having suffered a series of strokes, she spent the last nine years of her life semi-paralysed in a wheelchair.

Is there such as thing as academic determinism? Does one's research shape, in a mystical, preternatural way, the course of one's life? Would Dr Kübler-Ross have made a more comfortable exit from this mortal coil had she not obsessed in her work about death and coping with the void that it leaves?

Could the same be happening to me? Was there any way of knowing or would I only find out at the end?

The more tangled I got in this web of interlocked existential binds, the less reason mastered my thoughts and the more reason retreated the less control I had over my actions. It is only the benefit of hindsight, of course, that allows me to know this. At the time, I was unaware that I was not acting on conscious decisions but on an automatic reflex. Maybe that's what we customarily call 'character'; the stored up experiences, previous decisions, unreflective intuitions that compel our default actions and raise a mental block that requires great effort to overcome.

My quest started from her office. The sight of the empty room made me want to go through the papers on her desk and as many of her computer files as I could. I had no idea what I was expecting to find. Probably, like many a forsaken lover in the past, I was yearning to be reassured of her feelings for me, even if erstwhile, and any evidence from any source, second-hand, intercepted or unreliable would do.

But I knew that if she caught me loitering, nothing could save me from her fury so I didn't succumb to the temptation.

As I backtracked out of the room I felt a hand on my shoulder.

"Looking awfully furtive, dear boy."

"Hi, Duncan. I was just looking for Catherine. Would you happen to have seen her?"

"I saw her this morning. Looked rather more choleric than even her usual self."

"I mean do you know where she is now?"

"I don't keep a register."

"I need to find her so excuse me."

"What's the rush? Have you had a wee spat?"

"What?", I asked.

"You know, a little contretemps of the kind that both tortures and delights young lovers."

"I've no idea what you're talking about."

"Don't you, now? You should ask around. Everyone else knows."

"There's nothing to know."

"Oh there is always so very much to know."

"You've lost me. Listen, I really need to go. I've no time for this."

"You've changed, dear boy, you've changed. I miss the gracious old Michael."

As debonair Duncan made his jaunty way down the corridor looking for someone else with time to waste, I knocked on the door next to Catherine's.

"Oh, I didn't expect you just yet after this morning's chat", Alison said.

"No, it's not about that, sorry. I was just wondering whether you've seen Catherine."

"Is that really the kind of query that should be addressed to the HoD, acting or otherwise?"

It would have been a luxury to be embarrassed, as I probably would have been had under normal circumstances.

"Whatever", I mumbled.

"Fucker", someone whispered behind me.

I turned around. In a choreographed revolving doors routine, unintentional but executed with splendid precision, Lucy was emerging from her office as Horst entered his. For a split second, they were perfectly aligned, standing upright, only the wall separating them, he with his back turned at me, she throwing me an insincere but also sad smile.

Thomas walked past and attempted a wave at me that was more like an involuntary spasm. He lowered his head and jogged the rest of the way to the stairwell.

Doreen was stapling together bundles of documents by the photocopier with the painstaking thoroughness of a skilled craftsperson while ignoring Duncan, who was chattering away at her leaning against the machine, his hands in his pockets.

Faced with a canvas encompassing almost all my colleagues (only Catherine was missing), I came to a realisation.

I pushed Alison's door open again.

"What now, Michael?"

If there were any residual qualms inside me, the feigned exasperation in her voice removed them instantly.

"On second thought, Alison, this is as good a time as any. I'm not doing it."

She got off her chair in a rush as if to deflect the news with her entire body.

"Michael, we have to discuss this."

It was remarkable how quickly her cockiness had dissolved into a froth of flustered fretfulness.

"Nothing to discuss. I'm not doing it."

"Michael, you're making the wrong call."

Addressing me repeatedly by my first name for emphasis had no effect on me. If anything, it made me even more aware and certain about my decision.

"It's my call to make. Not doing it."

Of course I wasn't going to do it. It's not that it wouldn't have a considerable upside, which is why I had been entertaining the idea. It would give me some freedom of movement, the upper hand you could say. I would be wielding an administrative power that would allow me, would allow all of us, to put everything behind us, to move on. And I would also secure promotion – how could I forget that?

But the truth of the matter was that I couldn't possibly manage these people. I found it hard enough to even deal with tangential encounters with Lucy's obstinacy, Horst's aggressive conceit, Thomas's social ineptness, Alison's blasé professionalism,

Duncan's indolence, Doreen's monomaniacal dedication. And that without taking account of the volatile body of deluded candidate PhDs and needy students.

"Not doing it", I repeated and shut the door behind me.

When I turned around once more, the scattered figures had disappeared from the landscape. The corridor was empty save for Catherine, who emerged from the corner office accompanied by a man with screwdrivers and cables hanging out of every pocket of his cargo trousers.

She didn't give me the light of day. Much worse, she actively avoided me. When I approached and called her by her name in as mellifluous a tone as I could muster, her look made it clear that I was inviting physical assault.

It was a risk I had to take.

"I need to speak to you, Catherine. I need to explain."

She marched on. I followed suit nearly tripping over her heels.

"Please, listen to me for one second."

I hadn't intended talking to her in any detail there and then. It would have been singularly inopportune. What I was hoping to achieve was to get her to commit to seeing me that same evening. My apartment would have been the ideal venue but the Montgomery Arms would do well enough for starters.

"Catherine, please don't run from me."

By unfortunate coincidence, the lift door opened just as we neared it. The sole passenger, Jeremy, on one of his aimless up-and-down journeys, showed no inclination to disembark.

"Hi", I said with a fulsome casualness designed to relieve the tension.

He waved. He was about to say something but Catherine's assertive entry and the force with which she hit the ground floor button startled him and he retreated to the rear, pressing his back against the far wall in a vain attempt to disappear from view.

"Hold on", I said as I grabbed Ian from IT Services from the arm.

"I have to...", he said looking at the closing lift doors with all the despair of someone missing the last evacuation boat out of a city under attack by a deadly enemy.

"You'll catch the next one", I said. "What were you doing in there?"

"In where?", Ian said.

"In Paul Digby's office. With Dr Bowen."

"Nothing, just some software stuff."

"Ian, you'd better tell me."

"I'm not called Ian."

"Of course you're called Ian. Everyone calls you Ian."

"Do they? I don't know why, because I'm not called Ian."

"Whatever. What were you doing in there?"

He looked sheepish. He had been doing something he ought not to have been doing. And something I particularly did not want him to be doing.

"Speak up", I snarled.

"Just checking some files."

"What files?"

"Just checking the properties of a Word document, that's all."

"What properties?"

"When it was saved and stuff."

"Everyone knows how to do that. Why did she call you?"

"She needed metadata, which not anyone can get."

"What's metadata?"

"Data about data."

"And you *can* retrieve data about data?"

"It's my job."

"And you retrieved them."

"I did. It didn't take long."

I could have strangled him with one of the cables that dangled from his pockets. It was not his fault. He was just doing what he was told by Dr Bowen. How could he resist? She was his superior. Moreover, she was renowned for her skills of persuasion. None of that mattered a whit to me; this not being a court of law. I had assumed that anyone looking into the history of the promotion recommendation document would be able to find when it was created and modified. The former would have been when Paul was alive and well. The latter when Alison edited it and saved it right there in front of me. But Ian from IT Services, eager to serve with his codes and algorithms and apps and daemons, had uncovered the time stamp of every change ever made to the document.

I left Ian standing there wondering what to do as I returned to my office. Having passed through the five stages of grief, I had now arrived at the first stage of panic. Again I paced up and down my room, moving books and papers about the place, trying to keep busy in hopes that by interacting with three-dimensional objects I would disperse the mental fog that was blurring my vision.

The fuzziness dissipated only to give way to shakes and palpitations. Then my office phone rang and the name of the caller came up on the small panel of my device: Amina Okafor.

Duncan's paper hat was disintegrating, soaked in sweat from his brow, the trickle becoming a flow with every bite of roast and every swig of wine.

"Seriously have you never watched it?", Horst asked.

Alison shook her head.

"I've never even heard of it", Lucy said.

"It is an age-old tradition in Germany. New Year's Eve would not be New Year's Eve without *Dinner for One* on the television."

"And is it funny?"

"Same procedure as every year, James", Horst imitated the aristocratic accent of an elderly, mid-20th century English woman.

"Sounds a bit dated", Lucy said.

"It is hilarious", Horst said. "You see, at the end he has to have sex with her. It's part of the procedure!"

He burst out laughing.

"I was just wondering whether our meeting is still on. I can't get hold of Dr Bowen on her extension", Amina said.

"No, it's not, Amina, thank you and sorry for the inconvenience", I said quickly. "We've wrapped up the project."

"But Dr Bowen said it's still ongoing."

"Things have changed. By the way, what did Dr Bowen say the meeting was about?"

"Oh, there she is now. Good afternoon, Dr Bowen. I'm just on the phone to Dr West."

Amina must have kept the receiver still up against the side of her face, because I could hear everything she was saying but Catherine's voice wouldn't carry through to the speaker.

"He's saying the project is off... I see, alright, no problem..."

"OK, OK, listen to mine", Doreen said. "How did the comedian fracture his humerus?"

"How did the comedian fracture his humerus?", a few of the others said in chorus.

"He cracked a joke!"

The roaring laughter of the group was interrupted by Duncan.

"Did we get homemade crackers from the Medical School bazaar this year?"

"I read a very interesting article about Christmas crackers in the *Annals of the Belgian Anthropological Society* once", Thomas whispered.

"Do the Belgians have Christmas crackers?", Lucy asked.

"I don't think so", Thomas said, lowering his eyes.

"Amina, listen to me", I said. "Dr Bowen is not authorised to do this. You must not disclose any information to her."

"I will only take a second to retrieve the data", she said to Catherine, blanking me.

"Amina, don't ignore me. If you give Dr Bowen the information she's looking for, you'll be committing a disciplinary offence."

She did ignore me but kept the line live nevertheless.

"Let me get all this paperwork out of your way."

Her eagerness to make Catherine comfortable increased my terror by a notch.

"Amina, I'm talking to you! Do not do this."

"You're in luck, Dr Bowen", she said. "Older data is automatically erased after a few weeks. It was going to happen any day now."

"Delete, delete, delete", I yelled down the line.

❖

It was when the Christmas pudding was being served that I realised that Jeremy was staring at me and probably had been for a while. He'd been sitting diagonally opposite me at the other end of the table, as always, next to Duncan, but, having arrived late to the Department Christmas lunch, I'd hardly noticed him. He seemed nervous.

"You're awfully quiet, Michael", Duncan said to me across the table. "Get some Yuletide cheer in you."

He raised his glass. I returned a spiritless cheers and proceeded to neck down a whole glass of red.

"That's better, isn't it? So much to celebrate", Catherine said to me.

Her lackadaisical, soft tone, likely calculated so as not to raise any suspicion, sent an apprehensive ripple down my spine.

I hung up and rushed from my office, almost tumbling down the stairs to the ground floor – waiting for the lift would have wasted several precious seconds. I dashed across campus. My overcoat was in the office. The bitter cold hit me like a million sharp icicles but I registered it as something external that didn't affect me directly.

I elbowed my way past students and staff making their way to or from lectures or, more likely, pre-Christmas parties. Reaching the Services Building, I raced up the stairs to the mezzanine.

I was light-headed from my exertions, fearful I might be having a stroke or a heart attack but this was not the time to worry about dying.

I pushed the door open. Amina was in her small information kingdom, crouched over her computer, hitting keys with her index fingers.

"Just a second please. And..., send", she said. "What can I do for you?"

Her face lit up when she saw me.

"Oh hello, Dr West. I was wondering what happened. I was chatting to a dead line for ages! I called back but there was no answer."

"What have you done?", I said, still panting.

"Pardon?"

"She asked to see some entry system records, didn't she?"

She looked taken aback at my lack of professionalism in referring to a colleague in such a manner.

"Yes, she did. I thought you both did."

She hadn't listened to a word I'd told her on the phone.

"I told you the project was off."

"Dr Bowen said you got that wrong."

"And why did you believe her and not me?"

"Erm, I don't know. I just did."

"What did you do with the records?"

"PDFed them and just sent them off as you walked in."

"Sent to whom?"

"To Dr Bowen. Would you like a copy? Happy to forward you one."

"Did you read the data?"

"She only wanted me to send the file on and I've got better things to do. What's on it anyway?"

"Nothing. You're right. Plenty of better things to do. Did you delete the originals?"

"No, I can't do that! But they're scheduled to be wiped tomorrow so you made it just in the nick of time."

I hadn't expected the beginning of the end to be so banal. Data collected by a system that no one really cared for and, once the initial excitement over its installation dissipated, everyone would stop caring about. An administrator indifferent to the consequences of her actions, responsible only for what her job description required her to do.

I fully expected to be met by the police when I returned to my office. Perhaps DCI Rahman would have been notified. How disappointed he would have been in his son's professor. And how worried about the kind of education Adeel was receiving.

But there was no blue light outside the McKenzie Building, no tape cordoning off my office, no uniforms to be seen anywhere. In fact, everything was just as I'd left it. Everything apart from my email inbox. Among the new messages from students and academic mailing lists was a one-liner from Catherine:

"My office tomorrow at 9am."

"It's been quite a term, hasn't it?", Alison said.

She had stood up to deliver the customary end of term speech. Paul's strategy on such occasions was to start with the Department's achievements, some of which he had to talk up and embellish, then proceed with plans for the future, and finally, the concluding afterthought, a stern admonition about 'areas for improvement'.

"Not the same procedure as every year", Horst said, intent on milking the story that had once already made him feel the centre of attention.

He was spot on; everyone laughed.

"Quite, quite", Alison continued. "I don't want to go on for too long, because then there won't be any wine left for me..."

Laughter.

"...but there are a few things I simply have to mention. First, our first term student evaluation has been sterling, so well done all of you."

A round of applause and a loud cheer from Duncan. The only one not participating in the merriment was Jeremy. He was staring down at his untouched dessert, perhaps wondering what had happened to his main.

"I very much look forward to the postgraduate away weekend, which promises to be a blast this year."

As the organiser of said weekend, I was probably supposed to smile and raise a glass at that point. I didn't.

"It's that kind of thing that builds a healthy and exciting environment for our students. Second, there's some research-related news hot off the press. Thomas has been awarded a six-figure grant for his project on the anthropology of bullying in the workplace. Well done, Thomas!"

Horst gave Thomas a pat on the back in a show of familiarity and friendship. It still wasn't enough to disguise the jealousy that distorted his features. Everyone else applauded, Catherine with the greatest enthusiasm and accompanied by a couple of American daytime talk show styled exclamatory 'wows'.

The following day I got to the office at six in the morning, having already taken a long walk. Sleeping had been out of the question so I saw little point stewing in my own juices in my flat. The workplace might be as inhospitable but at least it didn't pretend to be cosy.

I'd struggled through the night to come up with a strategy but to no avail. In all honesty, I never really did have any strategy so it would be pointless to start devising one that late in the day. Since the fateful night of the reception at the Scrote, everything had been a haze and my actions haphazard and disconnected, my intentions imprecisely defined.

I was equally unprepared for the time of reckoning. That Catherine had not contacted the police was a relief yet a cause for concern at the same time. I didn't expect her to let me get away with it, not after my academic treachery had been exposed. So, I had no doubt that she would make me pay for it. All that was unknown to me was the precise form and severity of my punishment.

I knocked on her door a few minutes before nine. She made me wait for at least thirty seconds before inviting me in. She was seated at her desk, arms crossed, hair tied back, glasses on.

"Good morning, Catherine", I said.

She didn't reply. Nor did she offer me a seat, which was just as well because I wanted to keep a distance and one of the easy chairs had already been taken by Alison.

"Third, our lovely Doreen has been nominated for a Chancellor's Excellence Award. Richly deserved, as she has been herding us so efficiently and completely single-handedly for so many years.

"Fourth, we have some fantastic publications coming up in top journals. Horst's foundational work on methodology will appear in *Modern Anthropology* in the new year and Catherine has secured a contract for her new book."

"You disappoint and scare me in equal measure, Michael", Catherine said eventually.

"You must let me explain, please", I said.

"Is there really anything to explain? Facts do all the talking. Let's begin from what we've established and you can't deny. You were there when Paul died."

"Liam said he didn't see anyone come in and out of the building."

"Liam didn't know Paul from a bar of soap. A 'very nice bloke' who 'always said hello'? As if Paul would so much as acknowledge the security staff. Also, Liam is never at his post. Why do you think I was in the building that evening?"

She had never trusted me. She was referring to that first night that we slept together. She'd gone to the McKenzie to double-check Liam's story behind my back. And then she made love with me.

She read the astonishment in my face.

"Your campaign against Horst was too transparent. It made me wonder so I made some separate enquiries."

I tried to put events in chronological order in my mind to check whether her narrative held and how I'd staggered the campaign against Horst, as she so harshly put it, but I was too nervous to think straight.

"So, you were with Paul at the time of his death."

"Hold on, even if I was in the building, why assume I was in his office?"

"To start with, because otherwise you would not have lied about going home early."

All my protestations would be shot down one after the other.

"Plus something happened with the Malinowski book but I still don't know what so I can only speculate. It troubled me that you and Paul would swap books. It made no sense. In light of all the new evidence, my guess is that you took it that evening, possibly because you stained it with his blood, and replaced it with your copy hoping that no one would notice."

"No, that's not how it happened", I said but didn't offer anything else by way of explanation.

"And there were the muddy prints, of course. You're the only person in the Department who ever walks across the mudfield. I've asked around and no one else does – I certainly don't – so no point arguing against that. You've said so yourself anyway."

She paused and stared at me as if expecting me to give her an excuse to maul me. I didn't oblige.

"But, as it happens, all that evidence is redundant. You wrote your own promotion recommendation either before or after you killed Paul. Actually, probably both. You probably started it before he caught you in the act, you killed him, and then just carried on.

The document was saved a couple of hours after the estimated time of death."

"Maybe Ian got it wrong", I muttered.

"Who's Ian?", Catherine asked.

"Never mind", I said.

"I am speechless, Michael", Alison, who really had been speechless until then, said.

"Please let me explain."

"Believe me, I would if I thought there's something worth explaining. It is crystal clear to me that you killed Paul. What's hard to fathom is the hatred that moved you to do it. Is it just because he wasn't going to put you forward for promotion?"

"It was an accident", I mumbled, suppressing the urge to say that undermining one's career is not a negligible motive for murder.

"And then you thought it wise to cover it up? What reason would you have for doing so?"

"I was drunk."

"Oh please, Michael", Catherine said. "Could you not at least have come back with a better excuse? Were you still drunk when you agreed to do the research project with me? When you tried to throw me off the scent at every opportunity once we started looking into how Paul died? When you pretended you had no idea what had happened? When you slept with me just to distract me? When you systematically attempted to incriminate Horst? When you nicked my ideas and sold them as yours? I thought you were a good one, Michael. Turns out you're the worst of them all."

"But, of course, the term has been marred by the untimely death of our good colleague, Paul. It is a tragedy that will take us a very long time to come to terms with, if we ever do. But we have to try. We must uphold Paul's legacy, build on his accomplishments. We must continue to set the same high standards for our Department that Paul did. We must guard and strengthen our community, support each other, be guided by collegiality and mutual care."

❖

"So what now?", I asked, sensing that the onslaught had come to an end.

"You know that you're facing a traumatising legal procedure and probably a lengthy prison sentence", Catherine said, colder than the December wind blowing through campus.

Alison nodded.

"I don't understand why you haven't called the police yet", I said.

"Oh, we considered it, make no mistake about that", Alison said.

"But, you see Michael, neither of us are great believers in the criminal justice system. If my research has taught me one thing, it's that formal punishment has very little to do with what one deserves. It also doesn't work."

I should have been relieved but instead I felt apprehensive.

"So", Catherine went on, "we've decided on a different course of action. One that you should see as a second chance, albeit one with certain strict conditions."

"To achieve all that, we will need the guidance and leadership of someone who personifies all of our Department's qualities and who enjoys the trust and admiration of all of us. I am therefore extremely pleased to announce today that the next Head of the Department of Anthropology will be Michael West."

Part 2

That unpalatable pill

I had not made any plans for the Christmas holiday, which was just as well, because I would have had to cancel them. Since taking over as HoD, I was kept busy in a way that I'd never known or wished to experience before. Overnight I had become a member of every imaginable Committee, both in the Department and at the University. I was obliged to endure long, painful hours of inconsequential blather disguised in managerial speak. The torrent of documents requiring review and my signature seemed to know no end. Doreen bombarded me with reminders of the meetings I had to attend, most of which I had been happily and entirely unaware of prior to being summoned to appear.

More people were now passing through my door than had ever crossed the threshold in the years of my former academic career. They would queue patiently in the corridor for the privilege of discussing their grievances and successes, their aspirations and career prospects, broken radiators, slow WiFi connections, erratic off-campus access to academic databases, everything and anything they deemed appropriate to bother their HoD with. I could hardly turn any of them down either.

Well, some I could – Jeremy, for one, topped that list. Every time we bumped into one another in the corridor, he seemed desperate to have a one-to-one with me. Invariably, I ignored him or asked him to email me, which pretty much amounted to the same thing. Over time, his attempts didn't so much wane as become limp and lifeless. I felt sorry for him but I didn't have time for his obsessive fixations.

When I was in the company of those who knew what they were doing, or at least put on a believable act, I fully fathomed how hopelessly out of my depth I truly was. I frequently had to keep my mouth shut, when my handlers had failed to give me explicit instructions about what to do and say, lest I embarrass myself. I would then have to wade through reams of past paper-work just to familiarise myself in retrospect with what had been said.

Occasionally, ignorance worked in my favour. At a meeting with HoDs from across the University, the Vice Chancellor, a portly figure, selected as the supreme leader of our institution on the basis of a Master's degree in Economics from Harvard plus a long track record of mismanaging various businesses to the point of bankruptcy while pocketing handsome bonuses along the way, addressed me directly. What, he asked, was Anthropology doing to help increase undergraduate student numbers? Not having the slightest clue, since I had never had to deal with such an issue and knew little about the numbers or the student types we recruited, I winged it with as much confidence as I could muster. I mumbled something about offering pizza to prospective applicants visiting the Department on open days. To my astonishment, the sugges-tion was met with a nod of approval from the Vice Chancellor, which in turn triggered an appreciative hum from among some of the other HoDs.

Perhaps I am being too harsh on myself. Sure enough others knew the ropes and were fluent in the admin jargon. However, with very few exceptions, the records of those assembled ranged from inconsequential at best (in some instance surely intentional; not making waves ensured staying below the radar, a non-target worthy of eventual reward) to outright failures at worst. The Medical School, for example, had an indeterminate number of well remunerated staff who cost the University a small fortune while offering very little in exchange. Despite generous handouts and the perks bestowed on it by the University, the Department of Law sustained precedent by managing to record the worst score in student satisfaction year in, year out.

What did make my out-of-depth floundering easier was that on the really important matters of strategy and policy I was kept afloat by Catherine and Alison since they dictated in no uncertain terms exactly what I was to do. Effectively, they got to run the Department without any of the exposure and headaches. So content were they to be puppet masters that they even allowed me to keep the measly bonus of a couple of thousand pounds that the University granted to HoDs for their trouble.

Their directions, or should I say orders, were always delivered orally. They were very careful not to leave any traces of their involvement in decision-making. Once a week we would meet after hours away from the campus, always in that same café in town, where I had first spotted the two of them together. My phone had to be placed on the table, lest I became tempted to record our conversations. The session would begin with my updating them on administrative matters. I was then told exactly what to do, what to say and to whom. Not trusting me to remember everything, they required me to keep handwritten notes, which they then checked for accuracy. The meetings were run with a ruthless efficiency that University Committees could only dream of approximating. They ran no more than an hour with everything covered in the allotted timeframe.

At first, I was shocked by their cynicism. The idea that they were prepared to sweep an awful truth under the carpet just to reap personal gain was disconcerting, to say the least. Perhaps I'm not in the best position to pass judgement of that sort, but surely their approach was not the decent way to go.

Then, the more I thought about it, the more I came to appreciate that their response was not unreasonable. Involving the police would cause disruption not only to my life but also to the Department. We would be one staff member short when we were already overstretched. Besides, there was a real risk the working atmosphere could turn toxic. Paul was not universally loved, no two ways about it. Perhaps in Catherine's and Alison's minds I was guilty despite my protestations that Paul's death was accidental, yet, doubtless, in the absence of any concrete and conclusive evidence, some were bound to take my side. At least they would not jump to conclusions blaming me. This would cause tensions which would only escalate during my trial. Then there was the collateral reputational damage to be considered if the whole affair spun out of control. Who would want to go study with homicidal lecturers?

Another advantage of the operative model, was the fact that it increased productivity. Three minds, well, two plus an executive pair of hands, were better than one. Governance by triumvirate, however surreptitious and unevenly balanced, also kept disagreement within the Department to a minimum. If Catherine and Alison did not take issue with a policy, then no one else was likely to.

Yes, I did get all that. What I couldn't get over was Catherine's lack of faith in me. She had accused me of being intimate with her for an ulterior and dishonest motive, something that was categorically not true even if I admit that appearances strongly indicated otherwise. Yet, I could easily level the same accusation at her. What was she thinking while making love to me? That she might be sleeping with a murderer? Had there always been a veil of suspicion between us? Were any of her touches, any of her kisses genuine? Had she merely been trying to keep me in check? How could she have been capable of such deception?

Worst of all was that she had shown a clear preference for Horst. She had witnessed him being horrible to me it and yet failed to take my side. Yes, I had tried to throw suspicion on him but my intention was not to get him into trouble, just to muddy the waters. In the process, he had proved himself to be nasty and volatile. Even that was not enough to turn Catherine against him, which I took to be irrefutable proof of her duplicity. That and the unforgiving way she had turned on me so vehemently. She showed no interest in hearing my side of the story. She was brutally dismissive, as icy and pitiless as a professional executioner.

It would have been easier to swallow that unpalatable pill had I been able to comprehend Catherine's behaviour, which I found impossible, mainly because it was so disappointing but also because something felt amiss. Perhaps if I applied myself I would be able to make sense of it all. But I hardly had time to breathe.

Beauclerk Mansion, a 45-minute bus trip south of the University, was one of those stately homes that "beautiful they stand, to prove the upper classes have still the upper hand". The Beauclerk family had turned their surviving piece of real estate into a charitable institution, an honourable subterfuge for cloaking bankruptcy with a do-good gesture. Now its mission was to host university events so as to *"promote knowledge and rationality, imbue students' minds with moral values, promote progress, strengthen the ties of the academic community"*. To my knowledge, no one had ever openly challenged the Mansion about the irreconcilability of some of these aims.

The grounds were magnificent. Deer grazed serenely in the shade of gigantic trees knotted and gnarled with age. Marble and bronze statues studded the landscape and crept up on you in unlikely places, their pedestals draped in creeping vines that left unattended would soon envelop the whole place. The Mansion itself, originally built in the 18th century, had undergone several refurbishments since, twice in the aftermath of catastrophic fires. (The rumour that a drunken scholar had been responsible for one conflagration had never been confirmed.)

Though refurbished, the premises had not been modernised beyond the installation of some basic amenities. Yes, there was electricity and hot water was on tap around the clock. However, while the Mansion retained something of its ancestral grandeur, it was permeated with a musty joylessness and gloom that likely caused many of its original tenants to suffer respiratory and mental health problems. The wood panelled walls, where trophies and crests once hung, now featured photos of more immediate and less interesting past events. The open fire crackling in the drawing room mysteriously never went out even though no one had ever been witnessed tending to it. Heavy velvet drapes, patchily threadbare, hung over enormous windows, their frames so porous that a permanent blizzard seemed to funnel its way into the room, cancelling out whatever comfort and heat the fire might have provided.

"Sir", an obviously disconcerted postgraduate student whose name I couldn't remember said to me.

"Yes?", I said.

"There are no keys to the bedroom doors."

"That's right."

"But, that can't be."

"It's a safety measure", I said. "To ensure access to rooms in case of accident or criminal activity."

I was surprised to catch myself using formal language with such felicity. Assimilation into the machine was moving very swiftly.

"But our belongings, sir...", said the boy.

"Are you worried someone will break in and steal your precious gems?", Duncan, who had been hovering behind me, asked.

I nudged him as discreetly as I could.

"There are personal safes in each room. They're big enough to fit a laptop computer. You'll be fine."

"If anything happens to my stuff, I'll hold you personally responsible, sir."

He walked away, a mixture of agitation and insolence covering his concern.

"Little shit", I muttered.

"What a fine start we're off to", Duncan said. "I told you we should stop doing this wretched retreat nonsense."

"We can't", I said.

Discontinuing Beauclerk Mansion had been explicitly ruled out as an option by Catherine and Alison.

I was standing by the enormous front door which, despite the cold, stood open allowing me to welcome and usher people into a modicum of sheltering warmth. Students and staff sidled over to the reception desk.

"Hello, Dr West", came the greeting from behind me.

I turned around to see our keynote speaker.

"Ursula!", I said. "How lovely you could make it! Please, no need for formalities."

"In that case, hello Michael", she repeated.

"Right, yes. Please, let's jump the queue and get you to your room. All should be ready for tonight's talk."

"Looking forward to it", Ursula said. "I hope my old friend is here."

She put quotation marks around "old friend" with her index and middle fingers.

"Of course he is."

Of course he was. After all, Horst was the reason why I'd initially invited Ursula to deliver the keynote. My intention was to goad him, knowing that her presence would incense him to such an extent that it would trigger his inner Mr Hyde. I had even scheduled her keynote for the first evening in hopes that this would make Horst stew in his own juice for as long as possible, increasing the likelihood of an eruption. My plan had since gone awry, and would no longer serve that purpose. Still, piquing Horst would cheer me up, trapped as I was in infernal gloom.

Horst might have been the prime reason for inviting Ursula but when it transpired that she had been responsible for forwarding my rough notes on phenomenology to Prof. Dr Dr Bakker, the very least I could do by way of thanks was proffer her a brief junket amidst the faded nobility of the English countryside.

Among the many non-negotiable conditions the Mansion set in exchange for hosting events was that the academic programme had to be rigorous and relentless. This meant that we had to kick off shortly after arrival and that each day had to be packed with 'educational' events. The only respite were the meals and end-of-the-day drinks from the sparsely stocked bar.

Once all the participants had been herded into the conference room, I took to the lectern to introduce Ursula. I listed her most notable publications, joked about not being able to pronounce the longer German words in the titles, talked up the significance of her research, and offered her the floor.

She swept the audience with one swift look accompanied by a faint smile. She had an air of authority about her that I certainly lacked. In truth, her presence was even stronger than Catherine's. She was also very good looking. Her high heels added several inches to her already considerable height. Her blonde, shoulder-length hair framed her pronounced cheekbones and her visage was softened by blue eyes and full lips.

"If we were going to have a second rate academic give the keynote, then I would have done it", Horst said.

No doubt he intended to be heard by the whole front row but I doubt that he intended his quip to come out as it did. I couldn't help chortling and he couldn't help swearing at me under his breath.

Ursula's lecture was outstanding. She had dutifully stuck to the brief. Considering that I had asked her to "address students who know nothing but think they know everything and staff drooling at the prospect of mauling you", that wasn't an easy task at all. She was informative without being didactic and she actually made some original points that not even Horst could deal with. He asked a question, which no doubt he thought was so astutely critical that it would embarrass Ursula. Instead, she shrugged it off it with an easy erudition and a delightfully calculated pinch of patronising condescension. At the end of the talk, the queue of students wanting to speak to her, ask follow up questions, share their own ideas with her and just be near her in case some of her brilliance rubbed off on them stretched from the edge of the stage all the way to the far end of the conference room.

I congratulated myself on an all-round excellent choice of speaker. So did Alison and Lucy. Catherine was too petty to do so.

My elation and the victorious sense of achievement kept me buoyant until dinner. I had been dreading the ordeal of sitting at the same table with all my colleagues under the watchful eye of my two ruthless mistresses. When the time came, however, I felt I had the upper hand and I was not going to relinquish it.

I dominated conversations by putting on my larger than life persona, a guise that normally didn't come easy to me but on this occasion felt natural and right. I jested, recounted academic anecdotes, spoke authoritatively about matters of urgent concern to tertiary education and opined informatively about the state of the discipline. It was as if, for the first time since taking over, I was effortlessly slipping into the HoD mantle.

As per normal, I helped fuel that sense of well-being with copious amounts of alcohol. That boosted my confidence even further and, in turn, I took that as a cause to celebrate so I drank more. I must have had more than a bottle of wine at the dinner table and then continued at the bar, where all the staff members and most of the students joined me at my persistent urging.

The institution must have wanted to discourage excessive drinking which is why the bar was, in contrast to the rest of the Mansion, cold and characterless. The tables and chairs, all-weather aluminium outdoor pieces, would have been more at home in a provincial train station cafeteria. The cream carpet, several steps down from the handmade Persian rugs that lined the plusher common rooms, was stained in places (the Mansion charged guests for any damages caused but they didn't seem to invest the fines in repairs), and the yellow light from the exposed bulbs made everyone, deprived of exposure to sunlight as we already were, look beige.

"Mr Head", Jeremy said to me.

He had taken to calling me Mr Head after my appointment and, despite my requests to desist, refused to stop. I was leaning against a wall having a glass of wine with Ursula.

"Sorry, Jeremy, now's not a very good time."

"Mr Head, I've been trying to speak to you for a long time. It's very important. It's a matter of...", he hesitated, "it's dead important."

"I'm sure it is, Jeremy. How about putting it all in an email first? As a heads up, you know?"

"I've tried. I just don't know...I've tried."

"Then how about we talk about it tomorrow?"

"Tomorrow will be alright, I suppose. It's very important. It's about the HoD, Mr Head."

"I look forward to your eulogy, Jeremy. I'm sure you'll do a sterling job."

He shuffled to the furthest corner where he slumped heavily into the only armchair in the room.

"He seemed upset", Ursula said.

"Jeremy's generally a little confused", I said.

I rested my arm on the bar and lightly touched hers with the tip of my fingers. Clearly not one for flirtatious innuendoes, she said:

"Let's have a few more drinks first."

I meant to return a meaningful, sultry look but it came across as gobsmacked.

"What are you working on at the moment, Ursula?", Catherine said.

She had appeared out of nowhere and her opening line was unabashedly confrontational.

"I have a multi-million euro EU grant to explore the anthropological aspects of attitudes of citizens of states under accession towards other European states and the EU itself", Ursula said.

I gave her arm a delighted squeeze and she gave me back a proprietorial but nevertheless sweet look.

"I see", Catherine said.

I couldn't recall ever seeing her lost for words before.

"I suppose that's not the kind of project that would concern English academics any longer", Ursula said.

"A multi-million grant would concern any academic even if it was about the anthropology of Martians", I said.

Catherine looked displeased.

"Anyway, I think I'll go to bed now", she said. "Long day tomorrow. Thanks for your talk, Ursula."

As I watched her leave the room, I saw that Duncan had joined Jeremy. Their conversation seemed sotto voce, almost conspiratorial and so did the look they gave me when they realised that I was staring at them.

And being, by my after-the-fact calculations, on at least my third bottle of wine, that is pretty much the last thing I remember about the evening.

"Wake up. Michael, wake up."

I managed a squint. My first thought was that the blurry figure standing over my bed was an apparition. But apparitions don't tend to shake you that violently so the possibility had to be dismissed.

"What? Who? What's going on?", I said, words trying to exit my mouth in single file.

"It's Duncan, dear boy. Wake up. Something terrible has happened."

On the scale of hangovers, this one was hurricane force. My brain was foaming and grey cells were violently sprayed up against the walls of my skull. The pain felt as if my soul was trying to escape its corporeal confines.

Still, I was faring much better than Jeremy.

Duncan's description of the scene on our way to our old colleague's room had conjured up the image of Jean-Paul Marat in his bath, arm hanging over the rim, quill in hand, his face lit up with the serenity of martyrdom.

It was nothing like that. Jeremy was submerged in water. His hair was floating like seaweed and his skin, loose and wrinkly, looked as if it had been hastily wrapped around his frame. In places it didn't even look like it fit his skeleton. His eyes were open and the expression on his face was bewildered; disappointed even. Had death not been what he was expecting?

No note in his hands either. He had left us no clues.

"What happened?", I asked Duncan.

"We had arranged to meet for an early breakfast to beat the insufferable crowd. When he didn't show up, I came up here looking for him. I knocked and knocked. No answer. I came in and found him like that."

"What happened?", I asked again.

Duncan looked at me as if he had already answered my question, which in a way he had but it was different information that I was after and in my confused state I was going to ignore everything that didn't directly supply that.

"Are you alright?", he asked.

"How did it happen?", I rephrased.

"I'm not a pathologist, dear boy", Duncan said.

"How did it happen?", I repeated.

"Seriously, are you OK? I said I don't know. He probably passed out in the bath and drowned."

"Was he drunk?"

"He'd had a little wine, we all did. He was certainly not as drunk as you were. Or should I say are?"

"Poor Jeremy", I said.

"He loved that bath", Duncan said.

We both paused to consider the extra tinge of tragedy that detail brought to the situation.

"Do you have any recollection of last night? Do you remember what you two talked about?", Duncan said suddenly.

His velvety voice was now tempered with a slight but unmissable coolness, a frostiness that was quite unlike him and so at odds with his earlier cordiality that I was taken aback. It took me a few seconds to appreciate the full implications of what he had said.

"Hold on, Jeremy and I talked last night?"

"Of course you did. You followed Jeremy out of the bar and when I headed to my room, some ten minutes after him, you were still having a heated conversation in the corridor."

"We did?"

"You did."

"What time was that?"

"Elevenish. He seemed fearful and upset by your one-to-one. And you seemed angry. Do you not remember any of that?"

"Not really, no. Do you have any idea what he wanted to talk to me about?"

"He wouldn't tell me in detail. He did say it was about Paul though."

"What about Paul?"

"I told you I don't know, Michael, but..."

"But what, Duncan?"

"Let's just say that I can't help wondering why Jeremy was so keen to talk to you directly and why he thought that that was the 'collegial thing to do'. His words, not mine."

"Duncan, we both know Jeremy was growing more and more confused the older he got."

"He seemed perfectly lucid to me."

"Lucid", I said vaguely. "Anyway, you know what he was like about authority and hierarchy. He would never take up an issue with anyone other than the person with the relevant jurisdiction."

Duncan remained unconvinced.

"Michael, what on earth is going on?"

If the change of tone was meant to make him sound friendly or to make me feel more at ease, it failed on both counts.

It took the police and the coroner two hours to arrive. I was grateful because it gave me some time to sober up and to consider how I should deal with the situation. I determined on a course of action. Once the dust had settled, I would summon everyone to the conference room to pay tribute to Jeremy and, more importantly, tell them to not worry or panic. I would ask them to carry on with the weekend as normal but to tone down the celebratory atmosphere. I had to find a replacement for Jeremy's slot, the irony of the person assigned the task of delivering a eulogy needing one himself impossible to escape. Still, I reckoned I could probably rope someone into doing it. Even better, I would ask Duncan to go through Jeremy's things and find the eulogy (there was no doubt that a neatly handwritten text existed) so that I would read it. If Catherine and Alison permitted me to do so, that is.

Once my alcohol-induced predicament began to subside, I was surprised to discover some indefinable and unusual feelings surfacing from within me. It was a mix of elation blended with guilt, not quite full-blown guilt but the sense of restlessness that the intuition that you've done something wrong leaves you. I tried to trace the origins, backtracking in search of a flashback.

And then I knew.

Every time Jeremy catwalked across my memory – stalking me to hassle me about his obsessions, looking lonely, lost and dishevelled in his old grey coat, a spectre of academia past – I felt what I can only describe as a pang of relief. On the one hand, I was glad Jeremy was out of the picture and there were no two ways about it. I just wasn't quite sure why. The only reason I could think of was that he really could be a pain. Not in the demanding-bordering-on-nasty manner of someone like Horst but rather like a distracting irritant.

Deep down, I knew that my sense of relief said something absolutely terrible about me. Was I really that kind of person? Did I have no sense of moral proportion? Had Jeremy really annoyed me so much that I was pleased at his death? How could such an irreversible loss make me happy? How could someone's demise make another happy under any circumstances?

My thoughts had been well and truly derailed. Instead of completing the planning of my next moves as HoD, here I was struggling to come to terms not just with Jeremy's death but with my response to it and sundry ill-defined philosophical problems.

Best to interrupt that inconsequential but searing introspection and go for a walk in the grounds to clear my head, I thought.

No sooner had I exited my room than I bumped into Mr Jonathan Aisthorpe CBE, the Director of Beauclerk Mansion. An erstwhile lecturer in medieval languages, of the generation that had landed an academic job on the back of little more qualification than being able to spell, he had taken up the Mansion post upon his retirement. So stuck up and old fashioned was he that he might well have been speaking a medieval language.

"Dr West", he said, adjusting oversized spectacles that would put most hipsters to shame, "I need to have a word with you."

"Of course, Mr Aisthorpe", I said.

"It is very distressing, very distressing."

"We are all in shock. Jeremy was the most respected and beloved of our colleagues."

"Yes, yes", he murmured, "be that as it may, you do realise that I will have to have the room deep cleaned and possibly the carpet replaced."

"I beg your pardon?"

"Well, I can't just leave a dead man's room in that state. Think of our guests. It would put them off."

"I'm sorry but this is not the best time to discuss this."

"No, no, you see Dr West, I find that such issues ought to be resolved immediately. Otherwise misunderstandings arise, which in turn breed unnecessary disputes. It's in everyone's best interest to form a clear mutual understanding about the situation as soon as possible."

"I'm not sure I follow, Mr Aisthorpe."

"Compensation, Dr West. Beauclerk Mansion will be charging your Department for the refurbishment of the room, in which your colleague passed away. Also, your students have been burning paper in the drawing room fireplace. That's strictly against the rules so we'll be levying the prescribed fine for that too."

What a vile creature the man was. A failed academic on a power trip as a glorified hotelier, he oozed banal heartlessness. He was a walking cliché, all veneer and no substance, a subservient snob. It wasn't the first time he was being an arse to me. Every little transgression by students in the past would trigger chastisement beyond all proportion. But this time he had surpassed himself. This was more than lack of empathy; it was pure cruelty. It was the last straw. I was not going to pay a penny for his sodding carpet (which poor darling Jeremy had not soiled in the least) and he could take us to court, if he liked. My Department would also never patronise his overrated establishment ever again. Apart from everything else, it was too bloody cold and there were no keys to the locks.

The trouble was that everything I thought of him I said aloud. His response was muted, baffled. He managed a vitriolic look before turning to stalk away from me.

"What was that about?", Ursula asked me.

The confrontation with Aisthorpe was right outside her door, so she couldn't help hearing it.

"Everything is a bit fraught currently."

"I'm sorry about your colleague passing away. Your Department is building itself quite the macabre track record."

She didn't mean ill. She was just being her forthright self.

"Yes, it was a terrible night."

"Not all of it", she said.

Her attempt at being sultry was a little forced but eloquent. Something had happened between us the night before. Something I couldn't remember.

I'm not a rambler. When I walk I want a destination, preferably in an urban setting with trouble-shooting public transport options nearby. That day I had no choice but to wander aimlessly in the Mansion grounds. I had given up on the possibility of reconstructing the events of the previous night, at least not in the state I was in at the time. So I tried to empty my brain of every memory and thought by letting nature's images register directly, unprocessed, invoking nothing other than their form. It was a long shot but it worked. Meaning was draining out of the world around me. Even the serenity that welled up inside me defied articulation, being at best akin to a sense of floating.

I should have known it wouldn't last. On my return, the first person to greet me at the door of the Mansion was Catherine.

"What the hell did you do?", she said.

That Aisthorpe character hadn't wasted any time.

"Listen, he's an abominable character and these weekends are even worse. We're better off not returning to this craphole."

"What are you talking about?"

"I thought you were referring to my spat with the director."

"What spat?"

"I pulled out of the Mansion."

"You did what?"

"He's just awful."

"Well, whatever you told him, you'll apologise profusely, do whatever he wants you to do and book our slot for next year."

"Catherine...", I protested.

"But that's not what I was asking you. I meant Jeremy. What the hell did you do to Jeremy?"

Dr Pepple, whose catchment area seemed to know no boundaries, was unavailable so it was his assistant who came to examine the body. The cause of Jeremy's death was drowning alright but the stand-in pathologist's expert gaze had seen more than was immediately visible to the layperson's naked eye. Although careful to reserve final judgement until after the full post mortem in the lab, he was particularly interested in the bruises on Jeremy's shoulders, which, he opined, might indicate foul play.

And Catherine was accusing *me* of having played foul. In her eyes, I had become the usual suspect, the member of staff assigned the murder portfolio, the man who not only had axes to grind but grind them he did by knocking off his colleagues' heads with them one at a time. I asked her what possible reason I could have had for killing Jeremy. She had her answer primed and ready. Jeremy had found out something about my role in Paul's death. He was going to reveal all he knew in his eulogy, which Duncan had been unable to find in Jeremy's things. Somehow I had found out his intentions, snuck into his room, caught him in the bath, grabbed him by the shoulders and submerged him until he died. He must have resisted or perhaps my rage and determination was such that I bruised his shoulders. I then stole the hand-written eulogy, confident that no electronic copy would exist.

I found the allegation preposterous and infuriating. What enraged me even more was that I was unable to protest my innocence for the simple and exceedingly frustrating reason that I had no recollection of the latter stages of the evening. Yet I couldn't just sit on my hands and take this from Catherine. I needed to piece the story together myself.

My first and only available stop in my trek backwards in time was Ursula. Extracting information from her would have to be done tactfully.

"That was fun last night, wasn't it?", I said.

It was an admittedly awkward first line in the circumstances but it seemed like the only option.

"It surely was", she said giving me that same conspiratorial smile.

"Yes, it was great."

"Your skills in bed far exceed your academic ones."

Always careful not to disturb the equilibrium of self-worth and self-loathing in one's soul.

"So good, in fact, that I am prepared to forgive your boldness of barging into my room", she continued.

"We didn't leave the bar together?"

"I assumed you were too drunk to continue the evening behind closed doors so I left by myself at around eleven. But how wrong was I to think I'd go to bed alone?"

"Yes, quite wrong, I suppose. In fact, so good was it that I completely lost track of time", I said. "What time did I come?"

She laughed. I hadn't imagined she could be so puerile.

"Around half past eleven or so", she said.

"And what time did I leave?"

"You mean, what time did I ask you to leave?"

Of course she would have asked me to leave. But that didn't matter. Whether I fled or had been kicked out, what was important was the timeframe. Pepple's assistant had placed Jeremy's death some five hours before his body was found. That would have been around three in the morning.

"Yes, what time did you bring proceedings to an end?", I said.

"It was about two in the morning, I should think. An excellent performance."

"And how was I when I left?"

"Content, though a bit annoyed that you were not allowed to stay over."

"How annoyed?"

"On a ten point scale? I'd say about five. Maybe six."

I made a quick excuse accompanied by a charmless smile and a peck on her cheek, which was graciously, if not enthusiastically, received.

❖

"It's a pleasure to meet you at last, Dr West. Adeel will not stop talking about your lectures. And good to see you again, Dr Bowen."

Ameer Rahman, who had become the Department's resident DCI, was a jovial, gentle man. His smile and run-of-the-mill style was comforting, although how he could maintain either in such circumstances was a mystery.

"Adeel is our most committed student", I said.

Parents will believe anything their children's teachers tell them. In this case, the glowing report on his son's performance was also fortuitously true.

"Oh he takes it so very seriously. He's already talking about doing a Master's after his first degree."

"Early days but I'm delighted to hear this", I said.

"Anyway, to our point", Rahman said bringing the parent-teacher conference part of our meeting to an abrupt close. "Your Department is going through a very unfortunate period, isn't it?"

"Very unfortunate", Catherine said.

"The situation here is a little more complicated than last time. That's why I wanted to speak to the two of you first, before hassling anyone else."

"Of course, I understand", Catherine said as though I wasn't a party to the conversation.

"On the face of it, everything is straightforward. Professor Allcock was of an advanced age. I wouldn't be surprised if he was facing health problems. If I understand correctly, he had a little bit to drink. Cases like this are usually open and shut. The poor man decided to have a bath, fainted or fell asleep or perhaps suffered a heart attack or a seizure of some sort, the pathology report will tell us that, and he drowned."

"He loved that bath", I said.

"That's useful", Rahman said.

"But?", Catherine asked.

"You could tell there was a but coming, couldn't you? Very perceptive, Dr Bowen, very perceptive."

We were proving ourselves worthy of teaching his son.

"The 'but' is the bruising. That kind of thing triggers a further investigation, you understand. But there's about fifty of you here currently. I can't well invite them one by one into the drawing room to ask about their whereabouts and their relationship with Professor Allcock. I'm not Hercules Poirot, am I now?"

He laughed out loud. Catherine forced a smile. I failed to do the same.

"So", Rahman continued, "I thought I'd narrow down the scope of the investigation by speaking to you two first."

"How can we help?", I asked.

"First of all, of the people present in the Mansion at this moment in time, are you aware of anyone who might have wanted to harm Professor Allcock?"

"No, of course not", I said hastily. "Jeremy was universally loved."

Catherine nodded. Whether she was agreeing with me or answering Rahman's question in the affirmative was not clear.

"I'd be surprised, if you'd told me he had any enemies, to be perfectly honest. Surely, academia is a place of friendship and good will after all."

"We're hardly the Quakers", Catherine said.

"Another possibility is rough play, of course, but I'm inclined to dismiss that out of hand. Unless you have any pertinent information regarding Professor Allcock's private life."

"That can be safely ruled out", Catherine said.

“Of course”, Rahman said. “I hope you don’t find that line of questioning offensive. It’s standard protocol.”

“Not at all”, Catherine said.

“Good, good”, Rahman said. “Trouble is we still haven’t made any progress. We have suspect bruising but no one who might have had reason to inflict it.”

“May I make a suggestion, DCI Rahman?”, Catherine said.

Was that it? Was that going to be the beginning of my end? If she intimated her suspicion of me, then she would have to give away my so-called motive too. And if she did that, then everything would be out in the open and I would be facing two charges. And then, with no defence to speak of, I would be facing two sentences for murder. My mind raced ahead. I was already picturing myself behind bars, when Catherine said:

“I think there may be an explanation for the bruising on the shoulders.”

Jeremy's funeral was much more low-key than Paul Digby's.

His next of kin was a distant cousin. It took her several seconds to register who I was and what I was talking about, when I called to break the sad news. She had not seen or spoken to Jeremy in several years, their last encounter being a brief hello at another relative's funeral. Jeremy, survived by no close relatives after the death of his wife, must have been at a loss as to whom to put down as next of kin in his human resources file when we had to update them a few years back. The cousin's name was probably the only one that sprang to mind. Small wonder that she went to no great pains to organise a fancy send-off.

No student, current or former, turned up and even Lucy, Thomas and Horst sent their apologies when I shared the funeral arrangements with the Department. There were no eulogies, no specially selected readings or music. The celebrant was the death equivalent of a legal aid lawyer, summoned at the last minute and paid minimum rates to go through the basic motions.

I was grateful that the whole affair was so run-of-the-mill, not wishing in the circumstances to be further upset by anything emotionally demanding. After all, my situation was now so precarious that I feared the slightest nudge would bring everything tumbling down.

At the outset I hadn't believed that Rahman would pay any heed to Catherine's explanation but I had been quickly proven wrong. Pay heed he did and promised to follow up.

He got in touch a couple of days later to confirm that Dr Pepple, who in the meantime had returned to work and conducted the post mortem, had concluded that the bruising on Jeremy's shoulders was consistent with the pressure exerted by the straps of his rucksack, as Catherine had hypothesised. The theory was further corroborated by the fact that Jeremy had been on anti-coagulant drugs, which thinned his blood and made him more susceptible to bruising.

I had to admit that it made sense. Jeremy did of course carry his rucksack to the Mansion. He would never part with it and its antiquated load. Perhaps that, along with his diluted blood, did account for the discoloration.

I desperately wanted to believe that version of the story. But I couldn't. The coincidences were too many for comfort. The look that Jeremy had given me the last time I'd seen him, or at least what I recalled as the last time I'd seen him, remained indelible in my mind. It was the same anxious expression that he'd been wearing for a while but this time it was topped up by something else that I couldn't quite put my finger on. Was it disappointment? Suspicion? Fear?

And what was it that he and I had quarrelled over in the corridors of the Mansion? Why was I angry and why was he scared?

Then there was the timeline. I could easily have slipped into Jeremy's room either before joining Ursula or after leaving her room. Could I really have shifted gears so easily? First murder a man, someone I thought I liked too, and then go play lover boy? Or first go play lover boy and then go commit murder?

Catherine thought me capable of such brutality. The trouble was that it wasn't all that implausible. The way I had handled Paul's death revealed a dark side that I didn't know or could never have imagined was there. The lying, the rumour spreading, the covering up of tracks, all were cause for concern. And that was nothing when compared to my readiness to resort to violence.

I had not quite admitted it to myself, not explicitly anyway, that the day that Catherine discovered my plagiarism, I was fully primed to do her harm. It was obvious that her discovery would snowball and I couldn't think of another way to stop her. I hadn't quite thought it through so I've no idea what lengths I'd be prepared to go to. Would I strangle her in my apartment, or, perhaps better, in hers, and then dump her body in the mudfield, giving it a thorough roll in the dirt to destroy any evidence? Or would I dismember her and scatter the body parts around campus? Come to think of it, as final places of rest go, that might have pleased her.

Chances are that I would never have got around to doing anything so vicious and cruel but it's undeniable that that's where my instincts were leading me that day. Clearly instinct unfettered by rational or ingrained inhibitions, arising from the consumption of a hell of a lot of wine for example, was quite capable of making one do terrible things.

As the days passed, it became harder to shake off these thoughts and I gradually went from self-doubt to believing that what Catherine had accused me of was true. And the more I swung in that direction, the more inclined I was to turn myself in. On a couple of occasions, I even picked up my mobile phone and scrolled down to Ameer Rahman's name, on the verge of tapping on his number only to change my mind at the last second.

What diverted me from being overwhelmed by a sense of conditional remorse for possibly having killed Jeremy and the brief impulse to harm Catherine was the realisation that where Paul was concerned, I not only felt that I had done nothing wrong but firmly believed that what I had done was much closer to being right. In fact, if everyone in the Department bothered being honest with themselves, they'd admit it was just what they would have wanted. If the past few months had taught me anything, it was that more people than I'd ever imagined had fallen out with Paul. Besides, Catherine had let me off the hook twice for the simple reason that ensuring the Department continued running as smoothly as possible was best accomplished by not rocking the boat.

She'd told me so herself when I dared to ask her why she'd volunteered the rucksack theory to Rahman. That and also that she couldn't be sure of my guilt because the evidence was flimsy and circumstantial. Not that she missed the opportunity to let me know that I was on a knife edge. One wrong step, one tiny act of resistance to do hers and Alison's bidding and she would take everything to the police.

So there I was, a pawn in Catherine's hands and a slave to my moral dilemmas. I was facing a lifetime of unfreedom, of internal tribulation and terror. The alternative, if I broke down and handed myself in, would be to spend the rest of my days exposed, humiliated and incarcerated.

Such was my tragedy until the day dawned that opened up a whole new perspective on what might await me.

A process for assessing university performance

The larger the university sector grew and the more state funding shrank the more pressing it became to devise a system for allocating resources in a way that appeared to be fair. Inevitably, government came up with a process for assessing university performance to determine who got what and how much of it. One assessment exercise relates to research. Staff members are required to submit the work they have produced during the assessment cycle. That is then judged by a panel of experts and each piece is awarded a score in the childish form of stars. Finally, each institution gets ranked according to the number of stars it has been awarded.

The reward is worthless compared to the pain involved, given the enormous amount of preparatory work required of each academic Department. All that time and effort could be so much more productively invested were it devoted to actually producing genuinely good work. But the system is what it is and there is nothing we active academics, the lowest rungs on the ladder, can do about it.

Most places designate an academic member of staff as a Director of Research, someone who is saddled with the task of monitoring staff research and preparing the departmental submission. Since our Department was small and Paul Digby was an obsessive concentrationist, not surprisingly he had reserved that role for himself. When I succeeded him, I also inherited yet another dreadful burden.

My task was made marginally more tolerable by the fact that every colleague's submission came with a note from either Catherine or Alison, which typically consisted of a number of stars and a laconic commentary: "derivative", "mildly original", "should never have been published", "lacks ambition", "passable", that kind of thing.

My margin of discretion in assessing submissions was precisely zero and my role went no further than pulling everything together and writing an inconsequential blurb about the brilliance of the Department's research efforts. Nevertheless, with all that material accumulating in my drawers, idle curiosity eventually drove me to thumb through some of the submissions, mostly, it transpired, those of one particular author.

Catherine was turning in her monograph and three articles that had appeared in prestigious journals.

The most enlightening part of an academic monograph is without a doubt to be found in the acknowledgements. That's where you'll get a sense of academic genealogy, an insight into how the network works, why the author is where she is, where she wants to go, why the book was published by one specific publisher and not another.

There was much more than that to be learned from reading the acknowledgements in Catherine's book.

"Many people have had a hand in shaping this book. It started off as a doctoral thesis and I am in debt to my supervisor Professor Sue Merryman. Her work and guidance have been and will always be a source of inspiration. For the lengthy conversations about anthropology, the criminal justice system and all things cultural and for putting up with my frequent crises of confidence, I am grateful to my colleagues from various institutions and especially Maria, Matt, Jonathan, Raheem, Sinead, Pasquale, Alison and Horst. This study required extensive empirical research and I cannot begin to list everyone, institutional players and private individuals alike, who took the time to respond to my persistent questions and helped me to refine my anthropological understanding of the criminal justice system in East London."

At first glance it was an unremarkable set of acknowledgements, modest even. Most younger authors are so excited about publishing a book that they thank everyone they've ever met and often people they haven't. However, in Catherine's case, self-importance seemed to outweigh the courtesy of gratitude.

What was particularly interesting about that relatively brief paragraph was what had been left unsaid. First of all, why had she singled out Alison and Horst to thank from our Department? Where was Paul, who had jumped her to the front of the queue? And did her chumminess with Horst, to which I had been oblivious, explain why she had believed him and not me?

All these admittedly trifling questions were soon pushed aside by a nagging recollection of a passing comment dropped in a recent conversation I had been party to. Triggered by the acknowledgements, I thumbed quickly through the pages, skipping to chapter nine: *Mortal, Morbid, Moribund.*

Much of the chapter was devoted to a detailed exposition and analysis of the experiences of an East London pathologist, who remained anonymous "for reasons pertaining to research ethics". He had talked freely about his relationship to death, to his subjects and their relatives, as well as to other agencies involved in the criminal justice system. He was very talkative and appeared to have spent a fair amount of time over several sessions with Catherine. Indeed, it looked as though she had been given access to sensitive information that would normally be subject to strict confidentiality rules.

I put the book down and pulled my computer keyboard in front of me. It only took a couple of clicks to locate my target.

"After completing his medical degree and his specialty in forensic pathology at the Royal College of Pathologists, Dr Pepple joined the East London Forensic Lab as junior pathologist. He later took over as Director of the Pathology Department, where he remained for fifteen years."

That could not have been a coincidence. When Catherine and I interviewed him, it had seemed odd how he went from outright refusal to engage with us to full cooperation with a fluency and precision as though he knew exactly what type of information we were after in our short-lived phenomenological research. Now I knew why. He'd done something similar before. He was an old hand in social scientific research. Catherine and Pepple already knew each other; they knew each other well. And yet, in my company, she'd gone through the charade of pretending they were meeting for the first time.

❖

There was no question in my mind that this new discovery was extremely significant but I still struggled to make sense of it, let alone to decide what I should do about it.

One thing I was sure of. I would not confront Catherine. If I did, she would likely spin some skillful yarn and while I might not fall for it outright, it would nevertheless shake my confidence, leaving me to question my assumptions and suspicions, perhaps to the point where I might sweep them under the rug while slapping myself for being so paranoid. No, I couldn't allow her to turn the table on me.

Nor could I approach Pepple directly. Not yet anyhow. In order to gain the upper hand, I would need more data. With that little bit more up my sleeve, I would be able to extract more from him.

The question was how to acquire that information. How would I go about asking potentially uncomfortable questions that people might be reluctant to answer?

No matter the strategy I dreamt up, I seemed to be hitting a wall. Only then did I realise that I had no need to know many people or have access to the right places in order to get what I wanted. All that was required was to know someone with those skills, a node, a person of a thousand handshakes, one of those people who make the six degrees of separation theory a reality.

"What's up, buddy?", he said when he answered the phone.

"You're an academic, Nikhil, you can't call people buddy and stuff", I said.

"And you can't say 'and stuff'. Anyway, you really must stop thinking so highly of our kind."

"I'm working on it."

"How can I help you? I heard you've had more fatalities in your Department. And you're now HoD? What the hell is going on? Are you hell-bent on becoming the third victim of the curse?"

"That's why I need your help."

"Mine? How can I help?"

"Indirectly. You grew up in Hackney, right?"

"Clapton."

"What's the difference?"

"One's Hackney, the other one's Clapton. Also there's nowhere near as much smashed avocado in Hackney as there is in Clapton."

"Right, OK, but you know Hackney. You know people there, I mean."

"I do."

"And you've done research there."

"Do you mean my council estate piece?"

"That's the one."

"Carry on."

"And you still know people and feel comfortable doing a bit of discreet snooping around?"

"Stop beating around the bush, buddy. What's this about?"

"I'd like you to ask some questions about someone."

An accidental click with my left index

The discovery of Catherine's suspicious connection to Pepple not only gave me a sense of advantage but also emboldened me in my role as HoD. I felt empowered to take initiatives, to start running my Department the way I saw fit and not as Catherine and Alison dictated. It was too soon to take any direct action but there was nothing to stop me from doing some preparatory work.

My first move was to go through all of Paul's folders. Everything that concerned the Department was right there, carefully and systematically filed, in folders with titles as concise as they were clear and informative. I had to give it to him. He had been a tidy administrator.

My knowledge and understanding of how computers work would rate as somewhere between elementary and nonexistent. I was a competent enough user of the basics like email, word processing and slide presentations. However, if you were to ask me what lies beneath, I would not even know what form the answer should come in, a number, a word, a sentence, a symbol or a combination of all of the above.

So, it was a genuine mistake, a slip and an accidental click with my left index on the right button of the computer mouse that inadvertently showed me the way. Trying to close a pop-up window that had appeared, I mis-clicked, landing on the 'Folder and search options' line, which listed an array of previously unobtainable options, one being to 'Show hidden files, folders, and drives'. The word 'hidden' proved irresistible. I ticked the dot next to the command and returned to the folder. Nothing appeared that hadn't already been there. But that was just one folder.

I repeated the procedure with every folder stored in the computer. In some cases I had results but they were largely uninteresting. Some were old, their contents already public knowledge.

There was, for example, a lengthy document containing a strategy for securing good feedback from students in the previous year's national satisfaction survey; a report authored by Alison assessing the relative advantages and disadvantages of other Departments around the country in comparison to ours; that sort of thing.

The real mother lode turned up in the 'personnel matters' folder. Here were documents addressed to central Human Resources about Jeremy's pension age (both sides conceded complete ignorance as to when the old man was due to retire); recommendations for discretionary financial increments to staff on grounds of exceptional performance (my name, of course, not among them); plus recruitment strategies including a list from a few years prior of anthropologists the Department might wish to consider poaching. Catherine's name featured halfway down, and, not knowing whether people had been listed in order of merit, I took some comfort in assuming that she hadn't been Paul's top choice.

One document stood out in that treasure trove. Entitled "Administrative support: issues and ways forward", it was addressed to the Secretary General of the University. Last saved a few days after the final Departmental Meeting that Paul was ever to chair.

"Dear Mark,

Following on from our conversation the other day, I am writing to set out my proposal for a strategy that will best address the administrative issues of the Department of Anthropology.

As we have agreed, the growth of the Department's operations has put considerable strain on our administrative arrangements. Doreen has been an exceptionally committed servant to the Department but coping with the new reality is regrettably beyond her abilities.

I am fully aware of the budgetary limitations that you have already laid out to me in convincing detail. Of course, the ideal solu-

tion would be to expand our administrative team but I appreciate that this is not possible, at least not at present.

I therefore propose the following: First, subject to approval by HR, that Doreen be transferred to a part-time contract (I have informally checked with them and there doesn't seem to be any legal obstacle); second, that her duties be restricted to 'front of house' such as organising events, being first port of call for students and so forth (the exact job description can be finalised in due course); third, that a younger administrator be appointed full-time to take over all substantive operations (to include accounts, administrative support to first-tier Committees and so on).

I would be grateful, if you agreed to this arrangement as soon as possible. I will be happy to liaise with HR and draft full job descriptions and terms. I will then notify Doreen and announce the new administrative structure to colleagues at the next convenient Department Meeting.

I am copying in my Deputy Head, Prof. Alison Davies.

Looking forward to your prompt reply.

With warm regards,

Paul"

Mark's reply, not as prompt as Paul had hoped, arrived a few days before the Department Meeting that the HoD and I had missed. His answer was, however, in the affirmative, and therefore a devastating blow to Doreen. The largest chunk of her life was about to be hacked off and thrown away overnight. To add insult to injury, out of the blue she would acquire a line manager to whom she would be answerable for her every move.

Had she been told about all this? If so, had Paul broken the news to her or had Alison tipped her off first? I'd no reason to suspect that she had since when she took over as HoD, she presumably had shelved the plan. The new arrangement was never presented to the Department at the meeting that followed Paul's death. At the same time, there was no other correspondence between her and Mark Weatherby nor had she made any mention of it in her handover notes to me.

With a start, I heard the lift bleeping as the doors opened and the automated voice advising passengers that they had arrived at the fourth floor. I looked at the time, only to realise that it had already gone eight thirty and that I'd spent the previous five hours trawling through the HoD's computer.

Corridor lights came on. Footsteps came to a halt after a few seconds. Suddenly I was in the grips of flashback, of the memory of a similar sequence of events a few months back, me standing over Paul's dead body and a bloody rock.

This time I had no reason to duck for cover. I pushed my chair back and rushed into the corridor. At the sound of my door opening, the silhouette at the other end of the corridor froze. I walked towards the motionless man who faced away from me me like a child pretending to be invisible.

"Thomas?", I said.

If there was a reaction, I failed to notice it. I approached until I stood right behind him and tapped him on the shoulder.

"Thomas?", I said again.

He turned around with small steps as though executing a clumsy on the spot bourrée en couru. Then facing me, he nodded hello but kept his head lowered.

"You're in late."

Another nod.

"Working hard, eh?"

Yet another nod.

"Do you work this late very often?", I asked.

To my surprise, he shook his head with unaccustomed vigour. I'd never seen him so singularly decisive before.

"It's OK, if you do. This level of commitment pleases a HoD."

He nodded again.

"I'm sorry we've not had the chance to chat since I took over. It is my intention to have a one-to-one with every colleague to go over things."

It wasn't. I was making things up as I went along.

Thomas shook his head.

"Sorry, Thomas, not sure what you mean. You don't want to have a one-to-one?"

He shook his head again.

"I just thought it'd be good for your career. I feel that the previous management was rather, how to put it, unforgiving and harsh with you. I want you to know that this will not be the case under my leadership."

He looked up at me, soulful as a hurt puppy.

"Besides, there's lots more we need to talk about."

This last remark was delivered in a jocular, semi-threatening manner, but with sufficient menace to rattle him. Not that it was directly personal. He just happened to be there as I began the deferred business of asserting my authority and challenging others. After all, here he was in the Department after hours, quiet as a mouse, tip-toeing down the corridor.

"I've been offered a job in Canada. I'm leaving in September", Thomas Lusignan said as he scurried to the stairwell, faster than the echo of his words.

The Scrote was still busy. I didn't know any of the patrons by name, which minimised the chance of unwanted conversations. Just to be sure, I opted for a bar stool.

Barry, Dom and Ed were lined up in their customary sentinel positions, looking like they'd been on bar duty for several hours already. Not drunk exactly – they never looked drunk. More like in recovery mode after a hard day's work. But that didn't strip them of their joie de vivre which manifested itself in relentless commentary about their surroundings. Philosophers and social theorists often say that stuff acquires meaning through its relationship to its environment. This certainly applied to those three.

The student behind the bar, new to me and further proof of the perfectly understandable high rate of attrition in Scrote staff turnover, poured me my 175 ml of the usual second-bottom supermarket shelf Pinot Grigio. I ripped open a bag of Thai sweet chilli crisps, settled myself comfortably on my stool, ready to enjoy my luxurious dinner for one. It was not to be.

"All by your lonesome tonight?", said Dom.

"Yep", I said cramming some crisps into my open mouth in the vain hope that this would deter them from seeking my company.

They didn't even notice.

"You Anthro lot never come alone. Always in groups", Barry said.

"Very observant of you", I said.

"Architects, they're always alone. And biologists. They're always alone too", Ed said.

"Not always. You know Miranda the architect?", Dom said.

"Which one is that?", Barry asked.

"You know, blonde, glasses", Dom said.

"Oh yeah, yeah", Barry and Ed said in concert.

"She's been in with others a couple of times."

Despite my initial misgivings, the banality of their conversation was mesmerising and, for that reason, welcome. I could do with something that drained my mind of anything of import, at least for a few minutes. They competed with one another in their efforts to name-check people who had been seen alone in the Scrote. Eventually, they must have noticed that I wasn't paying attention.

"Not having your fancy stuff tonight?", Barry asked, nodding at my wine.

"I'm a man of the people, Barry. And besides, there's only one kind of stuff on offer in this fine establishment."

"I'm a bitter man myself", Ed said.

The other two laughed.

"What?", Ed said, oblivious to his double entendre.

"Could've brought your own again", Dom said.

"Pardon?"

"You could've brought your own again", Ed echoed.

"Brought my own? When have I ever brought my own to the Scrote?"

"Not you personally", Barry said. "Your Department."

"Have we?", I asked.

"You did last time", Dom said.

"Yeah, that party of yours", Ed said.

"You know", Barry added. "*That* party."

Come to think of it, they were right. We did have two kinds of wine at the party. Lucy was doing the rounds with two bottles in hand, a house Pinot Grigio and a Sauvignon Blanc.

"Doreen came in and arranged it", Dom said.

"Did she?", I asked.

"Aye", Ed said, "struck a deal with Angela from catering. Paid a bit of corkage and she brought a couple of bottles in."

"Just a couple of bottles?", I asked.

"I guess it was for the select few, not for the plebs", Barry said.

"One day you too will get to drink the good stuff", the voice had said that evening. I still couldn't be sure that it was Paul. There was also something else, some vague memory that felt pertinent, that could have answered the question but refused to come back to me fully formed.

Why serve two wines at the reception? It'd never been done before, as far as I could remember. Doreen hadn't said anything to me about it, not that she ever consulted me on such things.

Doreen. Twice in the same evening, her name was stepping out from the dim shadows.

"There she is again", Barry said.

"Fifty three days in a row", Dom said.

"She comes already made up and has a few nightcaps here", Ed said.

The three sots were staring past me at a new arrival. I turned around and saw her pull up a chair, her eyes as red-rimmed and bloodshot as they had been for the past couple of months.

"May I?", I said.

Victoria Alvarez had been staring at the tabletop. She raised her eyes.

"Hello, Professor. Yes, please."

"Let me get you a drink first. What would you like?"

"Double vodka, please. Thank you."

When I returned with her drink and sat beside her, I caught the whiff of alcohol in her breath.

"Are you sure you don't want a mixer in your vodka?"

"No, it's good like this."

"Should I be worried about you, Victoria?", I said.

"Why, Professor?"

"I understand you patronise the Scrote a little too often."

"Who told you that?"

"What matters is whether it's true."

"I just pop in for a little drink before bed. It helps me to sleep."

"Have you been working from home?"

It was difficult for a woman like Victoria to look dishevelled. No matter what she wore, the look was always calculated and fashion-conscious. Yet on this particular evening, her appearance bordered on scruffy.

"I find it easier."

"Let me rephrase. Have you been working?"

Again, she lowered her eyes.

"Not very much", she whispered.

"Victoria, I'm rather concerned about you."

"Thank you, Professor."

"It's not your gratitude I'm after. We have to find a workable way out of this."

She welled up.

"It's so difficult."

"Have you sought any help in coping with the loss?"

"No one can help me."

"Well, you won't know until you try it. Listen, I know I've told you previously that I can only provide academic help and I'm not qualified to serve as a mental health counsellor but it would be derelict of me now that I'm Head of Department, if I didn't offer you some pastoral assistance."

She looked at me, more in resignation than anticipation.

"I need to understand how you feel."

She took a gulp of straight vodka.

"Your relationship with Paul was, how to put it, more intimate than that of a student and her academic hero."

She necked back her drink.

"May I have another one?", she asked.

I couldn't tell whether the brief respite would make her feel more at ease or whether she would clam up but I had no real choice. Without another drink she would not say a word.

"You're right", she said as soon as I put the tumbler down on the table. "We were lovers."

I had expected the answer but not the grown-up choice of vocabulary. I remained quiet, hoping she would elaborate.

"It began, well, it began at the beginning. I mean when we first met. He had come to my University to give a seminar. I was a Master's student but I attended every research event. A lot of it went over my head but I found everything so fascinating. His talk was brilliant. Simple, accessible..."

In other words pointless, I thought.

"...and mind-blowingly insightful. I approached him after the talk. We had a long chat about my dissertation. He invited me to the dinner. That had never happened before. Doctoral students were sometimes invited out with the speaker and academics from my Department but Master's students? Never. He said he was impressed with my research and that he wanted to hear more. I sat next to him at the dinner table. My Professors were not pleased, I could tell, but I didn't mind. I wanted to spend as much time with him as possible. Between main and dessert, he put his hand on my knee. I know this kind of thing is considered unacceptable these days but I didn't mind. On the contrary. I put my hand on his knee too."

I wanted to put my hands on a toilet bowl and throw up.

"Anyway, we spent that night together in his hotel room. Then we stayed in touch and saw each other as regularly as we could."

I felt the urge to scream. How could she possibly have brought herself to sleep with that abominable man? For starters, had she failed to notice that he was obese and was missing a quarter of his teeth?

A generous sip of wine helped me to keep my mouth shut.

"Eventually I came here as a PhD student. That was on merit, Professor, I don't want you to think that I received preferential treatment."

"Of course not", I said.

I was sure she believed that. It might not have been entirely untrue either.

"From then on, we saw each other every day. At the office, at my apartment, sometimes at his home. We were a couple. And then he was gone."

I had to step in before she broke into tears again.

"And you took trips together too, didn't you?"

"No", she said with a shake of the head and a sense of regret.

"Are you sure?"

"Of course I'm sure."

"Did he have any nicknames for you?"

"Sometimes he called me Vivi."

"Not Carmencita?"

"No, why would he call me that?"

"Because you're Spanish?"

"What a cliché."

"Sorry. And how about you?"

"I called him BigDig. But only during sex."

I felt some of my Pinot Grigio and fragments of crisps travel back up my oesophagus. I pushed my rebellious meal back down with a gulp.

If they didn't take trips together, then who had written the note I'd found in his library? I had assumed it was from Victoria because of the Spanish references but I was wrong. She could be lying to me, of course, but what possible reason could she have when here she was spilling the beans in all their spicy, intimate details?

"Victoria, do you think, and please don't take this the wrong way, that Paul might have been involved with anyone else too?"

Her first response was a sniffle. The second was a growl.

"People talk", she eventually said.

"And what do they say?"

"That he was a philanderer."

It was lost on her that their affair was conclusive proof that he was a philanderer.

"But that's nonsense. I was the first one."

How was it that Alison had put it in her eulogy? "I still remember his visits, on evenings that we both worked late, to my office to talk about my research and administrative contribution when my time had come to apply for promotion."

But that was a long time ago. Who was the Carmencita who called Paul Digby "mi amor"? The note was undated but it had been placed between books published less than five years previously. Unless he had stored it elsewhere, pulled it out to have another nostalgic read, which would have been out of character, and then squeezed it between the books, it was reasonable to assume that the note had been hidden there all along.

"May I have another drink?", Victoria said.

"Fine", I said, "but this will be the last one for tonight. And there's something else I want us to discuss; your future."

Duncan had been standoffish with me since the weekend at Beauclerk. Every time our paths crossed, he greeted me with a show of mistrust.

At first, that stung a little. After all, he was the closest thing to a friend I had in the Department and now that bond was broken, gone up in smoke. Even though the loss of this presumed friendship had almost stopped bothering me, I was left to deal with a much more troubling concern. Duncan had played a part, not as big a part as Catherine but still not a negligible one, in causing me pain and guilt over Jeremy's death to the point of doubting myself and practically taking on the mantle of the serial murderer.

But now my disposition was beginning to change. I was taking things into my own hands as had been advised to do a long time ago.

Duncan's word was the only evidence that I had argued with Jeremy in the corridors of Beauclerk Mansion shortly before his death. His word alone attested to the very heated nature of that purported exchange that had supposedly terrified our colleague, who so soon afterwards was to be found drowned in a tub. And his word was the only word available. There being no other witnesses to this alleged row, I was at an impasse. I could not question Duncan yet I had no reason to believe him. My academic instincts told me that the onus of proof rested on him and that there was no reason why I should take his account at face value but there was so much at stake that I could hardly leave the matter to a technical rule of argumentation.

What I could do, and was now determined to do, was press him to flesh out his story with more detail.

"Thanks for coming, Duncan", I said.

I remained seated in my HoD chair, unwilling to relinquish any symbol of my authority. It didn't faze him. He made himself comfortable in an easy chair facing the shelves rather than me. He crossed his legs and rested fat hands on plump knees.

"You wanted to see me", he said.

"I did, yes."

"Are you going to let me know why or is it a secret?"

I resented the insinuation that I was the one to keep secrets.

"Do you have somewhere else to be? A ground-breaking research project that needs wrapping up perhaps? Or updating lecture notes to reflect developments in the discipline in the past thirty years?"

He rotated his chair in my direction but still had to turn his head to face me properly. The discomfort this caused him served my purposes very well.

"That is below the belt, Michael. You know very well that if my research output has stalled a tad, it is because of health reasons."

He was getting defensive, just as I wanted him to be.

"We'll talk about your performance another time, Duncan, although you should know that it is a cause for concern."

I didn't give him a chance to say anything. The second wave of attack should follow swiftly after the first.

"I've been thinking about what you said at the Mansion", I said.

"What exactly are you referring to?"

He was buying time.

"About Jeremy and I quarrelling in the corridor."

"OK."

"I feel terrible about it. I've no recollection of it and it's obviously too late to make up with Jeremy."

"Yes, it is", Duncan said.

"I cannot hope for closure but perhaps something can be done to help me to come to terms with it."

"And how might you hope to achieve that?"

Confidence had returned, his voice was more assertive. He thought he had regained the upper hand.

"Well for a start, you could tell me more about what happened that evening."

He cocked his head, staring at me motionless, then hunched further down in his chair before switching his gaze to the corner of the room on my right.

"I've told you everything there was to tell."

"You said I looked angry and Jeremy looked fearful."

"He did."

"Fearful of what?"

"And you did look angry."

"Was he fearful *because* I was angry?"

"What?", he said.

"Was I angry at him?"

"You were angry."

"You keep saying that but do you have any idea what I was angry about? Did you actually overhear any of the conversation?"

"Are you suggesting I tend to eavesdrop on people's conversations?"

"I'm not suggesting it. It's common knowledge that you're a horrific gossip."

He sulked with a frown.

"I only caught the odd word."

"Such as?"

"I don't know, I can't remember."

It was time to drive home what the stakes for him were.

"Perhaps you'd rather talk about a request from HR that landed on my desk yesterday."

"What HR request?"

"Apparently there's a drive to rationalise staff allocation. There are plans for restructuring and what not."

No such plans were afoot but the threat was far from implausible. He considered his position. Could he trust me to put in a good word, if he gave me the information I required?

"It would be irresponsible of me to reconstruct a whole conversation on the basis of a few words."

"We're going around in circles. What words?"

"'Shocking', 'unbelievable', words to that effect."

"And who was saying those words to that effect?"

"One or the other, I can't remember."

"At the Mansion you tried in a rather unambiguous way to give me the impression that Jeremy and I had been rowing."

"I wouldn't say unambiguous."

"When, in fact, perhaps I was angry and Jeremy may have been scared about the very thing that angered me."

I bet he was regretting that the version of events that he had given me at the Mansion left so much room for interpretation. He could hardly change his tune now or add any new pertinent information. My small victory didn't, of course, definitively mean that I had not been quarrelling with Jeremy, much less that I hadn't killed him in an inebriated moral blur.

All it meant was that I was reclaiming the narrative. Even if Duncan was to be believed, which in itself required a leap of faith, and Jeremy and I had indeed had a heated conversation, what the combustion was about remained an open question.

My mobile phone rang. Nikhil's name flashed on the screen.

"Go, we're done", I said to Duncan.

"What?", he said, offended.

"Just piss off!", I shouted.

"What do I get in return for my incredibly fast and efficient delivery? Not to mention the favours that I used up for your sake."

"I bet you have a bottomless pit of favours to draw from. Also, you get eternal gratitude."

"Eternity is a nonsensical concept, buddy."

"And yet I bet that's how long you'll make me wait before you tell me what you found out."

"Alright, so here goes. Pepple did indeed rise through the ranks at the East London Forensic Lab. He enjoyed universal respect for being meticulous and efficient and there were no rumblings when he took over as Head of Pathology. But then the Ellis case happened."

"What's the Ellis case?"

"Teddy Ellis was a Hackney teenager. He was stabbed to death in broad daylight five years ago. There were some eyewitnesses but their testimony was inconclusive so it all turned on forensics and the pathology report."

"And?"

"Well, Pepple cocked it up. He was accused of contaminating the samples – nothing was proven you see – so the three men who everyone knew had killed Teddy Ellis walked free."

"And how about Pepple?"

"There was disciplinary action. Had he been found to have violated protocol, his name would have been mud forever. His career would have been effectively over."

"Go on."

"As it happens, he was acquitted."

"I have a feeling there's something important coming up."

"Quite right, buddy. Apparently, it all turned on how carefully Pepple stored material."

"Did he?"

"Some former employees and colleagues testified that he tended to be overconfident and sloppy at times. His defence tried to character-assassinate them. The line was that all these people were disgruntled and dishonestly misrepresented normal practice."

"So their word against his?"

"Until another person's word decided the case. A student had been working with Pepple. Not quite working, sort of shadowing.

According to her, he'd been doing everything right. She was asked detailed questions about his practices and she gave all the right answers."

"What do you mean she was shadowing him? Surely she was a medical student or whatever kind of student works with pathologists?"

"Nope."

"You're not saying..."

"I'm saying, buddy, I'm saying."

Their suffering is justified

Knowing things that your interlocutor doesn't know you know about them imparts a sense of power that is enjoyable to the point of being well nigh addictive. You can toy with them. You can give them the chance to confess their wrongdoings, admit their moral failings, ask repentance and atone.

Best of all is when they fail to do the right thing, then you get to administer that punishment with a clear conscience. Their suffering is justified and self-induced.

"Let me just say before we begin, Dr West, that I consider this meeting entirely pointless. I don't understand why my secretary took it upon herself to allow you to see me and I'll be having words with her."

"I doubt it, Dr Pepple", I said.

"You doubt what?"

"I doubt you'll do anything so ill-advised as to 'have words with' your secretary."

"Perhaps you should be cleaning your own backyard before you meddle in my lab's affairs."

"Make no mistake, my visit has very much to do with my backyard."

"You're wasting my time, Dr West. Please state your purpose, if indeed such a purpose exists."

"Very well. Dr Pepple, you conducted the post mortem examinations on my two unfortunate colleagues, who so tragically passed away over the past few months."

"I did. So?"

"I need a little more information on both cases."

"This really is a waste of my time. Read my reports. You can show yourself out."

"You're being tedious, Dr Pepple. I'd like to see the photos of Jeremy Allcock."

"That's out of the question."

"I thought you might be in a disobliging mood. Do you know what else is generally considered out of the question, Dr Pepple?"

"Can I help being enlightened by you?"

"Not really. Offering surreptitious access to classified and confidential data and material to unauthorised third parties, that's what's out of the question."

"I've no idea what you're talking about."

"Especially when said access is provided in return for perjury."

Not knowing what to do with himself, he jotted something on the notepad resting on the leather blotter on his desk.

"Dr Pepple, you've gone silent."

"What do you want?", he growled.

"I told you. I want to see the photos of the body of my late colleague Jeremy Allcock."

"Is that all?"

"More or less."

He pushed the notepad on the ground as he dragged his computer keyboard in front of him. The man knew when to cut his losses.

"It was not perjury", he said as he typed.

"It's not a question of whether it was so, the question is how it looks. And it looks pretty bad, Doctor."

He stopped typing and looked at me.

"What evidence do you have?"

"Do you really want it to come to that? It's a simple thing I'm asking you to do in return for not rocking the boat. You have my word that, as far as I'm concerned, you'll have nothing to worry about afterwards."

He turned the computer screen in my direction.

The first time around, whatever feelings the sight of poor old Jeremy's dead body was meant to induce were far outstripped by my hangover. This time I could take it all in.

His head was immersed in the soapy water, his sparse hair floating like kelp, his face discoloured and his eyes wide open, frozen in the same blend of alarm, distress and bafflement.

For what it was worth, encountering him made me feel that we were on the same side. There was no guilt nor animosity. I had let him down, yes, but only in that I had not pulled my weight to achieve a common goal.

"I want to see the photos of his shoulders", I said to Pepple.

"Very well", he muttered and swiped through photographs with his mouse.

The marks were conspicuous, aggressive, angry.

They were also very wide. I instinctively looked at my hands.

"You opined that these marks were caused by the straps of Jeremy's rucksack."

"I opined that if he habitually carried a heavy bag over his shoulders, that, in tandem with the anticoagulant in his blood, which I understand he took in combination with hypertension medication, would account for the bruising."

"Did you find any other bruises on his body?"

He saw immediately where the conversation was heading and he looked embarrassed in anticipation.

"I didn't."

"If all it takes is a little pressure or a slight knock in combination with the anticoagulant to cause bruising, would it not be reasonable to expect there to be more discoloration elsewhere?"

"Maybe."

"But the shoulder marks were the only ones."

He didn't say anything. I leaned closer to the computer screen. I grabbed the mouse from his hand and enlarged the image.

"Are these gaps?", I asked.

"Hard to tell."

"Come closer, Pepple. Look carefully."

He obeyed, if with visible reluctance.

"Maybe", he said.

"The rucksack straps wouldn't have ridges like that, would they?"

"I wouldn't know."

"Have you ever seen rucksack straps with indentations that might leave streaks?"

"I'm not a fashion expert", he huffed.

"Look at my hands", I said.

"What about them?", Pepple said.

"How do they compare to the marks on Jeremy's shoulders?"

"In terms of what?"

"In terms of size, Pepple. It's really not in your best interest to be so obstinate."

"They're smaller."

"Yes, they're smaller."

"What of it?"

"Never you mind."

"Are we done here?"

"We're done with Jeremy. There's still Paul Digby."

"What about Paul Digby?", he said in a panicked voice.

"When I came in with her", I said, taking pleasure in not speaking Catherine's name but letting it linger like a threat, "with our research questions, you were very keen to stress that, and I quote you almost verbatim, the event was contained in the room. That's where everything had happened."

"So?"

"I didn't make much of it at the time but the more I think about it the more the emphasis perplexes me. What alternative were you trying to preclude?"

"I must ask you to leave now, Dr West."

"And I must ask you to remember what's at stake here."

"You have no idea what the stake is."

"Do you really want to risk being derided and cast out by your profession?"

"When one finds oneself between a rock and a hard place, one is only left with a gamble."

Blackmail only works on those who fear losing what you threaten to take away from them. Pepple was already past that stage.

Adeel Rahman was apprehensive when I asked him to come and see me about his dissertation. He rightly expected our first session to take place much later and he was all apologetic about how little work he had done towards it. He shouldn't have been. As it turned out, he'd already covered impressive ground. He had collected all the relevant secondary material and he was also making progress getting empirical data from his father's files.

That afternoon I spent such a long time going over his essay structure that I risked being accused of favouritism. That was partly because I was genuinely interested in his work. But it was also because I wanted to urge him to get one particular piece of information from his father, which, I told him, would be instrumental to the success of the whole project and which he should share with me immediately.

Work was already a chore. In the circumstances, it had become a dreary distraction. Nevertheless, duties had to be faced and tasks and assignments completed.

The most urgent business was drafting the agenda for the upcoming Department Meeting. It would be the first I organised and chaired and not surprisingly I felt like a fish out of water. Doreen had been ambushing me with documents, reminders, details and queries, even throwing in not so subtle hints about what to discuss at the meeting, what to refer to Committees, what to sweep under the carpet. Reluctant to turn to anyone in my Department for assistance, I enlisted the help of some other HoDs from across the University to talk me through expected practice. I had made some friends among those administrative echelons and I was admired for the good work I was doing in Anthropology despite the odds.

The only agenda item that allowed me some initiative was the HoD's report and that was not because it was some expression of unconstrained HoD power but because it was oral. Doreen of course expected to be told in advance what I was planning to say but no written record was required.

The morning after my meeting with Pepple I was subjected to the tedium of reviewing Committee minutes, University regulations and government reports. Unable to withstand sustained bouts of intellectual torture, I broke away periodically for forays on the Internet.

Many of my searches drew blanks, some led me to things I already knew, some were rather informative though the usefulness of that information wasn't yet entirely clear. For example, what was I to do with everything I learned about home pickling?

But it was another search that yielded particularly interesting results.

“I thought I was done with all that. What is the purpose of this call?”, said Geraldine Whitmore-Digby.

“Won’t take a minute.”

“Less than a minute is all I have.”

“The charity to which Paul donated his books.”

“What about it?”

“Why?”

“Why what?”

“Why that charity? Why did he donate his books to it?”

“I’ve not the faintest clue.”

“Anything else you can tell me about it?”

“Well, as a matter of fact, since you’re asking, yes. Going over his bank accounts after his death, I discovered that he had set up a monthly standing order to the charity up until a year ago or so.”

“How big an amount?”

“Just fifty pounds. Still, I thought it was odd.”

“Maybe not that odd.”

“Is that all?”

“One more quick thing.”

“Very quick.”

“When did you go to Seville together? Or Spain at any rate?”

“Never.”

“You never went to Spain?”

“I’ve been to Spain, he’d been to Spain. Just not together.”

“I see. When did Paul go?”

“You don’t want to know when I went?”

“It’s fine if you want to tell me.”

“I don’t.”

“I didn’t think you would. So when was Paul there?”

“Five years, maybe a bit less. Some conference or other.”

“Do you remember where?”

“Madrid, I think. That’s all now. I have to go.”

She hung up.

❖

I located four internationally active Universities in Madrid. Only three offered social science courses. Of these, only two had Anthropology Departments. And of these two, one had organised an international conference in the spring four years ago.

The competitive drive for Universities to brag about their accomplishments, however small and insignificant, means that information remains available on institutional websites in perpetuity. That includes conference programmes.

I scanned the schedule. There were papers on the anthropology of pet ownership, an application of Baudrillard's theory of the simulacrum to Jean Baudrillard himself, a comparative study of public toilet use in three European cities, an empirical account of the mating rituals of a hippy community in Canada. A veritable smörgåsbord of academic achievement guaranteed to make the world a better place.

Paul's name was not on the menu. There was another one though. A young researcher fresh out of her doctoral degree was presenting a paper on "*No drawing room scene: institutional synergy and dissonance in dealing with violent crime in a London borough*".

I picked up the phone.

"Doreen, I need to see personal expense claims of the past five years, please."

"Why?"

"We have to review the research allowance amount. Central HQ directive."

"That's the first I hear of that. Why was I not told it?"

"Because you're not the bloody Head of the bloody Department, Doreen, that's why. Now."

She appeared at my doorstep at superhuman speed. She dropped six ring binders on my desk.

"I think I should give you my feedback in the review process."

"Not necessary. Thank you."

I dismissed her with a wave of my hand. Flabbergasted and irritated, she loitered for a few seconds before turning on her heels and leaving in a huff.

Being afforded a yearly amount for research funding for attending conferences or doing empirical work is one of the few perks of the job and most academics devour it right down to the last morsel.

I went straight to the year that interested me. There it was; a claim for 'conference attendance'. A receipt from a hotel in Madrid for one night; one from a hotel in Cadiz for two nights; a flight from London to Madrid, one from Madrid to Seville, and one from Seville back to London; a two-day car hire contract from Seville airport; three meals including a couple of bottles of wine at each.

Paul Digby was certainly living the good life. At least he had the decency to not include the Sevillana doll in his claim.

That particular jigsaw puzzle was all but complete. There was one last piece to put in place.

I locked my office door behind me and walked briskly down the empty corridor. I stuck my head in the office to make sure it was empty and headed straight to the photos on the wall.

The bottle of wine in front of her was a Spanish Verdejo. She was wearing a floral dress and a lightweight cardigan. Her sunglasses were resting on her head, pushing her curls back. She looked healthy and happy. Scattered pebbles, cobbles and rocks dotted the sandy beach behind her.

Bright, smooth, round, heavy, white rocks.

Ian from IT Services II

The point of research in the social sciences is rarely ever to solve problems. It is to invent them. The first step is to read the available literature, which, more often than not, has accumulated into an autonomous entity, separate from the actual social data that it was meant to help to understand in the first place. Then one must find a gap even when no gap is to be found. Finally, one must fill that gap with an argument that passes the buck to others to start the whole cycle over again.

So accustomed was I to thinking like that, it was small wonder that I was at a loss as to what to do with the information I had collected since deciding to be more proactive. New data was floating around in my brain in a disorderly jumble. Much as I tried, I couldn't piece it all together into one coherent story.

Catherine with Paul Digby enjoying a chilled bottled of wine at a Spanish beach before, or maybe after, going for a walk and picking a small memento; the marks on Jeremy's shoulders; the plan to effectively demote Doreen, packaged as an honorary promotion; Horst's anger at Digby for undermining his research and controlling his doctoral student; Victoria's blind adoration; Catherine's link to Pepple; the pathologist's terrified reluctance to disclose anything about Digby's death; Paul's unsteady steps when he came into his office that night; the rock landing on his fat, bald head; Jeremy desperately trying to gain my attention; the look in his eyes during his tête-à-tête with Duncan at the Mansion.

To add to my frustration, all these disparate data bites were joined by recent throwaway comments, momentary vignettes, fleeting impressions, vague memories that refused to reveal themselves fully and fall into place in shaping the bigger picture.

I knew that what I had to do was to trace all those crumbs back to their origins.

A task far easier said than done.

I emerged from Nigel's office laden with a boulder-sized criminal law textbook, out of date but still serviceable for my purposes, and a load of ciphers.

To a social scientist uninitiated in the discipline of law, making head or tail of what it's all about can be daunting. I attribute this to a profound confusion of identity and purpose. Academic lawyers are not judges, they're not practitioners, they're not simple citizens, they're neither sociologists nor philosophers.

Whatever they think they are, they nonetheless held the keys to the knowledge that I needed.

"*R v White* is a classic case", Nigel had said. "Criminal law 101 stuff."

The index was a little easier to navigate than the body of the book, although the variety of case citation styles added an extra layer of complexity.

The case of White was indeed early on in the book. A man had tried to poison his mother. She died but, as it transpired, of a heart attack. The question was one of causation. What counts as having caused someone's death? Which strike is salient in the eyes of the criminal law?

That was easy enough to grasp. The sections on attempted murder, reckless homicide, and complicity in crime to which Nigel had referred me, less so. I did my best in hopes it would prove enough.

Why did he need all these cables hanging out of his pockets, when all he actually did required no interaction with anything in the three-dimensional world but a keyboard and a mouse?

I would have to ask him another time. On this occasion, I needed him to do what I required him to do without distraction or further agitation.

"Dr West, what you're asking me to do goes against the code of ethics", Ian from IT Services said.

"Which article?"

"Pardon?"

"Which article of the code of ethics does it go against?"

"I don't know the exact article", he mumbled.

"Which section?"

Amazing how even the slightest exposure to law can turn someone into a pedantic automaton.

"I don't know. Something about personal data or something."

"Who told you this?"

"They did a seminar a few years back."

"Who are they?"

"You know, the University Secretary's office."

"And they talked to you about data protection?"

"There was a slide presentation with dos and don'ts. And I'm sure that snooping into staff email accounts without permission by the authorities was in the list of don'ts."

"OK, let's take things from the beginning. First of all, you do realise that Jeremy Allcock has passed away, right?"

"Yes, very sorry about that."

"So we're faced with a conceptual issue here, Ian, aren't we?"

"Are we?"

"We most certainly are. And the conceptual issue is this: is Jeremy, sadly deceased, a person in the sense of the data protection regulations?"

"Isn't he?"

"Think about it, Ian. All these rules protect people from the police and big corporations and such like. They give people peace of mind. The dead don't have much use for peace of mind, do they? Nor do they need protecting from the Man."

"I guess not."

"So, there you go, Ian. The slide presentation you speak of does not apply to Jeremy."

"OK, but..."

"Then there's the other thing. You're not allowed to access staff email 'without permission from the authorities', you said."

"That's what the slide said. I think it was the fifth or sixth one in the presentation."

"So, when Catherine Bowen asked you to access Paul Digby's files, why did you oblige so zealously?"

"That was different, those documents were University business. Plus, the Dean had green-lighted it."

"So the Dean is an authority?"

Ian from IT Services hesitated.

"Isn't he?"

"Have you stopped to ask yourself who else counts as an authority?"

"I've not given it much thought. The police? The fire brigade?"

"The fire brigade?"

"Isn't it?"

"Fine, perhaps the fire brigade is an authority too but do you know who else is?"

"Who?"

"Heads of Department. I will refer you to Regulation 154 issued by the Joint Committee of Heads of Department and the Vice Chancellor's Policy and Development Steering Group."

"Erm, could you please refresh my memory because I can't remember it off the top of my head?", Ian from IT Services said.

"Gladly. According to Regulation 154 of the Joint Committee of Heads of Department and the Vice Chancellor's Policy and Development Steering Group, Heads of Department may gain access to staff personal data stored on University-owned devices, if they suspect wrongdoing."

"What wrongdoing do you suspect?"

"I don't have to tell you that."

"Says who?"

"Regulation 155 of the Joint Committee of Heads of Department and the Vice Chancellor's Policy and Development Steering Group."

Ian was a conscientious, if unadventurous, employee. He knew that the surest way of defending his actions should anything go wrong would be to follow the rules. So, I gave him rules to follow. That regulations 154 and 155 or indeed the Joint Committee of Heads of Department and the Vice Chancellor's Policy and Development Steering Group didn't exist and that I had made them up on the spot was beside the point.

"OK, OK, I'll do it. Give me a minute, I need to get admin access so I'll have to log out and in again and then out and in again."

"Do what you need to do", I said.

While he logged in and out twice over, hitting keys that did magical, secret things unimaginable to the layperson, I scanned Jeremy's shelves. Meeting him in his old age and the state of abandon in which he had ended up, it was easy to forget that he once was a very well respected scholar and a significant player in the field. Some of his doctoral students had gone on to take up important academic posts around the world and largely determined the agenda of the discipline. They had all failed to look after him. No Festschrift for Jeremy, no valedictory lectures, no journal issues dedicated to his work. In a way, he'd been killed off a long time ago.

"What's this all about?", Alison said, rushing into Jeremy's office.

Ian got startled and knocked the mouse off the desk.

"Carry on, Ian", I said. "Alison, what can I help you with?"

"I said, what's this all about?"

"Departmental business."

"What kind of Departmental business?"

"The confidential kind."

"Are you forgetting that no Departmental business is confidential from me, Michael?"

Ian couldn't help peering up to fully witness the escalation of the exchange in-between typing his codes into Jeremy's computer.

"Alison, I'll have to ask you to return to your desk now."

If there's one thing that can throw academics is to treat them like regular workers, especially if you do it with the arrogant disdain of a ruthless employer. They don't know how to react when the special status that they think they enjoy is brought into question. Alison thought she'd try to assert some authority one more time.

"Ian, stop whatever it is you're doing. Who gave you the right?"

"Article 154 of the Joint Committee of Heads of Department and the Vice Chancellor's Policy and Development Steering Group. My name is not Ian, by the way", Ian muttered.

"Ian, just carry on. Alison, I demand that you leave this office immediately."

If nothing else came of all this, seeing Alison on the verge of a stroke, helpless with indignation, was more than worth it. She stormed out of the room.

"All done", Ian said. "I don't know what the fuss was about though. There's not much to see here."

The Department Meting was quorate, a full house in fact. Alison Davies, still gobsmacked and peeved from the way I'd treated her the day before was sitting with arms and legs crossed. Catherine, next to her, was swiping on her electronic tablet through documents attached to agenda items. Judging by the look on her face, everything was to her satisfaction. Lucy Warburton was staring at the white-board behind me and Doreen was at the ready, her defensive missiles armed and prepared to be launched. Thomas Lusignan was keeping his eyes shut; either asleep or daydreaming about his move to Canada. Duncan Erskine-Bell had stretched his arms over the backs of the vacant chairs next to him, his obese thighs spread wide. Horst had taken off his right sandal and was dusting the strap.

"No apologies, all present", Doreen said to kick off the meeting.

The first item on the agenda was, as ever, approving the minutes of Committee meetings. With Jeremy not in the room to raise any objections, the process took less than a minute, the silence broken only by the rustling of printouts, Duncan's heavy breathing and Horst's clicking of his fingers.

The Meeting disposed of the next three items with the same efficiency and expediency. We decided unanimously that we would call in an external assessor to give our research output a preliminary going over to make sure we were on the right track; we agreed to push the University for a common room for our students; and all concurred that we should make milk freely available to doctoral students.

"Well, it looks like we'll be done in record time", Doreen said. "A brief oral report by the Head and that'll be us."

"Thanks, Doreen", I said. "There's a couple of things, one more important than the other. First, just to let you know that I'm making all the necessary representations to the University regarding increasing academic posts in the Department. I think our request is being listened to favourably. It'll be discussed at the next meeting of the Vice Chancellor's Policy and Development Steering Group. I will report back in due course."

Doreen tapped the stack of meeting documents on her lap to square them up.

"Right, that's it. Unless there's any other business, we can call it a day", she said.

"I'm not done", I cut her short flashing the palm of my right hand at her.

Everyone drew in a sudden breath, startled by my curtness. Doreen for one looked aghast and I could see surprise rapidly turning into rage in Catherine's face.

"There's a few things I want to say", I said.

"What's this about?", Alison asked.

"You'll find out soon enough. Doreen, you might want to stop taking minutes now."

"That's very inappropriate", Doreen said.

"Just put your pen down."

"We have jobs to go back to", Horst said.

"If no minutes are kept, the Union needs to know about this", Lucy said.

"The sooner we do this, the better so everyone just shut up."

The rumbling died down after a few seconds; they had obeyed.

"Colleagues, lately I've been wondering when was the last time that everything in our Department was normal or near normal at any rate. And you know what? It was the night of the postgraduate reception. Didn't we have a great time that evening? As ever, Doreen planned everything so efficiently. Snacks abounded, all kinds of wine flowed freely, students were having a blast and we all got to hang out together. A proper sense of academic community, don't you agree? Good times, good times.

"But that same evening Paul Digby tragically died and then everything turned sour and, if I may add, considerably weirder.

"I'm sure you've often wondered what happened to Paul. Well, maybe not so let me tell you anyway just to be clear on events. I know exactly because I was there."

I paused to gauge their reaction. Catherine was looking at me wide-eyed. The rest looked numb.

"I shouldn't have been but there you have it. I was drunk thanks to Lucy's surprisingly expert wine pouring skills but also because I was trying to drown my frustration. You see, earlier that day Paul had announced to me that I'd not been put forward for promotion. Again! I mean, nothing I ever did was good enough. So, spurred by lovely Catherine's – our incredibly able and successful colleague – encouragement to take things in my own hands, I left the party early, I snuck into Paul's office and started to forge my own promotion recommendation. Don't judge me yet, it's about to get worse.

"To my great surprise, Paul came back to his office. He was very drunk. And I mean very drunk indeed. His speech was slurred, he was losing his balance, he seemed hardly aware of what was going on. It's a miracle he made his way back to the McKenzie, to be honest. Anyway, my first reaction was to try to deflect suspicion from me and my, admittedly dodgy-looking, demeanour. In an unfortunate turn of events involving Malinowski's *Crime and Custom in Savage Society* – no need to go into the details now – a beach rock ended up on Paul's head and he fell dead. Terrible, I know."

"Dear boy, that is a shocking confession", Duncan said.

"Just imagine how I felt at the time."

"How the hell can you be so blasé about it?", Horst said.

"Trust me, I was not always so blasé. The realisation of what I had done tortured me. It tortured me when, shortly after Paul had died, someone came to the Department but left without saying anything. It tortured me the following day, when I stayed at home and tried to make sense of it all. It tortured me the first time I returned here for the Department Meeting two days later.

"And it was because of this internal torment that I let slip to Catherine that something was untoward about Paul's death. In retrospect, it was just a throwaway comment to vent some of my anxiety, the kind of thing that one would dismiss without second thought. Not Catherine though, not that brilliant, inquisitive, bright young thing who so adeptly jumps the professional development queues – Paul's words, not mine. She wouldn't let that comment drop. She saw a research opportunity, she said. We should map the discrepancies between official and unofficial perceptions of crime, she said. We should apply phenomenological methodology, revolutionise anthropological research, she said."

I sensed that I was beginning to get angry. I took a deep breath to calm myself down. My audience was captivated and that gave me a sense of power.

"Who was I to say no? I was excited beyond belief. To have a scholar as formidable as Dr Catherine Bowen offering me a collaborative research project. Wow, just wow. Mind you, it all did feel a bit on the bullshit side. I'm no expert in phenomenological anthropology but I was a bit sceptical when all we seemed to do was go around campus trying to record our intuitions as to how Paul had died. Maybe it's because we both had more than an intuition; we both had knowledge.

"Anyway, the whole thing proved quite successful, at least for me but let's not go into that now. You can read about it in the next volume of the State of the Art series."

"What?", Catherine snarled.

"I didn't pull out. I'll give you a signed copy, Catherine, don't worry. Gratis, of course.

"Very soon, Catherine, a rigorous observer of human behaviour, noticed certain things that led her to the conclusion that there was someone in that room with Paul at the time of his death. That must have come as a surprise to her so I guess I was one step ahead in that particular line of enquiry. Our academic project was suddenly transformed into a full-blown criminal investigation. I found myself in an extraordinarily awkward position. I was, you understand, investigating my own actions. I'm sure you'll all agree that that's taking phenomenology one step too far and that no one in their right mind would want to succeed in an endeavour of that peculiar nature. The rational thing to do would be to pull the wool over my partner-in-crime's eyes. And I never knowingly shy away from the rational thing to do.

"My task became much easier when it came to my attention how much hatred one of you harboured for Paul Digby. Yes, Horst, it's you I'm talking about. Paul had been sabotaging your research, cutting off your access to journals because you had been critical of his work. He was planning on embarrassing you in front of staff and students at your Mansion weekend presentation. Petty stuff, I'll give you that much but I was hardly going to care about whether your disgruntlement was justified. The point was that, if anyone looked for a suspect responsible for Paul's death, the first question they would ask is who had motive. So, I made sure that, should it come to that, the finger would be pointed at you first. It would not have been implausible either. You proved to be of a volatile enough nature to be capable of anything. Not to mention your lengthy one-to-one with Paul at the postgraduate drinks, a perfect opportunity to give him a piece of your mind for a last time. You were told off about that, weren't you?"

"No one tells me off", Horst said.

"No one tells you off enough", Alison said.

"And yet, I was unsuccessful. Catherine could see the facts and what they suggested, I've no doubt about that, but she just refused to reach the obvious conclusion. She showed more faith in Horst than she did in me. I found that very puzzling and disappointing. You would think that with the only suspect eliminated, that'd be the end of it. The hypothesis has been falsified. No one was responsible for Paul's death, it was an accident. But no, things got worse. Against all methodological imperatives, Catherine refused to give up. And that's because she had no trust in me whatever. It took the slightest excuse for her to turn on me, to probe *my* moves instead of asking questions of Horst."

"Michael, are you forgetting that you actually did do what you did? You just confessed to it", Catherine said.

"That's beside the point", I said.

"How is it beside the point? What's there more to say?"

"Just for once, get over yourself and listen."

"How dare you?"

I blanked her.

"So, as I was saying, Catherine turned on me and, aided by some miscalculations on my part, she detected my involvement in Paul's death. Now, what would you expect of one who comes across evidence of that sort? Call the police? Let it drop in the interest of friendship? And what would you expect from someone who was romantically involved with the person in question?"

There was a gasp or two.

"I thought everyone knew. Yes, we had a thing, Catherine and I. It was a good thing too. It felt genuine despite everything. It clearly wasn't. She was using me. I guess in a way I'm guilty of the same.

"Whatever a reasonable person would expect her to do in the circumstances, they would be disappointed. Because what Alison and Catherine did was to offer me their silence in exchange for my taking over as HoD but one who would be their proxy and act as their puppet.

"Alison had approached me about it before. No one wants to be HoD but everyone wants to run the place and that's a bit of a bind. So the idea was to find someone to dump all the work on and control him at the same time. I guess she always thought I'd make a malleable pawn so I can only imagine hers and Catherine's delight when all was revealed. What else could I do but accept? I had my back against the wall."

"I said it was a stupid idea", Alison scoffed.

"You said nothing of the sort", Catherine said.

"Too big for your boots, that's what you are", Alison said.

I continued:

"Let's put to one side why Alison would have agreed to something so, let's say, unorthodox. We'll come back to it later. The plan would have worked smoothly for them had it not been for Jeremy. His death came as a shock to me and filled me with considerable guilt."

"Is this another confession?", Duncan said.

"You'd sure wish it were. But it isn't.

"I felt guilty, first, because I had been ignoring Jeremy. He'd been wanting to tell me something, something he considered to be of the utmost significance, something that he stumbled upon while doing research, meticulous as ever, in order to write Paul's obituary. I ignored him. I treated him the way we all did; as an irrelevancy handed down to us from the past.

"What was worse was that I was made to believe that I did have a confrontation with Jeremy that evening at the Mansion, that we'd had, and I quote, a 'heated exchange'. Catherine then accused me of having harmed Jeremy. There were bruises on his shoulders, bruises suggesting that someone had held him under his bathwater and drowned him.

"I fell for it. I had no recollection of that evening and the timeline checked out so it was not implausible that Jeremy had revealed to me something I couldn't afford him divulging to anyone else and so I killed him. That the police filed it as an accident offered me no comfort. Catherine effortlessly convinced them that the straps of his rucksack had caused the discoloration on his shoulders. Her speculation was confirmed by Dr Pepple, who, as you all know, also examined Paul Digby's body.

"Which brings me to the most interesting part of today's oral report to the Department. Dr Pepple used to work in East London. He was a well-regarded pathologist until a cock-up of his let the killers of a young man by the name of Teddy Ellis walk free. Pepple got away with it. And do you know how? On the testimony of a doctoral student who had been doing anthropological research on criminal justice practices in East London at the time. No prizes for guessing who said researcher was."

"Who was it?".

"Do I have to spell everything out, Lucy? It was Catherine.

"Catherine's support was perjurious and it came at a price. Pepple granted her unlimited access to confidential data in return for her silence. He was not off the hook yet but this time it was a different hook. He'd never be free so long as Catherine had incriminating evidence against him. And the time to pay off the second instalment of his debt came when he started working in our area."

"Nonsense", Catherine said.

"You're becoming tedious.

"In the autopsy results Pepple confirmed the rucksack theory. He lied. I saw the bruises close up. They had been inflicted by human hands. There were gaps in the marks, gaps that could only have been left by fingers bursting the arteries under Jeremy's old, fragile skin."

"And whose hands would that have been?", Horst asked.

"Must you ask questions all the time?", Duncan said.

"I'm a scholar, that's what I do. Not like you, you good for nothing layabout."

"I'd told them you're unappointable but they wouldn't listen", Duncan said.

"All in good time, Dr Neuberg, all in good time.

"Once I established Catherine's relationship with Pepple, all sorts of other things started revealing themselves to me.

"There was always something sleazy about Digby but I hadn't quite realised the extent of it. I didn't, for example, know that he was involved with Alison many years ago. You just couldn't help alluding to that in your eulogy, could you, Alison? I also didn't know that he had been involved with one of our doctoral students, Victoria Alvarez. Poor woman was quite smitten. She's still utterly inconsolable. They have to replenish their vodka stock daily for her down at the Scrote.

"It also would never have crossed my mind that he used to have an affair with Catherine. I was too naive to suspect as much even when she said to me that she had hoped that her relationship with me would be unlike previous ones she'd been in with work colleagues. I mean, this is her first academic post. She never had any colleagues, not strictly speaking, anywhere else. But even I couldn't be blind to the conclusive proof of their holiday together in Spain. They both had kept memorabilia of it. She, a photograph. He, a Sevillana doll and a rock from a beach and a note from Catherine, signed 'your Carmencita'. In case some of you haven't made the connection, that's the same rock that landed on his head. I hope you'll enjoy the delightful irony in that as much as I do.

"There was also the charity to which Paul left his books. The same charity to which he had been donating 50 pounds a month until a year ago. The charity set up by the parents of Teddy Ellis in his memory. I assume he did it on Catherine's behalf. Perhaps she even gave him the money. Did that alleviate the guilt, Catherine? Was it that easy?"

"That's terrible", Thomas said.

"It's true, Thomas. That's pretty shocking.

"I also assume that the relationship came to an end at around the same time that the bank transfers ceased. Which was also the time that he started his affair with Victoria.

"For the life of me, I still don't see how any of you could bring yourselves to sleep with that vile creature. For what it's worth, here's my theory. You actually *fell* for him. He somehow *wooed* you. You were young and he had made a name for himself so you took that as evidence that he was an important scholar. Perhaps you took his attention as a compliment, as proof of your scholarly value. He probably convinced you that he was advancing your professional careers. A good word with an editor here, some feedback on an article there. Maybe some of it helped, that's the regrettable nature of the game, but certainly not as much as you thought. And he certainly was never going to stick his neck out for you. Catherine, do you know that you weren't even his top choice for your post?"

"That's not true", Catherine protested.

"You weren't", Alison said with evidence-based conviction.

"He wouldn't even supervise Victoria. What does that tell you? He had no interest in her academic progress. That's why she got saddled with Horst."

"What do you mean 'saddled'?, Horst said.

"He's putting it too mildly", Lucy said.

"But, more importantly, he made you feel special, made you feel that you were the only ones ever. You once felt the way Victoria feels now. At some point, however, you, Alison and Catherine, came to the realisation that you had simply been the most recent ones in a long line of women in the same position. Perhaps you talked about it in one of your regular meetings outside campus over tea and scones. You knew, however, that there was little you could do about it. He hadn't done anything that could be considered wrong by any formal rules. Any confrontation would have made him feel uneasy and, although he didn't make your careers as he liked to claim, he would have been able to destroy them as he came close to doing with Horst. And if Alison didn't have much to lose, Catherine did. Then she was put forward for a Chair and Paul had served his purpose."

"What are you suggesting?", Doreen asked.

"You're getting impatient so I'll cut to the chase. When I confronted Pepple, he refused to say anything about the circumstances around Digby's death. He wouldn't even explain why he was so adamant that whatever had caused Paul's death had taken place in the office. No, Pepple was too scared of Catherine to spill the beans. But a very keen first year student of ours, who also happens to be the son of the police officer who investigated both Paul's and Jeremy's deaths, provided some invaluable information, obtained in the course of his research for his dissertation. Let me assure you that it was, of course, all done in strict observance of our code of ethics. Pepple had not submitted any toxicological tests to the coroner nor was there any evidence that he had carried out any. He assured DCI Rahman that there was no need for it, because the cause of death was clear and further tests would be a waste of resources."

Adeel had done outstandingly well extracting that information from his father and imparting it to his supervisor without any delay. When I told him that that was precisely the kind of empirical evidence that would make his work stand out, the excitement in his voice was touching. He was all but guaranteed a first class mark for his sterling work.

"But Pepple made the mistake of telling me and Catherine that he *had* performed a test and that Paul had been drinking a large amount of wine. White wine no less. How could he have known that?

"Because he knew all along exactly what Paul had taken that evening. Catherine had told him. And it was Catherine who had made sure that he would be on call that evening to rush to the Scrote and give a false natural death diagnosis. And when Paul didn't die at the Scrote but managed to make his way to his office, it was Catherine who instructed Pepple to vouch that the cause of death was the impact with the rock."

"Why would she do that?", Lucy asked.

"Because the impact wasn't the cause of Paul's death or at least it wasn't the only one. I had a very enlightening chat with Nigel Cole, Professor of Criminal Law. He explained to me the basics of causation in law, pointed me to the relevant cases. Even if the rock had played a part in Paul's death, it's still the case that he would have died anyway. And that's because that evening, when Paul came into his office all wobbly and sweaty and slurring his words, he was not drunk. He had been poisoned."

"What the hell is that crap?", Horst said.

"Better believe it. Obviously, my first thought was that Catherine had been up to no good. She'd had ample opportunity; she'd spent a good deal of the reception with Paul. She had tried repeatedly to mislead me, although, truth be told, I was trying to mislead her in the opposite direction at the same time. It was all a bit of a mess for a while, to be honest. But that story didn't seem complete. Why would Catherine do it in public? She'd have nothing to gain from that and she could easily have met him privately somewhere else.

"And then I realised just how much you *all* hated Paul. Alison, on top of everything else he made you the Deputy Head and turned you into his puppet. For years you've been nothing but a glorified secretary. Catherine, you were infuriated by his duplicity and thirst for power. Horst, you couldn't abide a vulgar functionalist treading this earth, especially given that he nearly destroyed you. Doreen, you knew he was going to take away from you your whole life by appointing another administrator and demoting you to an essentially decorative post. You knew because Alison, the only other person in the Department privy to the plan, had told you. Duncan, you hated him because he had reprimanded and belittled you for being discourteous to Victoria and that was probably only the latest occasion, the last straw. Lucy, he had taken your precious course away and he just generally ignored you. All your fractious demands, say moving the noisy doctoral students further away from your office, fell on deaf ears. Thomas, he bullied you. He bullied you to the point of your pretty much losing your speech altogether. You'd rather keep quiet than say something that would give him or anyone else a cue to humiliate you again.

"All I had initially was a hunch but it was confirmed in two stages. Shortly after Paul's death, Nigel told me something, which

I didn't immediately find significant. He said that I had not been the only anthropologist seeking advice on criminal law matters. At the time I thought he meant advice on academic issues but when I asked him for details in our latest conversation, I was left in no doubt that it was practical tips that people had been after. A couple of you, whose names Nigel had already forgotten, had been asking questions about complicity in murder. I assume you had to pay him two visits, because the first time around you couldn't make head or tail of what he was saying. My guess is that you wanted to make sure to allocate the right tasks so that responsibility would be equally distributed among you. Then if one of you decided to snitch on the rest, they'd do so at their own peril. Let me add in passing that I commend you for the academic rigour with which you worked out the legal aspects of your deed.

"The final confirmation was given to me by Jeremy."

"Obviously impossible. This is all nonsense, dear boy", Duncan said.

"Every time Jeremy tried so desperately to attract my attention and tell me what he'd discovered over the past couple of months, I got him out of my hair by asking him to email me", I said.

"Jeremy couldn't email, we all know that", Doreen said.

"That's only partly true. What he couldn't do was *send* email. He was, however, able to compose one. The gods only know how long it took him. If he'd sent it, things would have been very different. He didn't. But it was still there, in the drafts folder, which is where I found and read it. Too late for Jeremy but just in time for me."

"Going through colleagues' email is highly inappropriate", Alison said.

"Piss off, Alison. How's that for appropriateness?

"You all know that Jeremy loved his bureaucracy late in life. It was the only thing he had left really. We all got irritated with his pernickety nit-picking of minutes and regulations, didn't we?"

Some of them nodded as if they'd forgotten what this was all about.

"It was thanks to his attention to tedious detail that I managed to piece together the whole story. You will all remember the Department Meeting before last. I wasn't there. I'd made up some excuse to avoid that ordeal. Paul wasn't there either. He was away. Yet Doreen had marked him as present in the minutes. A very unlikely mistake to make. Jeremy had made a note of it though. He'd be lost without his notes. So, he picked up on that at the next Department Meeting. And when he trawled the minutes once more, he picked up one more thing. In Paul's absence, Alison had given the oral report that day. Some of it went on record, as it ought to, but a large part remained off. Now, to Jeremy reality was exhausted in official records. If I hadn't asked him to write the eulogy, he would never have remembered what he did remember and had begun to write to me.

"Mr Head,
I have been carrying out with the thoroughness that the circumstances allow me the task that you have ascribed me. I believe I have almost completed a biographical note of the late Professor Digby.

There is, however, something very important missing. Much as I have tried by going over all recent minutes and formal communications, I simply cannot find the details regarding Professor Digby's early retirement. And yet, my notes clearly suggest that the plans of his discharge had been discussed, all the way down to the choice of wine for his valedictory party. I am exasperated to find, however, that none of that has been minuted. Alas, my memory fails me and further details refuse to come back to me. I cannot, however, believe that I would have been so mistaken in my perception of what was being said at the time. I have tried to take this up with Doreen but she will not afford me the time I need to explain. I am also obviously loath to address my concern to any other colleague for the fear of by-passing you. Only official information will do, you understand.

I am at a loss. I fear that my speech will remain incomplete. It is with considerable embarrassment that I have to admit this to you and with unmitigated regret that I must apologise in advance for disappointing you.

Yours sincerely,
Jeremy Allcock (Professor)"

"Early retirement? A fine euphemism for murder. Complete with a valedictory party too. You even discussed the choice of wine. At last, a Department Meeting with actionable decisions."

"What the hell are you suggesting? You've already confessed to killing Paul", Horst said.

"I'm suggesting that what I did was accidentally finish off a dead man. *You* had already killed Paul. All of you, in unison. Catherine came up with the plan and probably brought you all on board one by one; I expect that was the easiest part considering how you felt about him. Alison finalised the plan and presided over the meeting that sealed it. Doreen supplied the wine, which *only* Paul drank. In fact, that was how he was lured to the Scrote that evening. He had been promised good quality wine and he was too greedy and cheap to pass on that. It was also Doreen, the mistress of minutes, who, after his death, added Paul's name to those present at that Department Meeting to deflect any suspicion. Lucy was pouring the wine that evening making sure that only Paul got the Sauvignon Blanc whereas the rest of us had the Scrote's Pinot Grigio. And it was Thomas who came to check that Paul was dead in his office. Only he was too timid to come into the room. He was too scared of being humiliated by Paul even posthumously. Had he seen me there, perhaps everything would have been different."

"Fuck's sake, Thomas", Lucy said.

"I'm going to Canada", Thomas replied.

"So what am I being accused of doing?", Horst said.

"You supplied the poison of course. I was certain that it had been administered with the wine but the details still escaped me.

Until I did some research on poisoning and it all clicked together. Paul's symptoms were perfectly consistent with acute botulism. Blurred vision, slurred speech, losing balance, a dry mouth. And do you know where clostridium botulinum bacteria are found? In various places actually but one of those is badly canned food. You're a pickle enthusiast, Horst, aren't you? But, like everything else, it doesn't always work out well for you. Sometimes a can goes off. Like that recent can of tuna. Well, that can was put to good use. Some of that deadly pickling liquid was injected into Paul's Sauvignon Blanc. I suspect it must have stunk but it goes to show you how much of a wine connoisseur Paul was."

"You've no evidence of any of this!", Lucy said.

"What are you going to do, Lucy? Lodge a complaint with the Union? Or call the police? The thing is, further evidence is not even required. You seem not to grasp that we're not in the rule of law business here.

"But we'll come to that at a later stage. First let me finish my story.

"There is, of course, Jeremy. The internal torture of not being able to perform his task as duty compelled him and my constant snubbing him made him intimate his predicament to the person he considered to be his closest friend in the Department. The same person who snuck into his bathroom and pushed him under the water bruising his shoulders with his fat fingers until he died."

"And, for the record, who was that?", Doreen said.

"Duncan of course. True to character, he had taken the back seat in the planning of Paul's murder. Always keen to reap benefits while contributing nothing. That didn't get him off the hook, of course, as his silent endorsement has already made him an accomplice.

"But then he was forced into action. Jeremy confided in him that evening at the Mansion. He told him that his eulogy was going to be incomplete but he also told him what he was going to include in it, that is the discussion about Paul's 'early retirement'. Duncan instantly knew that none of that could be aired and, most importantly, that Jeremy should not be allowed to speak to me. He spoke to the leader of your gang about it and the decision to kill Jeremy was made. He snuck into his bedroom, and only he would have been able to do so without raising any suspicion as he'd taken Jeremy under his wing, knowing that his victim would be in his beloved bath. He pushed him down until the poor soul died. He then found his notes and the manuscript of Paul's eulogy in his rucksack and burned them in the drawing room fire. The Mansion is fining us for that, by the way, and the fine will be docked from your pay, Duncan. Doreen, you may minute this."

"That's fair", Doreen said.

"The following day, when Duncan realised the extent of my alcohol-induced memory loss, he saw the opportunity and seized it. He made up the story of Jeremy and me rowing. That never happened, of course. If Jeremy had had the chance to tell me anything, it'd be me floating dead in the bath, not him. Duncan told Catherine about it and they decided to make the most of it. If I felt guilty for Jeremy's death I'd keep my mouth even more firmly shut than before and I'd continue to be the servile puppet HoD that Catherine and Alison had the ingenuity of turning me into.

"But then I pressed Duncan to tell me more about the imaginary conversation with Jeremy. That caught him off guard. He was unprepared, as ever, thinking it was all over. If he made up more lies, he'd only expose himself further. You never could see anything through, Duncan, could you?"

The stunned silence rang like music to my ears.

"Any other business?", I said.

Crime and custom in savage society

What have we learned from the facts of crime and its punishment recorded in this and the foregoing chapters? We have found that the principles according to which crime is punished are very vague, that the methods of carrying out retribution are fitful, governed by chance and personal passion rather than by any system of fixed institutions. The most important methods, in fact, are a by-product of non-legal institutions, customs, arrangements and events such as sorcery and suicide, the power of the chief, magic, the supernatural consequences of taboo and personal acts of vindictiveness. These institutions and usages, far from being legal in their main function, only very partially and imperfectly subserve the end of maintaining and enforcing the biddings of tradition. We have not found any arrangement or usage which could be classed as a form of 'administration of justice' according to a code and by fixed methods. All the legally effective institutions we found are rather means of cutting short an illegal or intolerable state of affairs, of restoring the equilibrium in social life and of giving vent to the feelings of oppression and injustice felt by individuals. Crime in the Trobriand society can be but vaguely defined — it is sometimes an outburst of passion, sometimes the breach of a definite taboo, sometimes an attempt on person or property (murder, theft, assault), sometimes an indulgence in too high ambitions or wealth, not sanctioned by tradition, in conflict with the prerogatives of the chief or some notable. We have also found that the most definite prohibitions are elastic, since there exist methodical systems of evasion.

Bronislaw Malinowski, *Crime and Custom in Savage Society*

Was it a coincidence that everything that happened happened in an academic Department of Anthropology? Had my colleagues internalised the informal systems of justice that they taught and researched? Had they lost themselves in their discipline a tad too much? Had Catherine, such a good student of humans, told them that the official system would never hold Paul Digby responsible for his wrongs and that administering justice was left to them?

My phenomenological anthropology project has been going spectacularly well. The State of the Art piece was received with great enthusiasm, generated a great deal of discussion and landed me a book contract with a most prestigious publisher. I'm not planning on including acknowledgements in it. I've also been invited to join the editorial board of the *Journal of Phenomenological Anthropology*. It is interesting, amusing even, that Catherine initially came up with the project in order to deflect all suspicion from them. The timelessness of death, the wrong being contained in Paul's office (amazing how she'd even made Pepple regurgitate that stuff), the pub being a topos protected from conflict; she probably thought it was all nonsense, making it up as she went along but there you have it; there was academic value in it after all. I'm just not sure whether that's testament to her brilliance or mine.

It's a great pity that my most interesting idea cannot be included in the book. Readers would no doubt find it as fascinating as I did that Catherine, Alison, Doreen, Duncan, Horst, Lucy, Thomas had planned and executed their informal punishment of Paul Digby in institutional settings. They agreed the details at the Department Meeting. They poisoned him at the campus bar. He died in his office, with his lanyard still hanging from his neck.

They were of course motivated by self-interest and there's nothing remarkable about that. They discussed it at the meeting because no one would question why they all got together there. They did the deed at the reception because then they would either get away with it or go down as a group. But when you look at it from an anthropological perspective, there's something fascinating about how the institution framed their crime.

I've been doing great as HoD as well. It helps that, in a way, we're all hostages to each other and this creates a balance of terror, the most essential precondition for the smooth running of an academic Department.

Having said that, I came out of this whole affair with the upper hand, because my colleagues collapsed under mutual recriminations and mistrust. They have each other to worry about as well as me. That's given me enough leeway to establish myself as the leader of the Department more or less on my own terms. Now I have friends in higher places too and that empowers me to pursue my own agenda. What Alison and Catherine hadn't taken into account is that University top management like to deal with people they see, people in the front line, not those behind the scenes. My performance in Committees has been so impressive that other HoDs and high-ranking administrators trust me and listen to what I have to say.

Doreen is now on a part-time contract. It was time she got some rest. I personally selected a new administrator as competent as Doreen if not more so, and so far, I feel I can trust her. It also helps that I introduced a three-year probation period for admin staff so I've got her treading on eggshells. I blocked Thomas's move to Canada. As if I would allow another University to pocket his research grant. I've been working on him too. I've been giving him more responsibilities and space to take initiatives. His self-confidence is growing and he's grateful to me for it. I also hired Victoria on a temporary lectureship contract. Her mourning for Paul has subsided (she's still in the dark as to what happened to him and I'll do my best to make sure that she so remains) and now that she's standing on her own two feet, she's quickly becoming a force to reckon with. It's a good thing that I can count her among my allies, at least for now.

Duncan's taking early retirement as of next academic year. He'd been surplus to requirements for a long time so he can't complain. I withdrew Catherine's promotion application (the University Promotions Committee, of which I am a much respected member, was agreeable to this). I explained to her that it was too soon and that she would have to prove herself a little more before we can take that step. I put myself forward instead and I don't expect any glitches in it being approved.

Horst was a little more difficult to tame. He remained cocky and obstreperous against all reason. We're making progress though. It helped that I appointed Ursula as the external assessor of the Department's research outputs. As it happens, Ursula and I have been seeing each other. One could go so far as to call us a couple. What with the distance separating us we don't spend as much time together as we could but perhaps it's better this way.

As for Alison, she's as professional as ever but largely does the wise thing and keeps herself to herself.

I've often wondered why it was that my colleagues left me out of their plan. Was it just coincidence? Would I have been included had I been present at that Department Meeting? I doubt it, because I expect that the plan had already been more or less formed and they only ironed out the details and committed to it as a group then. Catherine had said to me that she thought I was a 'good one'. Perhaps that was it. Perhaps they all thought so and questioned whether I would go ahead with it.

That thought gives me some comfort, especially when I recall the events in Paul Digby's office that fateful evening. When I picture him wobbly and weak, holding on to the shelves right there next to me, *Crime and Custom in Savage Society* in my right hand and the white Spanish beach rock that crushed his skull firmly clutched in my good hand, the left.

Acknowledgements

I am grateful to the friends who read early drafts of *Peer Review* and helped me to improve it with their feedback: Zelia, Jo, Maria V., Jill, Lesley, Judy, Margaret S., Liz, Dimitris, Jonathan, Fiona, Bernard, Stella, Maria I., Margaret M., Roxanna, Lena, Ian (not from IT services).

Thanks are also due to Brian Kelly for editing *Peer Review* into a tighter book and Dean Gorissen for designing the wonderful cover, which tells the story itself.

Lindy read every word many times over and patiently endured me throughout the process. I owe her more than I can put into words, not least the very opportunity to do what I love.

As the academic disclaimer goes, all remaining errors of fact or judgement are mine.

Manolis Melissaris
December 2020

Manolis Melissaris was born in Athens, Greece. After studying law in his home town, he moved to Edinburgh, Scotland, where he completed a postgraduate degree in criminology and sociology of law and a doctorate in philosophy of law. For several years he taught philosophy of law, criminal law and anthropology of law at various universities in England (Manchester, Keele, LSE), publishing academic books and articles on a number of topics.

In 2017 he moved to Cyprus and seized the opportunity first, to thaw out, and, second, to give up academia and concentrate on the two things he truly enjoys doing: writing fiction and cooking. He now works as a personal chef and runs a popup restaurant (thelonelyolive.com), and writes.

Manolis blogs at http://manoliswrites.wordpress.com

Printed in Great Britain
by Amazon